Also by JJ Spain

Last Night in Sturgis

Three Days in Daytona

IT STARTED IN LAUGHLIN

A MIKE SALAS NOVEL

IT STARTED IN LAUGHLIN

A MIKE SALAS NOVEL

JJ SPAIN

HMS PRESS

This publication contains the opinions and ideas of its author. It is intended to provide helpful and informative material on the subjects addressed in the publication. The author and publisher specifically disclaim all responsibility for any liability, loss, or risk, personal or otherwise, which is incurred as a consequence, directly or indirectly, of the use and application of any of the contents of this book.

HMS Press
PO Box 2
Valentine, NE 69201

MikeSalasNovels.com
1-402-322-9197
jeffreyaspain@gmail.com

Ordering Information:
Quantity sales. Special discounts are available on quantity purchases by corporations, associations, and others. For details, contact the publisher at the address above.

Library of Congress Control Number: 2022923381
ISBN-13:   979-8-9872733-2-6   [Paperback Edition]
                  979-8-9872733-5-7   [Digital Edition]

CHAPTER

1

"Salas!"

A scratchy, high-pitched voice echoed across the detective's floor. Professional singers called the voice a mezzo-soprano. Salas scowled under a smile as he pictured the red-haired Bonnie Riatt.

The voiced barked, "My office in five." Not exactly Bonnie crooning, *"Let's give them something to talk about."*

"You have got to be shitting me," Salas said under his breath as he rubbed his bald head. He stood from his chair, which rolled away from his desk, to face the music.

"Man, Salas, that woman has only been here three weeks and you are already under her skin," the detective in the next cubicle said while typing away on his keyboard – one finger, one letter at a time. "Usually, it takes a few months before people don't like you."

"What did you do to piss her off, Mike?" Ronnie Higgenbotham asked as he took a sip of coffee. He was leaning against Salas's five-foot-tall gray plastic cubical wall, his elbow resting on the upper ledge.

Ronnie had his hair pulled back in a ponytail. He wore black jeans, black lace-up steel-toed boots and a long-sleeved black T-shirt proclaiming that the Daytona Bike Week was in March 2017.

"Must be my charming personality," Salas said, walking to the voice's office—the same office once occupied by former Captain Tom Green. Green was now a permanent resident of the Indiana State penal system.

It was Salas's first time in her—Captain Toni Harrison's—office. He recognized Green's desk, which was in the same location, facing the same wall of windows that oversaw the same cubicles. The view of the detective's floor was now masked by frosted windows. Gone were the wooden blinds.

After Toni's third day of slamming the door and the third time the blinds fell to the floor, she had them removed and the windows frosted. Now the detectives could not see in and she could not see out. Everyone was happier.

Salas entered the office and sat on the edge of her desk. Like Green, Toni had a credenza laden with pictures. Unlike Green, Harrison had photos in different frames. Like Green, the pictures were of famous people. Unlike Green's, they were not all of Larry Bird.

Scanning the pictures left to right, Salas saw they were of Toni standing with Theo Epstein, Toni arm-in-arm with Mike Ditka, Toni and Oprah smiling, Toni with the actor from *Hell on Wheels*, the guy who went by one name—like Prince. Toni with Sammi Sosa. Toni with Bill Murray at Wrigley.

Toni must be from Chicago. The far wall was more pictures; these must be of her family. A young man in a cap and gown standing next to Toni. The same young man in a blue-and-white football jersey snug tightly over shoulder pads and a helmet under his arm. The young man and a smiling Toni. Toni standing between two men—one who was the same kid and another one, perhaps her father, who was graying at the temples.

Salas thought Toni looked like Gabrielle Union, her son like Reggie Bush, and her dad resembled Thomas Sowell. All three with vibrant smiles, athletic-looking, in great shape, and attractive.

"What the hell, Salas! Get your ass off my desk!" the captain screamed as she slammed the door to her office. The windows shook; if the blinds had been there, they would have been on the floor already.

Toni's face was animated, a contrast to her generic, off-the-rack business suit: black blazer over a black skirt, and a white shirt—rather, a blouse—under the blazer. She, like Ronnie, wore black leather shoes; no heels, no steel toes, but dressy.

The men and women on the detective's floor looked at each other.

"Poor bastard."

"What did he do to her?"

"What was he thinking?"

"Why would he sit on her desk?"

"I bet he quits or takes early retirement. He has age plus years served."

These were comments from the floor.

Salas did not move. He was still sitting on the desk; if anything, he scooted back, his entire butt on the desktop, his feet dangling above the carpet, one leg swinging up while the other swung down. He was smiling.

Captain Toni Harrison walked towards Salas. She faced him as he placed both hands on the desk, pushing her notepad and granite coffee coaster to the side. His triceps were flexed as he sat upright, his white T-shirt taught over his chest.

She wedged her hips inside of Salas's knees, placed the palms of her hands on Salas's biceps and kissed him. A long, tongue-filled, erotic Netflix kiss.

"Oh, Mike," the captain, his captain, groaned softly in his ear. "I can't get you out of my mind. I've tried, but I don't want to." She kissed him again.

It was decision time.

Salas responded. He took her in his arms, pulled his head back for a moment as they looked into each other's eyes, then his tongue went into her mouth. He placed both feet on the floor. They briefly embraced before their hands explored each other.

Salas briefly considered the frosted windows, let the thought pass, and hoped they worked.

They changed positions. Toni was now on the desk, her skirt bunched above her hips. She was less formal under the business attire. She had gone commando. That made Salas even hotter.

They made love on that desk. Captain Green's desk. The same desk where he and Green shared coffee, whiskey, and bullshit.

She wanted to scream. He wanted to let her. The room was quiet.

"Mike, we can't do this," Toni said after they finished. Her skirt was back to normal. Salas zipped and buttoned up his pants as she adjusted her hair and makeup with a hand-held mirror. They were both breathing hard. They were both smiling.

"Toni, I told you that last night. You called me then and you called me again today." Salas kept the grin. "And, by the way, thanks for calling."

The couple had been going at it like this for the past three weeks. Their first time was the evening they met, a formal reception with the mayor. That evening, Salas had worn a suit, minus the tie. He did not know it was a reception to meet the new captain until after he had kissed his new captain in the kitchen.

Their attraction was immediate and their passion was intense and growing.

"I don't know what has gotten into me," Toni said, sitting in her executive leather chair. "I've been divorced for eight years. Focused only on raising my son and my career. And now look at me! Like a college girl away from home for the first time."

"Eight years? Without, you know, sex? You got to be shitting me!" Salas exclaimed.

"Yes. Eight long, very long years. You felt like the first time all over again," Toni said.

"Toni," Salas said, standing next to her desk. They held hands. Even after their session, he still glanced down her blouse. "How is this going to play out? We get caught. You get fired? You dump me? I file a sexual harassment suit?"

"Quit checking out my boobs." She was smiling. "I don't know, Mike. I have never done anything like this before. I can't believe I'm doing this in my office." Toni was rubbing Salas's arm. "I applied for this position to be near my son. I never thought I would get hired. He, James, is finishing his freshman year at St. Francis. He plays football there and I have never missed a game. And, Mike, I want to do it again."

"This minute? My team needs a rest," Salas said.

"Not now, silly. But later. Right now, I need you to take over the Peterson case." Her attention went to the papers on her desk. The papers Salas had pushed to the side.

"Uuugghhh. You have got to be shitting me. Not that one. It has been a cluster since day one."

"I know. But you taking it shows no favoritism. I believe you are the only one who can figure this mess out. I had to have the kid arrested. They posted bond. The parents are super pissed off."

"I bet they're pissed. They should be. We totally messed this up."

"Glad you feel this way. So, lucky you. Good news is, it gives you an excuse to see me and me an excuse to yell at you. We need to keep this—us—under wraps for a while longer," Toni said.

"So, you *are* saying there is an 'us'? I like the sound of that. Captain, oh my Captain."

"Get out of the office, Mike," Toni yelled, then said softly, "Rest your team."

Toni gave Salas a manila file. She turned to her laptop and gazed at the screen. "I will call on you later."

Salas checked his fly with his free hand and blew Toni a kiss with the other. He walked out of the door, slamming it as he exited. Again, the window shook, a mini earthquake in the making.

"Damn!" yelled Salas. "That bitch," he said much softer as he walked toward his cubicle.

"What is it, Mike?" Ronnie asked.

"I got the fucking Peterson case," Salas said loudly.

Groans came from the cubicles.

"Glad it was you," came from an anonymous voice.

"Great," said Ronnie. "You get to tell the court how we mishandled evidence. How we dropped the ball. How one of our officers killed himself and how we let a rapist and murderer walk free."

"Salas! What did you call me?" Captain Harrison was standing at her doorway. Her hip was cocked to the side, with her right palm resting where Salas recently had a firm grasp.

"Nothing, Captain. Nothing at all. I said, isn't this just rich?! I play the game by the rules and I get the Peterson case," Salas replied. "Why not give it to Blumenthol? He has less cases than me."

"Hey, don't get me involved in this," a voice, minus a body, came from a cubicle.

"Salas, this is yours. Don't question me again," Toni said. "Why don't you rest up for a few hours, Mr. Salas, and we will talk later in my office."

The captain stepped back into her office. She then stopped and turned. "What the hell are you all looking at?" Captain Toni Harrison asked as she shut her door.

CHAPTER

2

RJ stood on the porch of his Boulder home, eyeing the rising sun on the eastern horizon. The Rocky Mountains were to his right, blocking out the blue sky from the west.

The front windshield of the Ford F-250 sitting in his driveway was covered with a thin sheet of ice. The truck's motor was running as the morning frost slowly melted off the glass. The smell of diesel fuel was in the air.

It was early April, and snow showers were in the forecast for midmorning. There would be skiing in the Rockies for a few more weeks.

In his hands, RJ held an atlas, the pages turned to the State of Colorado. With his index finger, he traced Highway 93 from Boulder to Golden, then Interstate 70 to Provo, Utah. Five hundred miles, one way.

His meeting was at three. He stepped on the running board and climbed into the Ford, checked his mirrors, backed out, and headed towards the mountains.

The Ford truck was accustomed to pulling a flatbed gooseneck construction trailer loaded with hand tools, scaffolding, and a skid loader. Now, minus the load, it climbed the mountain elevation with ease.

RJ would have preferred to ride his Harley through the twists and turns of I-70 but with the coming snow and freezing temperatures of the high altitude, riding a bike would not be as safe. Besides, he had not had a chance to drive the new/used Ford. It was the Club's latest business investment.

My Three Sons Construction had cash flowing in its first quarter of business. Three members of the Sons of Silence were doing flat concrete work, dry wall, framing, and bidding on decks, retaining walls, and residential roofing projects.

RJ and the club provided the funding. The three members worked hard to support their families.

The Ford sped past Georgetown and Silver Plume, through the Eisenhower Tunnel, down the mountain to Silverthorne. Outlet stores and Lake Dillon were to his left.

He stopped at the Frisco exit for coffee, where carloads of men and women clad in European ski wear headed to Breckenridge, Keystone, A-Basin, and Copper Mountain.

Traffic thinned further west. Near Vail and Beaver Creek, the mountain homes grew larger and more grandiose, with Range Rovers and G-Class Mercedes replacing Ford Explorers and Chevy Suburbans. Both locations seemed to be hoping for one more mountain run before the slopes were closed for the summer.

RJ stayed on I-70, following the Colorado River and cresting the last of the Rockies with the slow descent to Grand Junction, Colorado.

He crossed the Utah state line ahead of schedule and turned north at Green River and Highway 191.

Two hours later, he pulled into the City of Provo and the heart of the Utah Valley. On both sides of the highway, RJ noted construction projects—something he rarely noticed or ignored before My Three Sons came to life.

Stopping for diesel at a Love's Truck Stop, RJ programed the meeting destination into his smartphone. The Ford was older, with no built-in navigation system, but did have a USB outlet to charge his cell phone. The voice on the phone told him to turn right in 100 feet, staying in the right lane. His next exit was five miles ahead.

The Utah Railway Yard is a primary interchange for both the Union Pacific and BNSF Railroads, and the meeting location for RJ and the motorcycle club named the Devil's Brothers of Las Vegas.

The rail complex, featured multiple rail lines running the length of the yard in parallel fashion. The pickup bounced and rocked as RJ slowly advanced the Ford to the railcar storage area. The main lines were served by multiple switches or turnouts where the cars can be rolled off and repaired or stored for later use.

The railcar in question was 12 cars in, a 60-foot insulated Sterling boxcar decorated with artistic gang graffiti. DBFFDB, the acronym for Devil's Brothers Forever, Forever Devil's Brothers, was painted in bright reds, blues, and glossy black on the railcar metal.

The Devil's stole the idea from the Mongols. Evidently, the Mongols failed to get a patent. Under the spray-painted graphic letters were more artistic designs: a red devil sporting a white goatee and wearing dark sunglasses. The little devil in the throes of giving any onlooker the middle finger.

Facing the little devil, RJ put the pickup in park and shut off the engine. As he exited the Ford, he scanned the area for other vehicles or bikes. He saw no one as he stood several minutes, looking right and left. No movement, no one on foot, no vehicles came or went.

He walked towards the railcar. The side door was slightly open, wide enough for a cat or a small dog to get through. A set of wooden steps connected the ground to the metal structure on wheels. Eight upward steps to the entrance of the railcar.

RJ took the steps one at a time. Using both hands, he slid the door open. A rusted-squeaking noise emanated from the metal rollers on the top and bottom of the door. The sound reminded RJ of his grandmother yelling at him as a child.

"RJ," a voice came from the back of the car. "Welcome to Provo."

"Manny. Long time no see. It has been a while, my friend," RJ said.

"Yeah. I was released a year before you. Sorry, I never came back to visit. It was a time I do not wish to remember."

A light switched on, a solitary blub hanging above a picnic table. The man speaking was sitting in a wooden chair at the head of the wooden structure. Manny's black hair dangled on both shoulders, a yellow bandana covering his forehead. Three men stood behind him.

The door cried and squeaked again as it was pulled shut. RJ turned. Two more Devils guarded the exit. The only exit. Five bodyguards for Manny, all with weapons at their sides: handguns, a long rifle, a shotgun, an AK.

"You look good, Manny. And well-armed," RJ said.

"And you look like you are still lifting weights. I should have joined you," Manny said, patting his belly. "Come sit." Manny pointed left, to the bench attached to the picnic table.

As RJ approached, one of the men behind Manny came forward, the long rifle hanging by a strap over his shoulder. He told RJ to "spread 'em."

RJ did as he was told. With both hands, the man patted RJ on the arms, the small of the back, down each leg.

"He's clean."

"Manny, you told me no weapons. I did as I was requested. But you? Five armed men. Should I be alarmed or flattered?" RJ asked as he stepped to his left, opposite of where Manny wanted him. RJ lifted his leg over the bench of the table and sat catty-corner to Manny. The two men shook hands.

"Just a precaution, RJ. I have had a very bad week. People I love are gone from me. And, after all, it was you who violated our agreement. Violated our trust," Manny said. "Fool me once, shame on you. Fool me twice, shame on me."

"Our agreement, Manny? I agreed we would not be hauling any— and I mean any—contraband in Utah, Colorado, or Nevada. We have lived up to our agreement. It was you who took my two men," RJ said. He placed both his hands on his knees and leaned into Manny's space at the table. RJ's nose was within inches of Manny's. "You violated my trust."

The three men behind Manny came forward. Manny waved them off with a flick of his wrist.

"Your two guys. They were in my bar, RJ. In my space. Wearing their colors. Why were they there?" Manny asked.

"Two guys out for a ride and a beer. We have a truce. You broke the truce by taking my men."

"They are mules. What are they hauling?"

"Did you search them, Manny?" RJ asked, then answered himself, "Of course, you did. You searched them and their bikes. If you found drugs on them or on their Harleys, then they are yours. I do not want them. But I know you found nothing on them, Manny. And that is why I am here. In person. They were clean. I have come for my men. And for an apology," RJ said.

"We can't believe you are clean, RJ. What are you hauling? Why were your men in Vegas? Did they take something they should not have taken? Are you making a move into Vegas?" Manny asked.

"Sounds like you lost something of value. But we didn't take it. We are legit, Manny. You should try it. Quit living on the edge, man. Give your men a life. Aren't you tired living like this?" RJ answered as he spread his arms, pointing at the men with guns.

"Get RJ his boys," Manny told the two guards at the door of the railcar. The sliding door loudly made it known that it was being opened as the two men left.

RJ, Manny, and the three bodyguards sat in silence. Within minutes, they could hear the familiar rumbling sound of Harleys approaching. Someone opened the door the entire distance of the side rail. Bright sunlight lit up the inside of the railcar.

RJ stayed seated, looking out the door. He watched as one of his men exited the back door of a white Chevy one-ton pickup. The other member of the Sons stood as he got out of the rear door of a black Lexus sedan. Each vehicle had a driver, most likely with more guns. Two Devils rode the Son's Harleys into the storage area and parked them by RJ's Ford.

"You good?" RJ yelled to his men.

Both of RJ's men nodded as they got on their motorcycles. RJ, Manny, the five guards, and the drivers all watched as the two bikers rode off.

Manny stood. He and his three men walked down the wooden steps, their backs to RJ. As their feet hit the dry ground of the railyard, they heard a tearing sound, the sound of tape being ripped off a surface. All six men turned to look at RJ. The drivers of the Chevy and sedan came out of their vehicles, their guns drawn.

"You still owe me an apology, Manny." RJ stood facing the men. He was in a shooter's stance, his legs slightly bent, his right leg forward, his arms extended, a six shot Kimber K6S (DASA) revolver pointing at Manny.

"How the fuck did this happen?" Manny asked, looking at his men.

"Now for my apology, Manny," RJ said.

"You cannot kill us all, RJ," Manny said, extending his arms wide. "That is just a six-shot and there are six of us. You are not that good of a shot."

"No. I'm not going to kill anyone, Manny, especially you. We spent two years together in lockup. The Feds, they wanted us to kill each other, that is why they put us in the same cell. We had each other's back then. I want us to have each other's back now," RJ said. He lowered his weapon. "I just wanted you to know I have connections, too." As he said this, he looked to the right and to the left of the railyard. He knew none of his men were out there, but he didn't want Manny to know that.

Manny's men formed a circle around him, their weapons at the ready.

RJ squatted, his rear on the heels of his leather boots. He held his weapon by the barrel. "Listen. There is no you versus me or the Sons versus the Devil's Brothers. It is us versus them, Manny. We should be able to ride into each other's turf. To go into each other's bars and not get hassled. I am not talking changing patches; I am talking supporting each other. I don't care if you are hauling meth or Girl Scout cookies. We have the same goal: to help our boys and their families." RJ stood.

"So, about that apology. You better make it sound sincere. And on the first try, Manny," RJ said.

"My apology to you, my friend, RJ. My error in judgement. Our truce continues. You have my word," Manny said.

RJ watched as the men packed themselves into the two vehicles. He stood on the steps as they drove out of the railyard, following the distant roar of the Harleys. He then got inside his Ford and drove back to Boulder.

3

Salas took over the conference room of the police station. He and Ronnie had crime scene pictures lined up on the table. The white board was a timeline in ten-minute intervals. The window was a maze of Post-It notes, the far wall a makeshift SWOT analysis of the case.

"Ok, Ronnie. Let me talk you through what we have," Salas said as he paced the conference room. Ronnie was seated at the end of the table, a yellow note pad on the desk and a writing pen in his hand.

Salas started, "Thursday, six days ago, Jacob Walker, the alleged murderer, gave Katie Novak, the deceased, a ride home from school. Several witnesses corroborate Katie getting into Jacob's car at approximately 4:30 p.m." Salas was looking at pictures on the table. He took a drink of water.

"At 5:15, Brian Novak, father of the deceased, came home from work. He owns Novak Custom Car Creations. His employees also confirmed that Novak had to leave early to get home. Novak left his garage at five o'clock. Mr. Novak tells us he got home and met Jacob. Jacob was alone in the kitchen. Novak said Jacob was washing blood off his hands. Novak said Jacob told him he cut his hand checking the oil on his car."

Salas continued, "We have the kitchen towel with Jacob's blood as well as Jacob's fingerprints on a glass cup and his fingerprints on the handle of the toilet in the kitchen. Novak said Jacob seemed, and I quote, 'anxious to get the hell out of the house.' Novak said the boy left immediately, going to great lengths to avoid Mr. Novak."

"Again," Salas said, "Novak said the boy was nervous. Novak then said he went to Katie's bedroom and found Katie dead. She was lying in her bed, under the covers. Her pants and underwear were on the bedroom floor, the pants were folded. She was only wearing a white button up shirt and bra."

Another drink of water.

"Ronnie, what do you have on Jacob?"

Ronnie took a deep breath and began. "Thursday night, Jacob was interviewed by Detective Dale Peterson at 7:30 p.m. at the Walker residence. Jacob's parents and attorney, a Mrs. Jenson or Jenkins, something like that, were present. Per Dale's notes, Jacob stated he dropped Katie off at home and went into the house to use the restroom and clean his hands. He related he scrapped the back of his hand checking his oil when he got gas. We confirmed he did get fuel at the BP on Wentworth at approximately 4:45. The station is three-point-five miles from the Novak home.

Ronnie continued, "Jacob stated he was in a hurry to get home, as a college recruiter was coming to his house. Jacob is a standout senior point guard for a Catholic school here in Fort Wayne. The 5:30 appointment with a Coach Daily from Indiana State was confirmed. Jacob stated Katie went to her room when her dad came home, leaving him in the kitchen alone with Mr. Novak. Jacob stated Katie said her dad would be mad that Jacob was there since she was a freshman and Jacob a senior."

"Did the coach say anything about the interview? Was Jacob nervous, agitated, anxious in any way?" Salas asked.

"Per Dale's notes, that is a no. The college coach said the interview went great and they are—were—leaning towards giving Jacob a partial scholarship," Ronnie answered. "Jacob stated Katie was fine when he left. He seemed visibly upset and was crying when interviewed. But— the huge 'but' here is—Dale noted a scratch on Jacob's neck. Jacob said he caught a nail from playing basketball. He is currently out on a $500,000 bond with an ankle monitor. What does 'caught a nail' mean?"

"Fingernail. You know, when hands are flailing around, like in a basketball game." Salas stood with his arms up, legs bent, and feet wide as if in a basketball stance. He then waved his arms back and forth as he shuffled around Ronnie. "You know, good defense, you get your hands in their face." His hand touched Ronnie's neck. He gently slapped Ronnie's face.

"Ok. Ok. I get it. Stop. No wonder I never played the sport."

Salas spoke next. "Thursday night, the criminal investigative unit got the prints we discussed, the bloody towel, the sheets off the bed. Katie's white shirt had blood on the collar and specks of blood were also on the pillowcase. The conclusion was that she was raped and choked to death."

"Yes. The blood on the collar," Ronnie said. "When questioned, Jacob said while in the car, he held Katie's face in his hands and gave her a kiss. That was when he noticed that the bleeding from the scratch on his hand was worse than he thought. Jacob said that was when the blood got on the collar. Thus, the reason Jacob entered the home was to get cleaned up. As far as the blood on the pillowcase, could have been from Jacob's hand or maybe it rubbed off from her shirt when she was on the bed. But Jacob did admit it was his blood on her shirt."

Salas continued, "Now the hard part. Detective Peterson was responsible for the rape kit, which was performed at the Novak's home. The father, Mr. Novak, wanted the test done in his home. Not in the hospital. He was adamant about his daughter not going to the hospital. The crime scene tech did the samples, but she had to leave early to get home, so Peterson was the person responsible for the evidence. In addition to the kit, her fingernails were also scrapped and cleaned. The evidence was all bagged and tagged, as per standard procedures in kit #175432."

"On the way back to the lab," Salas said, "Peterson stopped at his home. Totally against protocol. Per the report, he locked the car and went into his house. He stated in his final notes that he knew he screwed up, but his wife was ill and he wanted to check on her."

Ronnie made notes, then interrupted. "Yeah. The crime scene was a cluster. The two normal, regular med techs were at a conference in Chicago. The person on duty was a temp from Indy. She had to leave early to get back to her kids. They called a doc, but Dale said he could take the evidence bags in."

Salas said, "The bad or worse news was that Dale's wife, Darlene, died Friday morning after a long bout with cancer. Dale called 911 Friday morning at 7:15. The ambulance came, as did other police officers. And that was when he, Dale, remembered the evidence. The arriving police officers advised Dale that the passenger side window of his Taurus was shattered, the glass on the inside of the car. It was a typical smash and grab. Dale said he was missing his laptop and the new set of golf clubs Darlene had given him for Christmas. He told the officers nothing about the missing evidence bag."

Salas continued, "Saturday and Sunday, Peterson tried to deal with the passing of his wife and then look for the missing evidence. He even tried to recreate the evidence that was stolen. He went to the morgue on Sunday, lifted what fingernail residue he could get, and tried to replicate the rape kit. He re-bagged and tagged, falsified the dates, snuck them into the lab, and hid them under other papers. We know this as fact because he wrote it all down on paper," Salas waived the suicide note, confession, and the apology in the air. He then laid the paper back on the table.

"We suspect he felt guilty about making up evidence and wrote the note. That and his wife dying were too much for him. He used his service revolver with one shot to his temple Sunday night. When he did not report for work on Monday, officers went to his home and found the dead body and the note."

"Monday afternoon, I guess word had gotten out about Katie because dispatch got a couple of calls," Ronnie said. "Two girls from Jacob's school. I need to go visit both. But the jest of what they said. Caller number one, a McKenzie Spence, said Jacob roughed her up once on a date, got physical with her when she denied his advances. Pushed and slapped her. Caller number two, Kelly Morris, stated that after a heavy petting session, she called it 'grinding,' he acted like he was going to choke her. With both hands on her throat. After that, she never went out with him again."

"Yeah. Monday, the DA and the lawyers of Novak and Walker were advised of the detective's death—the apparent suicide of Mr. Peterson—and the lost evidence. Tuesday, no one touched the file. Wednesday morning, we get the case," Salas finished. Both men stood over the table and looked at the pictures.

"Where to start, Mike?" Ronnie asked.

"Jacob's blood on Katie's collar, and on her bed. A history of similar behavior, especially the choking. Looks pretty open and closed. Got to be the kid," Salas said, then waited for Ronnie to say something.

"What's the first thing you noticed, Ronnie?" Salas asked, to get Ronnie thinking.

"The bedroom, well, the bed. I am new at the dating game, but Doris and I really mess up a bed. I would think these kids would too, especially if it was a rape. In the pictures, she is lying there like she was asleep. And her pants were folded. I never fold my clothes before sex. And don't you think the bed and covers would be thrown around, on the floor? This bed looks like it had just been made. What about you?"

"Jacob's demeanor. The boy was home by 5:30. Jacob's mother and the recruiter both attest he was at his house on time. Jacob's attitude and conduct were not of someone who had just raped and killed a young woman. They said he was excited about the going to Indiana State and that the interview went great. For him to rape and kill someone and then act normal, we are talking about one smooth psychopath. Another question: If Jacob left at 5:15, as Mr. Novak says, then why did Novak wait to dial 911 until 5:47? That was the time dispatch says he called in the death," Salas said.

Ronnie was holding up the pictures. "Statistically, 90% of rape victims know their attacker, with a rape happening every 98 seconds in the United States. Two of five rapes occur in the victim's home, yet less than 5% are by a family member. Per your logic, all evidence points to Jacob."

"Yeah," Salas said. "Yeah, probably the kid. Like Dale figured, the hotshot jock gets any girl he wants, right? But like the Spence girl, Katie says no, so he snaps, rapes, and kills her."

"Well, probable versus possible. Or think about this. Could be Jacob closed the deal and had sex with Katie. That would explain why the kid was nervous and wanted to get out of the house," Ronnie said, looking at the file. "Then dad goes to the bedroom, sees his naked daughter, figured they had just been doing it. The dad goes postal—super upset—and kills his daughter in a fit of rage. All by accident."

"Then why was the scene so serene? No sign of teenage sex and no sign of a fight or a struggle. There was nothing in the bedroom—no furniture knocked to the floor or out of place." Salas wondered out loud. "Ronnie. Get the bed cover, comforter, whatever they call it. See that it gets tested ASAP."

"Never thought of that. Could be sex on the bedspread, then Katie was placed under the covers. I'll go get the bedspread and get it tested for DNA."

"Agreed. Also let us re-examine the body. Get the rape kit redone, this time with the proper authorizations. Has anyone asked any basketball players if they scratched Jacob? So, recheck Katie's nails. If she had scratched him, we need to know."

"I can question some players, but no can do on Katie," Ronnie said. "Parents had the body cremated yesterday morning. Funeral service is tomorrow at 10:00 a.m."

"That was fast," Salas said.

"Yes. Parents pushed it."

"Interesting. Two things for now. I am going to go talk to Mr. Novak. Ronnie, you get the bedspread. If we want to get to Laughlin on time, we got to get this case wrapped up fast. Be thorough. Make no mistakes. Pressure is on us. The case has been a cluster. Let's do it right."

"Yeah, 15 of 16 rapists walk free. But murders? We got to get this kid."

4

Manny Escamilia slapped the man on the face. An open-hand slap, aka a bitch slap. The man's head snapped to the side. A red welt quickly formed. The man, taller and heavier than Manny, didn't try to fight back. He took the blow to his face without expression.

"A gun? You did not look for a gun in the railcar? You only had to search a picnic table and a fucking chair."

Another man spoke. "The car was locked up tight, Manny. I locked it myself. I don't know how they could have gotten in and planted a gun."

There were five men in the room. All wore their colors, black leather vests with red emblems, again the devil with sunglasses with the middle finger extended. Four of the club members had beads of sweat on their foreheads and upper lips. Manny was not sweating.

"I was made a fool! How can I have credibility with your incompetence? The Devil's Brothers will be a joke. First, someone kills Ramon, one of our friends, one of our brothers, one of our leaders. Then, they steal my daughter, my 17-year-old baby. And we do not make amends? We don't strike back? Now... Now you let the Sons plant a gun on our own property. I know RJ. He wanted to show me he was in charge."

Manny kicked the end table next to him. Magazines and an empty water bottle fell to the floor.

"And you, Johnny," he was pointing at the man he had just slapped, "you oversee my security. You are lucky you are still breathing."

The room went quiet. You could hear passing cars and trucks through the open windows, the hissing sound of tires on the pavement, the dull thunder of engines working. There was no breeze; the air was stagnant and stale.

The Las Vegas heat was early this year, over 90 degrees in mid-April. One of Manny's men sat the end table upright, re-stacked the magazines, and threw the empty water bottle into the trash.

"After meeting RJ, I do not believe the Sons have anything to do with my Maria. We beat his men. They were clueless," Manny said. He sat down hard on a brown leather sofa. His eyes were red with large dark bags sagging under each, victims of hours of no sleep, hours of excruciating pain only a parent can experience from the loss of a child.

"Rojas, what news do you have for me?"

Rojas was built like a wrestler, the opposite of Manny. He was lean, with broad shoulders and a small waist.

Rojas said, "As we had before, Manny. Maria was at a party with friends. She was there, then she wasn't. Her friends thought she went off with a boy to talk. She never returned. After two days, her mother called you. We went to the house where the party was held. Nothing. No witnesses. No one could recall her. We talked to twenty kids who were at the party. No one could remember seeing any bike colors. They said it was all kids their age."

The man Manny slapped said, "We have an Aztec, like we took the Sons. He is not talking. The Bandidos, we are inside with them. They are clean. We have seen the Pagans in east Vegas and the Brotherhood. Word on the street is, the Outlaws are moving in. The Angels, they went underground on us. We have not seen or heard anything of them this past week. I say it's the Angels."

"It has been over a week, Manny. No demand for money. No demand for products. No threats have been made. No one has taken accountability for taking her. If it were a rival, they would be bragging.

They would want money, or product. I do not think it's a club," Rojas countered the head of security.

"I am fully aware of how many fucking days it has been since my daughter has been taken from me, Rojas. I agree with Johnny. It's a club. A club that wants to see us fail. A club that wants us out of Vegas. Connolly, Johnny, find me a Pagan, a Brother, and an Outlaw. Rojas, get me an Angel," Manny said. He lowered his head in his hands. "My Maria is gone. Someone must pay."

CHAPTER

5

"Mr. Novak?" Salas held is badge for Brian Novak to see. "Mike Salas, Fort Wayne Police."

He was standing in the showroom of Novak's Custom Car Creations. The showroom featured a wall of windows. Driving east or west, Novak's work was showcased. Today's museum piece – a 1970 cranberry red Chevy Chevelle with tuxedo black stripes. Salas's mouth was watering, looking at the classic.

"Frame-off restoration. A 396 V8 with a TH350 three-speed auto. Less than 100 miles on the engine. Stamped serials. Maybe my best work. Fifty-two thousand dollars and you are driving it home," Brian Novak said.

"Well, beyond my paygrade, Mr. Novak."

Salas thought to himself, *Kind of a cocky guy for just losing his daughter.*

The two men shook hands. "My condolences for your daughter. I realize this is a hard time for you, especially with the funeral in the morning."

"Yes, it is. I came to work to get away. To paint. Gets my mind off my troubles. My wife is with her mother. Do you have anything new for me besides you screwing up the evidence that would lock away the kid that killed my daughter?" Novak took out a soft cloth and began buffing the Chevelle.

Salas ignored the comment and switched his attention to a bright-yellow Pontiac GTO Judge. He walked around the car, his finger tracing the outline of the vehicle. He looked at the pictures on the walls: muscle cars, old Chevy, Ford dealership signs, before and after restorations. A wall of golf course pictures seemed out of place with the mood of the showroom.

"Your showroom is immaculate. For older cars, the place has that new-car smell," Salas said.

"Yes, I am a stickler about our shop. We have a break room for food, but no smoking. And notice the air exchange system. You can't even smell paint when I am painting."

"So, you a golfer, too?" Salas asked, pointing at the pictures.

"Yeah. Played in college. Purdue. I am scratch. Area champ five years running," Novak replied.

Salas raised his eyebrow again, thinking, *Maybe Novak is displacing his anger and remorse by talking about how good he was.*

"Never took up the sport," Salas commented. "Not much into finesse. Question for you Mr. Novak," Salas said as he walked past Novak and opened the metal door to the garage. He could see two men leaning over the front quarter panel of a car, the hood acting as a shield from the overhead lights. Salas thought it was an old Ford Mustang.

Novak followed. Both he and Salas stood in the garage. An overhead heater blew hot air towards them. If Salas had had hair, it would have blown sideways in the hot current like Novak's did.

"So, Officer. Your question? I want to get back to my work. My time is valuable. As they say, time is money." Novak had his arms crossed over his chest.

"The delay. Walker left your home at 5:15. You called 911 at 5:47. A man is in your kitchen wiping blood off his hands and thirty minutes later you call the police?" Salas stated and asked.

"When I found my daughter, I was in shock. I didn't realize that much time had gone by," Novak responded.

"I couldn't imagine," Salas said quietly.

"I tried to resuscitate her. Mouth-to-mouth. I know CPR. I was just too late." Novak had a tear in the corner of his eye. "I am the head trainer for CPR in this part of the state of Indiana. Probably the best instructor they have. I do not charge a fee, though. My way of giving back to the community."

What a pompous ass, Salas thought as Novak wiped his eyes. The two men working on the Ford were looking at a carburetor. Their hands were black with grit, grime, and grease.

"I told you it was the carburetor," Novak yelled at the two men. He looked back at Salas, saying, "Geez, if you want something done right, you have to do it yourself. Right, Mr. Salas? Actually, I was frantic when I saw my little girl. I screamed at her, trying to wake her up. She would not listen. She just wouldn't listen."

The two mechanics took handfuls of a yellowish liquid from a can. They rubbed their hands with the goo and then with paper towels. The black coloring disappeared and the color of their hands went back to normal. They threw the towels in a fifty-gallon barrel with the lid missing. Cigarette ashes were on the floor. The barrel was near to overflowing with trash.

"I'm sorry, Mr. Novak," Salas said as he went to the door, exiting the garage. He and Novak walked outside. Salas stopped beside a jet-black Pontiac GTO. It was pristine.

"Wow."

"This is my ride," Novak said with pride. "A 65 Goat. Numbers match. PHS documented. You cannot find many GTO convertibles. Power seats make it even rarer. Only the best. And, by the way, all my own work."

Salas bent from the waist, looking inside the restored classic. "Even the inside is pristine."

"Of course. We are the best exterior and interior restorers in the state."

"Where your clubs? Your golf clubs? You don't carry them in the car?" Salas asked.

"Of course not. Clubs are expensive. They need to be in a controlled environment when not in use. I would never keep them in a car or at the country club, where someone could mess with them." A slight pause. "You are some detective."

Salas left Novak standing by the GTO and walked to his Ford Taurus. He said to the car, "This is my ride. A 2015 faded blue Ford Taurus. The numbers match. And all my own work."

⎯ɯ⎯

Salas's cell phone rang. He hoped it was Toni. It was not.

"Salas," Ronnie said, "I got the bedspread. The mother questioned why I was asking for it but was ok when I told her it was standard procedure. Took it to the lab. Initial test under UV light. Get this. Five different areas positive for semen. As you are aware, seminal fluid is a complex mixture of secretions from four male glands. The seminal vesicle gland, the prostate, the epididymis, and the bulbourethral glands. The average male ejaculates like 3.5 milliliters with up to 50 million sperm cells."

"Spare me, Ronnie," Salas said. "Did you say there were five areas on the comforter where fluid was found?"

"Ah, yeah. Five," Ronnie confirmed, his finger on the paper file.

"Jacob Walker said they had only been seeing each other for a week. He was a busy boy. Found a good girl and took advantage of it."

"Maybe the bedspread was a hand-me-down from mom and dad?" Ronnie asked.

"Go back to the house. Ask Mrs. Novak in a polite way. You know, 'was this a new or used comforter, a hand-me-down?'"

"Will do. I have the lab scrapping each location and will be testing. Perhaps some DNA will match it up."

"Ronnie. Do me a favor. Canvas every dumpster within a three-mile radius of Novak's business."

"Sure. What am I looking for?"

"Golf clubs and a laptop. Get me a warrant to search Novak's office and garage. And, Ronnie, see if you can get Brian Novak's medical records." Salas swiped the phone to end the call.

6

RJ's cell phone vibrated in the cup dispenser of the Ford, notifying him that a text message had just arrived. He continued to back the pickup into the driveway. A 20-foot flatbed trailer led the way.

Two men from the Sons of Silence were rolling their hands in circles, encouraging him to continue. RJ struggled with backing up using just the side and review mirrors. Everything was opposite. He had his right-hand palm up under the steering wheel. He vowed, as he had promised before, to practice backing up later that night in the Walmart parking lot.

Putting the gear shifter into park, RJ signaled he was done. He turned the key to the Ford to off and grabbed his phone. The two Sons were wondering why RJ had stopped in the middle of the driveway. Shrugging their shoulders, they released the pins holding the ramp upright and lowered the metal gate to the asphalt. They had to walk an additional thirty to thirty-five feet to the worksite.

The men then began unloading lumber, concrete blocks, hand tools, shovels, and electric cords. The morning temperature was in the mid-fifties; the men did not mind the extra work.

The text message was in black words against a gray background. The sender's name, also in black, was at the top of the screen above a number with a 702-area code. It was Nellie from Vegas, club president of the Outlaws.

The text read, "Heard you had a round with Manny. He has got one of my boys. What is his deal?"

RJ texted back, "Let me handle it. Give me a couple hours."

The response was "K."

The phone buzzed again as RJ opened the door of the Ford. He could see his men unloading the lumber. He glanced at the screen. Another Vegas number, another familiar name.

The man named Soldier was best known from his enforcer days with the Pagan's. Now he was trying to insert himself as the club's future CEO.

The text: "WTF is with Manny? He got my man. We are taking him out."

RJ felt his pulse rise. After years of relative peace between the clubs, Manny was starting a war. Why was Manny kidnapping club members?

He texted back, "Give me a couple of hours."

"U got 2," was Soldier's response.

He informed his work crew he had to go. Club business was calling. RJ did not tell them of the abduction of two different club members by the Devil's Brothers. For the most part, the Devils never ventured out of Vegas or Salt Lake. For the most part, the Devils stayed in their own lane, minded their own business, and never caused trouble. For the most part, Manny was respected by all the clubs.

In club circles, everyone knew Manny and RJ shared the same cell in prison. They knew the two of them took care of each other, thus the text messages were out of respect. While most of the clubs were staking claims in Vegas, RJ pulled his charter and his men out of Sin City, opting to stay away from potential conflicts. Conflicts like today.

Using his phone, RJ ordered an Uber. As he waited, he called Manny. It went to voice mail. It was full. He called again. No answer. He sent a text.

"Manny, we need to talk. Now. Call me."

The text back was immediate. "Got no war with you, my friend. Got to find who's fuckin' with my club. Will interrogate one at a time."

RJ responded as he entered the Uber, "Manny, don't. No one has a beef with you. If they did, I would know."

"You don't know everything, or you would know about this."

"Let the Pagan and the Outlaw go, Manny. I will take responsibility for them."

Manny did not respond. RJ waited. Ten, fifteen, thirty minutes, an hour passed. It was brutal, like watching junior high girls' basketball – lots to watch but no scoring.

Nellie texted for an update.

Soldier left a voice mail that simply stated, "You got 30 minutes."

RJ packed his travel bag, strapping it to his Harley. He checked the weather. If he hustled, he could be over the mountains, the same trip he had just completed a few days ago, before the temperatures dropped. This time, no snow in the forecast. He wanted Manny's response before he got on the bike. He received nothing.

He called Soldier. The phone was answered before the first ring ended.

"Yeah."

"Asking for a favor, Soldier. I am on my way to Vegas. Be there tonight. Give me till tomorrow morning. They will rough up your boy. They beat my two guys around. Manny has lost something or someone. He is searching. I can handle it, but I ask you, don't go to war yet. We don't need a war."

The line was quiet. More waiting. RJ's stomach churned. He had skipped breakfast and knew he would miss lunch. He was thinking of the 800 miles and 12-hour ride he had ahead of him. If he left now, he would roll into Vegas at midnight.

"Ok," Soldier responded. "Out of respect for you, RJ, we will wait. Call me in the morning. By 10. But there will be repercussions. Last night, one of my men was taken out, a street hit in Vegas. RJ, he was shot sitting on his bike at a stop light. I am not kidnapping others to find out. But now, we must issue a counter measure regardless of what Manny is missing."

"Sorry to hear about your boys. I get what you're saying, Soldier. I will broker the counter measures, too. Tomorrow." RJ cut the line.

RJ texted again. "Nellie, I'm on my way to Vegas. Will meet Manny tonight. Stay cool."

Another text. "Manny, I will be at your club tonight by 2 a.m. Text me the address."

From Nellie, a text that read, "Got it."

He got an address from Manny.

Another text. This time from RJ to Scooter, the Vegas chapter president of the Angels. "Scooter, Manny will be trying to take one of your men. He has lost something and thinks a club took it. I am on my way to Vegas. No war yet. Meet me at Lucky 13 at midnight."

Scooter's text: "Yeah, we are monitoring. Glad you're coming. Hell will break loose soon. Lucky 13, forgot that place. Fun times. See you there."

Before RJ slipped the phone into the pocket of his jeans, he scrolled through the names in his contacts. He found the name he was looking for and sent a text.

"Salas, will meet you Saturday night at Harrah's in Laughlin."

RJ started his Harley. The rumble felt good between his legs. He could feel the cold barrel of his Glock against the skin of his lower back. He wore a neck gator and pulled it over his mouth and nose, his helmet on, more for warmth than safety. Under his leather jacket he had three layers and wore insulated leather gloves. The windshield was snapped in tight. The saddle bags were full of additional gear, oil, a tool kit, a box of 9 MM shells, and his rain suit.

Forty minutes later, RJ was riding on I-70 with his cruise control set at 85 miles per hour.

CHAPTER

7

Standing in the conference room, Salas asked, "Ronnie, what's the lab say about those jack spots on the comforter?"

"Nothing yet. Takes four or five days to get DNA back."

"You got to be shitting me. Ronnie, we must be on the road tomorrow by noon. Can they tell if the spermatozoa were viable? Were they swimmers?"

"No, Mike. Spermatozoa die within minutes in the open air. They need a warm moist environment. Thus, the rape kit would have been the evidence we needed to close this out. We should focus on the murderer. His blood on her collar, his blood on her sheets, the scratches on his neck and hand that both look like defensive wounds. Of course, that evidence was lost, too. By the way, I cannot find anyone that said they scratched Jacob playing basketball. Jacob's coach said the same."

"Anything in the dumpsters?"

"Yes, but no to the laptop. Found the golf clubs behind a Firestone Tire store about two miles from Dale's house. Clubs, bag, golf balls, a left-handed golf glove."

"They stole the clubs then threw them away? That makes no sense."

"The name tag on the bag said Dale I. Peterson. The logo was from USA Golf here in Fort Wayne. We called, verified the purchase. Gold clubs are expensive. I did not know golfing cost so much. The putter alone was like $250.00. We cleaned out that dumpster. Nothing was left. Clubs are in evidence."

The two men walked shoulder to shoulder. The hallway was painted light blue to soothe their emotions. With each step, the leather-soled biker boots squeaked in rhythm on the linoleum floor. Salas swiped his name badge on the security panel, like a key to a room at the Marriot, then opened the metal door.

The word "EVIDENCE," plastered in bold letters, looked Salas in the eye of his six-foot frame. Ronnie penned his autograph on a clipboard. The desk clerk glanced at the clock perched above the door. The uniformed officer followed protocol and wrote down the time next to Ronnie's name, adding his own initials.

The room, missing windows, shone like the sun under rows of fluorescent bulbs. The bright light glared down on the stacks of cardboard boxes hogging the metal shelves. Each carton proclaimed the familiar "EVIDENCE" insignia, with yellow tape securing the box seams, adding additional reminders that evidence was inside.

The evidentiary golf clubs stood out like Waldo in the confines of boxes and plastic bags. The golf bag was wrapped in a clear plastic tarp; it, too, covered with multiple black EVIDENCE logos.

Ronnie pulled his tactical folding knife from his back pocket, locked the blade, then cut the tape.

Salas stood the leather bag on end. With his right hand, he touched each club; driver, three- and five-woods, pitching wedge, nine-iron through two-iron, an additional sand wedge. Taking the seven-iron out of the bag, Salas inspected it then tried his best golf swing, a mix between Mark McGuire and Paul Bunyan. He would suck at golf.

Salas looked over each club. "Look here," Salas pointed to the end of the club, where the shaft entered the head. "Old Dale put his initials on every club. D.I.P. Dale Irwin Peterson. That guy always cracked me up."

They re-wrapped the golf bag and clubs. The evidence file clerk would reseal after he has inspected and confirmed with the original inventory sheet.

"Now what?" Ronnie asked.

"You get the warrant for Custom Creations?"

Ronnie nodded a yes as Salas led them out the side door of the police station and to his Ford. They drove to Novak's auto shop, parking where the GTO once sat. They walked into the garage. No sign of Brian Novak. One of the mechanics Salas remembered from his previous visit also recognized him.

"Hey. You just missed Brian. He went home for the day. The funeral is tomorrow," the mechanic said.

"Damn. We need to look at a few things. We have the paperwork," Salas said as Ronnie waved the warrant in the air. "Mind if we look around?"

"Not at all. If it helps with your investigation, go ahead. Hope you arrest that bastard Walker soon. Katie was a great girl. I feel so bad for Brian and his wife," the mechanic said as he returned to the motor he was working on, the same Ford Mustang as before.

Donning plastic gloves, Ronnie went to the front office. Salas donned the gloves as well but headed directly to the barrel stuffed with trash. Paper towel by paper towel, Salas emptied the container. He found what he was looking for at the bottom. He picked up a burnt piece of plastic with his thumb and index finger and placed the burned residue in a Glad plastic bag, along with a handful of ashes. He re-filled the barrel with the trash, smashing it down with his hands.

Salas thanked the mechanic who waved a return gesture, his head still under the hood.

"Ronnie, let's roll!" Salas yelled as he exited the front door. Ronnie came running out the front door.

"But, Salas, I hadn't gotten through the first desk drawer, much less looked at the computer."

"Waste of time. Your bike packed? We're headed out at noon tomorrow. Doris have her bike ready?" Salas asked as he steered the Taurus out of the Custom Creations parking lot.

"What about the Peterson case? Captain Harrison will be really pissed if we leave."

"We put in our vacation time weeks ago. It's already approved. She cannot make us stay. And she cannot tell us when to take vacations. Are you packed?"

"Yup. Doris says she's ready, too. You know she got her bike repainted. Should be ready today. I can't wait to see it," Ronnie said.

"Good. It was embarrassing riding that thing in Sturgis with that damn paint job."

"What," Ronnie asked, "you didn't like the pink fenders and pink gas tank with the words 'Crazy Bitch' painted on it?"

"My first ride on a motorcycle and it was that bike. In my nightmares, I still see the weird looks I got riding that damn thing."

CHAPTER

8

Rojas was watching Fox News. A local politician proclaimed himself to be the new sheriff in town. The political candidate named Orlando promised more gun control, to rid the city of gangs and offer sanctuary for all illegals.

Johnny walked in, twirling a pistol in his hand. The weapon was a Taylor .45 LC single-action six-shooter revolver. It twisted awkwardly on his index finger. He caught it by the grip and slipped it into the holster dangling by his side.

"Hell, yeah!" Johnny yelled. "Like Billy the Kid!"

"Put that away before you shoot yourself or, worse yet, you shoot one of us!" Rojas yelled at Johnny.

They were standing in the kitchen of the clubhouse. Manny had called all the Devils to the main place for a meeting tonight, informing them of the meeting with RJ from the Sons of Silence. It was a historic meeting, a first for a rival club member to meet in their facility. Manny wanted the place to be in top shape and his men in their best colors, a show of force and power.

"If we are going to go all cowboy and round up the Indians, I am going all out." Johnny did a quick draw and mimicked shooting Rojas.

Rojas stepped to Johnny and slapped him on his left cheek.

"You ever do that to me again, I will shoot you myself." Rojas stopped. He grabbed Johnny by the cheeks of his face. "Your pupils, your eyes. You are stoned, Johnny. Are you cracking again? You fucking idiot."

Johnny stepped back, swatted Rojas's hands off his face. "I was just teasing. Don't be such a drama queen, Rojas."

Manny entered the room. If possible, he looked worse today than the day before. He sported swollen, raccoon eyes. Junior dos Santos looked better after fighting Cain Velasquez.

The room got quiet.

"Rojas, what have you learned from the Outlaw and that piece-of-shit Pagan?" Manny asked as he tilted his head back. Drops of Visine fell onto his cheeks; some made it into his eyes.

Rojas once again went through the motions. They know nothing, they saw nothing, they have no idea what and why Manny has them.

"Manny, we need to let these men go. You are asking for retaliation. The Outlaws and Pagans will strike back. We do not have the firepower to take them on." There was pleading in Rojas's voice.

"I take it you do not have my Angel then?" Manny asked.

Rojas wanted to buy more time. Time for the Son to come and talk sense into Manny.

"I thought you and I, Manny, the two of us, would grab an Angel together. Tomorrow after the meeting with the Son," Rojas said.

"We can take them, Manny. We can take them all. Let us start a war. Let us kill them all. Vegas will be ours," Johnny yelled as he jumped up and down. He then did another quick draw, twirled the pistol on his finger, and slammed it back into the holster.

Manny stepped back, the clear liquid of the eyedrops running down his cheeks like tears.

Manny grabbed Johnny by the throat. "You think this is a game, Johnny? You think this is all for fun?"

He slammed Johnny against the kitchen wall. Pots and pans fell from the shelves, clanging loudly on the concrete floor. Manny pressed Johnny harder against the wall, lifting him off the ground. The drywall cracked and white dust filled the air.

"Someone took my Maria, Johnny. Someone must pay. You, you fucking junkie. You piece of shit. Because of men like you, my Maria is gone. My only child is missing."

Manny's grip was turning Johnny blue. He had both of Johnny's feet off the ground. Manny reached for Johnny's gun and pulled it from its holster. He jabbed the barrel of the gun into Johnny's ribs. He drove the barrel upward. Johnny's skin broke open. Johnny screamed. Blood ran down the barrel onto Manny's hand.

"Fuck you, Manny. You are the piece of shit. Because of you is why your daughter is missing. While you rotted in jail, she was a little whore," Johnny yelled into Manny's ear.

A shot rang out, canceling the yelling and screaming. Manny tossed Johnny's body to the floor. Blood dripped off his hands.

Johnny's body quivered, shaking as if he were naked on the streets of Fargo in December.

Several men ran into the kitchen, their guns drawn. They stared at Manny and Rojas.

"Rojas, clean this shit up. We have business to do," Manny said as he stormed past his men and out of the room.

9

The ride on I-70 was different on his Harley than in the F-250. The wind, the cool air, the smell of emerging evergreens. RJ noticed more birds. More deer and elk lounging on the slopes. More snow on more mountain peaks.

If it was cold, RJ did not notice. He forgot about Scooter, Manny, Nellie, and Soldier. He just rode, his mind on the next curve, the next car he passed, the next mystic view of the Rockies.

RJ loved the Eisenhower Tunnel, the descent into the basin, the view of Lake Dillion.

He stopped for fuel in Frisco, enjoying the strange looks from the snow bunnies in rented four-wheel drives. The ride by Vail and Avon looked expensive, a lifestyle he would never know and did not care about. The faster he rode, the better he felt leaving the Vail life on his mirrors.

Cresting the last highway peak in the Rockies, RJ flew past wineries promising unique varietals—reds and whites. He got more fuel in Grand Junction and then he was off to Green River. The turn to I-91 and Moab was tempting but would add three hours.

He stayed on I-70, stopping again to shed some layers of clothing, the helmet, and gloves. He would like to toss the windshield, but it was his trusted friend through the cold and rain.

A Porsche 911 passed on the left as if RJ were still parked on the side of the road. He fed his bike more fuel. At 95 mph, his front end was a little light, but he stayed with the silver-haired, midlife-crisis man behind the wheel of the Porsche. Evidently, this guy was in a bigger hurry to get to Vegas than RJ was.

The sun was setting as I-70 merged with I-15 near the city of Beaver. Past St. George, RJ crossed briefly into Arizona, entering Nevada at Mesquite, the interstate nearly empty.

As the moon came in full view, the rocky, dry, barren land switched to casinos, billboards, and people.

RJ was well north of North Las Vegas when he rode into the parking lot of the Lucky 13. Streetlights highlighted the entrance to the Shadow Creek Golf Course, still a few blocks west.

He dropped his kickstand and swung his leg over the back of his bike. He made the 12-hour ride in just under 10. He texted Scooter that he was early and to stop by as soon as he could.

He packed the saddle bags with his leather jacket. His choice of attire, the leather vest. The Sons patch was proudly displayed on the front left side of his chest. An even larger Sons of Silence patch covered his back, shoulder to shoulder. He wore no shirt, just his blue jeans, which were ripped at the knees, and his steel-toed work boots, as always. He pulled his hair back into a ponytail, locking it in with a rubber band.

Opening the door of Lucky 13, RJ stepped back into the seventies. Vinyl chairs surrounded low-top tables. The side walls were lined with Naugahyde-clad booths, each fronted by cracked laminated tabletops. Only thing missing in this seventies re-run was a shag carpet.

The newest addition to the bar, taking it into a new era, was a large flatscreen TV mounted near the hallway. The light from the television illuminated the restroom sign. Its sound was on mute, and captions from Chris Como spewed CNN's personal opinions versus actual news.

Bad Company was pounding out Shooting Star over the loudspeakers. At the bar, sitting shoulder-to-shoulder, visiting, were four patrons and a waitress listening in. The four drinkers had their backs to RJ, but he could see their faces in the bar's back mirror. Each looked at RJ tentatively in the same reflection.

RJ chose the last booth near the rear exit, the opposite side of the bar from the urinals. A wall sconce with a 30-watt bulb lit the tabletop, exposing more cracks on the surface. The waitress approached. She had a pretty smile. Her hair was also in a pony. Her tank top was a little tight.

She asked, "Feel lucky?" Her boobs were enhanced as they rode high minus a bra. Bob Seger sang it best – *way up firm and high*. Her smile was better the closer she got to the table.

"What can I get you, handsome?" was her opening line. RJ smiled back. Her smile grew wider.

"Hi. I'm RJ."

"Yes, I bet you are. My friends call me Shelli."

"May I call you Shelli?" RJ said softly.

"We'll see. What can I get you?"

"Grill still open?"

"Not really, but for my friends I can make something up."

"Seems your friends get all the perks."

"Yeah, I guess they do." Shelli's smile lit up the dark room.

"You have got to get me in with the owner."

"We'll see. Maybe I can come up with something."

"Dozen wings? And a Miller Light."

"I'll have to bring them one at a time."

"Wings or the beer?"

"Both. That way, I can see you more often." They were both still smiling.

"I would like that. Treat yourself to a beer. On me," RJ said. "Start me a tab, please, Shelli."

She walked away, then stopped and turned. She caught RJ looking at her butt, which looked nice in her Lucky jeans. She knew it, and now so did RJ know that she knew.

Shelli returned with two beers. They clinked the long necks. RJ took a deep swallow, then wiped his chin with the back of his hand. He watched as his new favorite waitress walked away. Again, she turned and looked. Again, she caught RJ staring. Bob Seger was now crooning on about Mainstreet. RJ liked this bar.

Two beers later, RJ was five wings into the dozen when the front door of the bar opened. A lone man walked in, his eyes scanning the crowd, now up to six. It was a quick scan.

It was Scooter. He was dressed like RJ, minus the holes in his jeans. The two men made eye contact. Scooter walked to RJ's booth. Shelli was at RJ's side before the Hell's Angel could sit down.

"Listen, boys, I don't want any trouble in here," she said rather loudly. Two of the four people at the bar exited stage right. She added, "You guys are hard on business."

"No worries. Sorry, Shelli. We are just two old friends reconnecting. Please bring my friend here a light beer. He looks like he could use it. Buy a round for the guys at the bar."

RJ handed Shelli a twenty-dollar bill. She returned to the counter. This time, she did not look back.

The two men shook hands as Scooter sat down opposite RJ in the booth. Scooter ate one of the wings before either man spoke.

The beers were served. Shelli gave RJ a WTF-is-this look.

"So, what's Manny's story?" Scooter asked, grabbing another wing.

"I find out tonight, after I leave here. He make any moves on you?"

"Not yet. I got my boys in groups of three. Heavy security. We are not going to fuck around with him, RJ. If he hits us, we hit him fast and hard. I don't care about your past with him. He means zero to me, bro."

"Manny has lost something or someone and he thinks it was a club move. Someone's trying to shut them down or get them out of Vegas," RJ said.

"Hell, one of my boys lost his girl a few days ago. We don't know if she left on her own, got taken, killed, or what. We're looking, but we didn't go after clubs."

"Soldier said two of his guys got hit. You know anything about that?" RJ asked.

"No. Hmmmm..." Scooter was thinking. "We had a drive-by the other day as well. Off the strip, broad daylight. Killed one of our prospects. The other still in the hospital."

They had another beer. Scooter finished the wings. RJ bought the two remaining diehards at the bar another round.

RJ continued, "I'm going to the Devil's club tonight. Meeting with Manny. I will get to the bottom of this. I hope to get Nellie and Soldier's boys back tonight and shut this down."

"The Pagans, the Outlaws, they will want more than a slap on the wrist, RJ. Can't believe you didn't take Manny out, especially when you had a gun on them."

"You heard about that?"

"Yeah, everyone has an in on everyone. I'm sure you got someone inside with my boys." Scooter said.

"Actually, I don't, Scooter. You do your thing, we do ours. No conflicts. Going a new way."

"Yeah, right. Us, too. Hell, we are so legit that we have a booth in Sturgis selling Hell's Angels paraphernalia. T-shirts and shit." Scooter licked the remaining barbeque sauce off his finger. "Call me when you get something. If they try and take one of my guys… Well, you know how I feel. It will be over quick." Scooter stood and left the bar.

RJ signaled Shelli for the check by raising his hand and pointing his finger to the table.

Shelli gathered the empty bottles and the red plastic basket the wings were in, now just bones and grease. She took them to the bar and returned with the check.

"All good in the world of badass bikers?" Shelli asked, her smile returning.

"Yes, all is good. The world is safe for another day."

RJ placed a wad of cash in her hand, holding her hand longer. It was softer than she expected.

"Hope to see you again soon. I have to go to a meeting, or I would stick around." RJ stood and walked to the door. He stopped and looked back at Shelli. She was looking at him, too. Another exchange of smiles.

"That's what they always say, '…be back after a meeting.' I'll be here tomorrow night. Hell, I'm here every night. I own the damn place."

10

Katie Novak's funeral was at 9:00 on Thursday morning. The ceremony was held at the parochial high school she attended. The gymnasium was filled. The Novaks sat in the front row. Her freshman classmates filled the floor seats behind the family. Neither Jacob Walker nor the Fort Wayne Police were in attendance.

Several people walked to the podium and spoke: the funeral director, Katie's best friend, Katie's youth pastor, the mayor. Brian Novak spoke last and talked about his loving daughter, her dedication to school, her love for her friends and family. Brian broke down in tears, crying uncontrollably, and had to be escorted from the stage by the pall bearers, most of whom were his employees. There was not a dry eye in the gym.

The funeral ended promptly at 9:30. A reception followed in the school commons area, then again at the Novak home for close friends and family.

Ronnie and Salas arrived at the Novak's at 11:10. They had to park several houses down the street, given the line of cars parked against the curb.

Sitting in the Novak driveway was Brian's prize GTO, an immaculate Ford Thunderbird from the sixties, a fully refurbished Ford Woody wagon, which Salas thought had to be vintage late forties or early fifties, and a bright-white Ford Bronco that OJ would have liked. Was Mr. Novak showing off his work?

The two detectives were admiring the classic cars when a burly uniformed police officer joined them in the driveway.

"I don't understand, Salas. What's your plan? We do not have anything to arrest anyone. It is all circumstantial," Ronnie said.

"Just go with me, Ronnie. I will know the truth when I see it," Salas said.

The three men entered the home. No one greeted them; in fact, they received scowls with rolling eyes from several of the family members. More people were leaving than those entering. The reception was winding down, letting the real mourning, sorrow, and coping with the death to begin.

As far as funerals go, everyone is there at the beginning, but few are there for support when the family really needs it.

"Mr. Novak. So sorry for your loss. Can we have a few minutes of your time?" Salas asked Brian Novak.

"Look who's here, the keystone cops. I take it no news as to the conviction of Jacob Walker?" Brian Novak led the three men to what they guessed was a den or study. The room was decorated with golf pictures, golf memorabilia. An autographed picture of Brian arm-in-arm with Tiger Woods hung above the mahogany desk. A set of golf clubs sat in the corner. Salas stood next to the clubs.

Mrs. Novak entered the room. She looked exhausted, pale, lifeless. "Can I get you gentlemen a coffee or tea?" she asked.

"No, thank you, Mrs. Novak," Ronnie said as the police officer shook his head no.

"Our sincere apologies, Mrs. Novak. I cannot imagine what you are going through. I have one child, too, a young lady like your Katie. I am so sorry," Salas said.

"Whatever, detective. I personally don't care about your daughter. I am sure you would have done a better job of detecting if it were your daughter laid to rest. What news do you have for me?" Brian Novak interrupted.

"Yes, let's get to the point," Salas said as he looked at the set of golf clubs. He grabbed a club and pulled it out of the golf bag. He examined it in front of Novak, then practiced his best putting stroke.

"Put that back, Mr. Salas. How rude of you. Do not waste my time with your childish behavior. Put the putter back now. And leave," Novak demanded.

Salas lifted the club and let the head of the club slide to his palm, he looked at the end of the PING putter.

"What is this here, Mr. Novak? On the end of the club. There is an engraving," Salas pointed the putter at Brian.

"I have no idea what you are talking about. Put the club away and get out of my home. Let us mourn in piece."

"Let me help you. The engraving appears to be initials. The initials D-I-P," Salas said D-I-P slowly, letting the letters hang in the air. He showed the end of the club to Ronnie, Mrs. Novak, and the police officer.

"D-I-P. The only dip here is you detective. Now take your skinny sidekick, the overweight officer, and go," Brian Novak talked louder with each word.

"Let me help you, Brian," Salas said. "D-I-P are the initials for Dale. I. Peterson. These initials just so happen to match the initials on an entire set of golf clubs we have in our evidence room. It would appear you have one of the golf clubs stolen from Dale I. Peterson's car the day of the rape and murder of your daughter."

"And, Mr. Novak," Salas added as he slid the putter inside the sleeve of the golf bag and then pulled a plastic evidence bag from his front pants pocket, "see this?" Salas placed the evidence bag on Novak's desk. "We got this from the trash barrel in your garage. And, yes, we had a warrant. And, yes, your employees invited us in to take a look around. This is an evidence identification tag, or what is left of it. Seems someone tried to burn it. Please read the numbers to me, Mr. Novak."

"It is charred and ruined. This is ridiculous," Novak said.

"Humor me. Read the numbers, Brian."

"Looks like a five, a four, a three, and maybe a two," Novak said.

"Ronnie, look at your notes. What is the evidence number of the rape kit Dale I. Peterson used? The one that was stolen from Peterson's car," Salas asked.

Ronnie sped through his note pad, not expecting this question. "Ah, well. Here, here it is. The official number was evidence tag 175432." Ronnie looked surprised.

"It appears, Mr. Novak," Salas said, "that perhaps you stole the evidence kit. And tried to burn the evidence bag in the metal trash can of your shop. Seems you put the fire out before it destroyed all the numbers. Plus, you stole the golf clubs. Why, I do not know. Just because they were there, I suppose." Salas paused for effect. "Then you saw the expensive putter and decided to keep it as you tossed the rest of the clubs behind the Firestone store. You just could not resist that nice putter. Only the best for you. Right, Mr. Novak?"

"Get out of my home, detective. You are planting this crap. This insane theory about me because your idiots botched the evidence. Instead of admitting your incompetence, you are framing me. Now get out." Novak pointed to the door.

"Well, just a minute. There is more. Seems, per your medical records—which, of course, we obtained legally, none of that HIPPA stuff—you had a vasectomy 14 years ago. Is that correct, Brian?" Salas asked.

"What the hell does that have to do with anything?" Brian Novak asked.

"The ejaculatory fluid taken off the bedspread was absent viable spermatozoa. Jacob is virile, you are not," Salas lied.

Mrs. Novak interrupted the scene. "A vasectomy? Brian? We have been trying to have another child for years. I have been taking Clomid and follicle-stimulating hormones. You said it was my fault."

Novak's wife closed her eyes. She hugged herself. "Oh, my Lord. It is true! Katie told me you had taken her. She said you did. I thought she was just fighting back because you would not give her a car or a cell phone or let her date. You bastard." Mrs. Novak slapped Brian Novak.

Brian Novak stepped toward his wife; his fist closed. Salas grabbed his arm, twisting it behind his back. Novak groaned in pain as he arched back into Salas.

Mrs. Novak slapped Brian again. And again. Salas let her. Novak's cheeks were hot pink, her wedding ring drawing a small slice of blood.

"She isn't mine, you bitch," Novak verbally lashed back.

"Not that again. We have been over and over that. I never slept with him. He is your brother, for goodness sake. You raped your own daughter."

"She wouldn't listen to me. She is a bitch. Just like her whore of a mother," Novak screamed.

Ronnie spoke softly. "Mr. Novak, the DNA tests confirm she is your daughter." Ronnie did not know for sure, but he went with it.

"No. No. No!" Novak yelled. The tears started to fall. Silence filled the room. The seconds dragged into minutes.

Salas let the silence do the heavy lifting.

Novak was first to break the silence. "I didn't mean to kill her. She just would not listen to me. She just would not listen. So, I showed her who was in control. I showed her. Then, then she just quit breathing. I mean, I tried CPR. It did not work. I have saved others, I really have. But I could not bring her back. I laid her in her bed and covered her up."

Mrs. Novak slapped Brian with a right, then a left. His body went limp as he slumped to the floor. The police officer cuffed Brian as he read him his rights. With great force, the arresting officer pulled Novak to his feet. The effort elicited a groan from Novak, along with a wail of tears.

Dragged by the elbows, Novak cried and screamed profanities. He tried to head-butt the officer. He kicked at Salas. He spit at Ronnie. The officer calmly released Novak, stepped to the side and tasered him. The flow of electricity blazed a path to Novak's chest. The impact dropped Novak to his knees. Another shot, another white flash, and Novak was face down, his body trembling.

Ten minutes later, the two detectives watched as the police cruiser escorted Novak out of the neighborhood, his face pressed against the passenger rear window. His eyes were glossy as the cruiser took the route to the city's lockup facility.

Salas knew Novak would get a high-priced attorney. He would probably have to sell a couple of "only the best" cars, but with the open admission of guilt and four witnesses, he would be going to jail for a long time.

"How did you know about the putter, Mike?" Ronnie asked as they walked to the Taurus.

"You told me. You said the putter was expensive. In the golf bag in the evidence locker, there was no putter."

"Ah. Shit, I never noticed that," Ronnie said. "What about the burnt tag? You never said a word about that. How did you know to look for that?"

"Just an observation. Things out of the ordinary. There were ashes by the metal trash can in Novak's shop. The garage was immaculate. Not a tool out of order. Yet there were ashes on the floor and no one that worked there could smoke in the shop."

At the police station, Salas, after a brief desktop interlude with his captain, was able to convince Toni of the need for a delayed report on the Novak case. Salas promised it would be on her desk within a week to ten days, most likely closer to ten.

Salas had planned a three-day ride to Laughlin, with stops in Joplin, Missouri, a Hyatt in Albuquerque, New Mexico, two days at Bally's by the river, one night at the Bellagio in Las Vegas, then a three-day ride home. All in total, a nine-day-to-Vegas-and-back vacation.

After a long kiss goodbye, Salas was on his bike and officially on his version of spring break. His first stop, a BP gas station where he was to meet Ronnie and Doris.

CHAPTER

11

"Abdul, get me our friend, Vegas Phil," Rashid talked into his iPhone. "Have him come to the compound. I wish to place a special order."

Abdul grinned, knowing what his boss was after. Abdul enjoyed his service for Rashid. The two men came to the United States a year prior with the money and influence to live and work where they wished. Rashid, the son of a wealthy oil family in the Middle East, was granted "diplomatic immunity" by the prior presidential administration.

They lived in DC for a few short weeks, staying at the Ritz, which was far too crowded for Rashid's tastes. After DC, they tried New York City, where they blended in well with the locals, but Rashid was not happy there. Rashid longed for a better life for himself and his habits.

A month later, after a weekend in Las Vegas, Rashid purchased a house on the edge of the sprawling city. It was in Vegas that he could feed his desires.

Rashid gave orders, Abdul carried them out. Both men were of large frames, dark skinned with heavy eyebrows, thick beards, square jaws, and broad shoulders. Abdul came from a family of peasants, people who spent a lifetime working hard with nothing to show for it. He left the family farm or, as he called it, "herding sheep," for the possibility of being a Royal Guard. With his unique ability to kill, to hurt and maim others, male or female, all without remorse, he quickly rose in the ranks.

Abdul was built like a fighter; his broad shoulders were accentuated by narrow hips and a flat stomach. Scars lined his face. His left ear was mangled—not cauliflower ear like in MMA but partially bitten off.

Abdul used to love to exercise. His morning workout was more than Rashid could do in a lifetime. However, over the past year, his exercise has consisted of his young girls.

In his early days, Rashid may have been built like Abdul, but years of excessive, expensive, and opulent food together with daily abuse of alcohol and drugs had made Rashid fat. He was obese, really, by any standard. He rarely dressed, opting for robes. He bathed in what most would call a hot tub. Abdul carried him around the house in a Home Depot cargo cart.

Abdul ordered in all of Rashid's favorite delicacies, from food and wine to women and children. When Rashid's father realized his oldest child had unique tastes and habits even the royal family could not hide, understand, or allow, he sent his only son to the debauchery of the United States. When Rashid's father finally admitted his son would be outed, perhaps imprisoned, or killed in a country of freedom and the second amendment, he arranged for special immunity by writing a large check to a phony foundation. For his son's security, he assigned his most deadly Royal Guard to watch over Rashid—that being Abdul.

Rashid was leaning back on a large specially built bean bag chair. The chair, made of leather, had the expanse of a king-sized bed and looked like an over-sized potato. The king bag faced a small stage complete with a three-inch diameter stainless steel pole anchored from the floor to the ceiling. Strobe lights highlighted a short runway that snuggled against the bottom of Rashid's belly.

Rashid wore his finest silk robe with the front always open, exposing a massive stomach that covered his private parts. The room smelled of body odor, sweat, and Febreze.

"Abdul, bring the twins. I wish to watch my twins." Again, Rashid gave the orders.

Abdul descended the light-gray-and-peach–colored stone steps into a wine cellar. The stone, the realtor said, was imported from Italy. The wine cellar featured an arched entryway also of stone, a stone floor, more stone on the ceiling. The walls were lined with cedar shelving designed to hold one thousand bottles of wine.

The north side of the cellar was used as intended: bottles of wine slid into each of the boxed crevices, mostly reds. The south side had been altered – *remodeled* is how Rashid termed it. The south wall, still with the cedar shelving absent of wine, was blanketed with a floor-to-ceiling chain link fence. The chain link was set up as six dog kennels. Each kennel separated by more of the fencing. Four of the kennels were occupied.

"Rise and shine, my babies." Abdul announced, turning on the lights. It was mid-afternoon but, given Rashid's habits, the inhabitants' days and nights were upside down. He could hear groaning, moaning, hesitation.

"Time for our medication, and guess who gets to perform today? Laverne and Shirley. You are on stage!" Abdul said, eliciting louder groans.

Abdul stood next to a red metal cart on wheels. A Craftsman Tools logo decorated the top drawer. You could find the same cart at garages where mechanics worked on cars – a large toolbox on wheels.

He unlocked the padlock, lifting the top, which folded down the back side of the cart. He opened the first compartment, removing four syringes from plastic wrappers. Out of the next shelf, perhaps where regular guys stored screwdrivers, Abdul took four alcohol pads from a blue-and-white box. Using the cart as a table, he went to the lowest shelf, unlocking another padlock. Here he removed what looked like a loaf of bread wrapped in heavy plastic.

Abdul slowly unwrapped the loaf, removing several spoonfuls of a fine whitish-brown powder. Using a small bowl, Abdul mixed the powder with distilled water, carefully swirling the concoction in a right-to-left manner. He then filled each syringe with the milky substance.

The dog kennels came to life. Standing next to each of the locked metal gates with their shoulders pushing through the two-inch gaps of the fencing were four young women. They yearned for the intermuscular injection. Abdul knew their tolerance would change soon. Their needs would grow stronger. Soon they would need the hypodermic needle to be mainlined, injected straight into their veins because they would be searching for that immediate high.

Soon their addiction would be so strong and their bodies so frail that Rashid would no longer find them appetizing, no longer pleasing to his tastes. Then Rashid would order Abdul to clean the kennel. Abdul did not enjoy cleaning the kennel, but he did enjoy new girls.

The women received their shots. Abdul relocked his tool kit, tossing away the used needles and used alcohol swabs. He cleaned the small bowl and spoon in the sink. The four girls rescinded to the back of their cages, content for now.

The first two cages contained the twins. They were dressed in black lingerie with lace and thong underwear that slid up their rear ends. Abdul had dressed them several days ago while they were passed out. They remained in the same attire.

The feisty Latina in the rear kennel was now subdued by the drug. Abdul enjoyed her. She fought him as he forced his sex on her. She fought him every time, even under the influence of more and more heroine. She had not yet performed for Rashid. Abdul thought of keeping her for himself.

The middle kennel held what was once a beautiful blonde turned skanky-looking meth-faced shadow. Vegas Phil had brought her in two weeks ago. Neither Rashid nor Abdul wanted her physically, yet Abdul did her anyway. Abdul had a large sex drive. This job was fulfilling his needs. Abdul knew the blonde would be gone soon. He would take her deep into the desert. Maybe do her on the sand then put a bullet in her head.

The girls had no access to a shower or a bath. When the stink got bad enough to where Rashid complained or Abdul could not have their sex, Abdul would drug them and bath with them in the large hot tub. He enjoyed playing with the girl's privates as he washed their hair – top and bottom.

Using more keys from a large key ring attached to his belt, Abdul unlocked the two cages housing the twins. Their bodies responded to Abdul's request, they walked forward with their chins on their chests, their arms extended towards Abdul, looking for him to provide support. The two zombies leaned on the large Arabic man.

Gently, Abdul used a warm cloth to take the sleepy tracts from their eyes. He washed their arm pits and led them to the bathroom. There, he helped them brush their teeth and use the toilet. Abdul cleaning their bottoms longer than necessary. They showed no embarrassment; Abdul worked with impunity.

As they left the bathroom, Abdul sprayed a vanilla scent perfume on them. The bottle said Britney Spears.

One of the twins – Rashid called her Laverne – gave Abdul a kiss on the cheek and said thank you. Abdul smiled. He had taken this 14-year-old's virginity. He was the first for both of the twins. Rashid did not know of their virginity or did not care.

Most of the time, Rashid did not want sex. He wanted to watch them dance, then hit them, beat them, poke objects into them, lick their own blood off of them.

The trio stumbled up the steps to the stage and the silver pole. The twins had been there before, over a dozen times now. They knew if they did not dance, if they did not perform oral acts on each other, the fat man would hit them with a cane. He would whip them from his huge bean bag chair while he leaned back, eating Domino's pizza and drinking wine directly from the bottle.

Abdul turned on music. Rashid liked Frank Sinatra, Dean Martin, and Tony Bennett. Rashid would watch them dance to "Just the Way You Look Tonight," poke them with his cane or a lit cigar to "New York, New York," and then licked them to "That's Amore."

What used to take two or three hours was now over in less than thirty minutes. Rashid's obesity drained him of any vigor or endurance. The twins got off easy. He watched them go down on each other, inserted his cane into Shirley, making her cry, and then drew blood from her vagina.

Laverne was told to take Rashid's manhood into her mouth, but her work was futile – there was no response from Rashid. He hit Laverne with his open hand, yelling at Abdul to remove the whores from his sight.

Abdul knew the twins would only last another week, maybe two. Perhaps he would keep them for a few days after Rashid told him to dispose of them. Not like Rashid could walk down the stairs to check on them. The twins were so fun to play with, but he knew their long-term future would be in the Nevada desert – to be eaten by coyotes, crows, and turkey vultures.

He escorted the girls back to their kennel, giving them several chalky white tablets of oxycodone. The young teenagers chewed on the pills like Jelly Bellies. Later, for supper, the girls would get Taco Bell, Wendy's, or maybe Arby's.

Abdul's iPhone watch signaled a text message. It was Vegas Phil. He was five minutes out.

CHAPTER

12

Captain Toni Harrison was not happy to see her favorite detective ride off into the sunset without her. She was even more upset that he left without the Novak case fully documented, signed, sealed, and delivered. She felt that, perhaps, just perhaps, Salas took advantage of her. Yet, she knew she assigned the case to Salas knowing she took advantage of him.

Their last chance for romance, on her desktop, was enthralling, satisfying, invigorating, and left her wanting more. She got online to check flights to Las Vegas. The two of them were in a desktop moment, committed to the relationship. As they dressed, they decided on letting Ronnie know first, in Vegas.

Toni booked a flight from Fort Wayne to Las Vegas. It was direct, non-stop flight. Every airport had a non-stop to Vegas. She then took her phone and held it in front of her and took a selfie. Toni with her smile, Toni in the mirror with her full figure, Toni with her smile and top off, Toni with her smile and clothes off. She did not think twice before hitting send to her new boyfriend. Had she had Facebook or Instagram, she would have posted her new status but, of course, with different pictures.

Salas sat under the canopy of the BP Station in Fort Wayne, waiting for a ten-minute-late Ronnie and Doris to arrive. He had met Doris once, at the Buffalo Chip Campground a few miles outside of the city of Sturgis, South Dakota. She had been intoxicated, having just tipped over her motorcycle. The bike lay on its side, the motor running and back wheel turning while Doris stammered, trying to stand.

Salas visualized her lowcut tank top with breasts pouting, the words "Crazy Bitch" emboldened on the front of the T. He recalled the bandana covering her forehead stating again this was certainly a "Crazy Bitch." One more advertisement of her abilities was the butt-less/crotchless panties proclaiming "Crazy Bitch" over her, well, lady area. Salas had flashed his badge, telling the intoxicated 30-year-old with her ass cheeks hanging out her leather chaps that he was taking her ride.

He was confiscating her motorcycle, for her own safety, or so that is how he remembered it. What he needed was a ride to downtown Sturgis where the serial killer he had been chasing was sitting in a jail cell. He did recall Doris protested the appropriation or her Harley, although briefly. She wanted collateral in return. Salas gave her Ronnie.

And so…the Doris-and-Ronnie romance began.

Salas's phone vibrated. Four texts from Toni. He opened each and smiled as he saved them to his photo album. He was liking this woman more and more, with a brief hesitation to stay crossing his mind. Should he miss Laughlin and stay with his new lady friend? He wanted this relationship. He wanted Toni Harrison. Salas was sure of it.

Toni Harrison—Captain Toni Harrison—was going to be the next Mrs. Mike Salas. A rumbling noise snapped Salas out of the image of his boss dressed in a white wedding gown and him in a black tux watching her walk down the aisle.

Salas heard them before he saw them. Doris's Harley had Vance & Hines Street Sweepers. He remembered the noise her bike made. The Harley exhaust, the *hupt-hupt-hupt* was intoxicating. Maybe that was when he knew he was buying a bike.

Doris rode into the parking lot, Ronnie her passenger. His six-feet-plus skinny-ass frame loomed over the miniature Doris. Ronnie, clad in brown and yellow, resembled a new wave United Postal Service delivery man. His protective headgear was an old football helmet without the face mask. The couple were a modern-day Jack Nicholson and a more-buff-yet-female version of Peter Fonda. Ronnie's feet were on the passenger foot pegs, his knees angled outward above Doris's head.

Salas admired the couple. Ronnie was perfectly content with Doris as the driver and he as the passenger.

Salas looked at the new paint job Ronnie could not wait to see. Still a pink tank with pink front and rear fenders. The new paint? Well, instead of proclaiming "Crazy Bitch," it now read "Ronnie's Crazy Bitch."

"Great new paint, Doris. Remind me not to ride your bike," Salas said as he pulled in front of the contemporary version of Easy Rider's George and Wyatt.

"Yes, Salas, not exactly what I had envisioned. I was thinking more of a black tank with yellow-and-oranges flames," Ronnie yelled as his sentence was cut off by Salas revving his engine and going full throttle down the ramp to the expressway.

Salas yelled, "Laughlin, here we come!"

The threesome were officially on vacation.

Their goal—well, Salas's goal—was Joplin, Missouri. At the speed limit, a ten-hour ride, they should be there by 10:30 Thursday night. Salas was counting on his badge and fellow police officer privilege, so he was riding well above the set limit. By his estimation, they would save ten minutes per hour on a ten-hour ride. That would be an hour or more saved.

He wanted Joplin by 9:30. It was a 28-hour three-day ride from Fort Wayne to Laughlin. Hit Joplin first, then Albuquerque, then Laughlin on Saturday night, where they would meet up with RJ.

Everything was on schedule until St. Louis.

Salas's favorite professional baseball team was the St. Louis Cardinals. He had been to a home game every year since he moved to Indiana. In April, the Cards were in spring training, preferring to play America's pastime in the warmer, more temperate climates of Florida and Arizona. He had not thought of why they did not do spring ball in Missouri until it started raining just northeast of St. Louis.

The two bikes pulled off the interstate to put on their rain gear. The black ominous clouds facing them on the horizon was not moving. The sun had no chance to break through. The next ten or fifteen miles were without a sprinkle. Then, at once, under the guidance of a sudden bolt of lightning and a thunderous boom, which sent both bikes into the right lane, the rain did fall. Not a light rain, not a gentle spring April shower that brings May flowers, but a torrential wind driven monsoon.

Salas led the way, ducking low, his helmet taking the brunt of the wind-driven rain. His face felt as if it was being diced with shrapnel, of skin-piercing rain bullets from the guns of heaven. Ronnie tried to scoot lower in his seat, Doris's windshield offering some level of protection. He, too, lowered his head, hoping for the helmet to protect his face.

There were no exits. The two bikes and three bikers trudged forward at 30 and 40 miles per hour. Water was several inches deep on the concrete interstate. Semi-tractors with 50-foot trailers sped by on their left, washing them with waves of water-soaked gravel and pushing them to the right, to the grass embankments.

As if the rain was not enough of an insult to the three, hail came next. Pea-sized, then dimes, then quarter-sized round hail stones jumped off their helmets and thudded hard onto their cheeks and hands. Ronnie tried to protect Doris, placing his hands on her cheeks while he was pelted, the blood drawn from his nose and hands.

Salas found an exit—one car, two, five, ten autos lined the downward ramp, each with a new comprehensive claim for their insurance company. At the bottom of the ramp, Salas turned left, going under the interstate. Doris followed as the two dropped their kickstands and cut their motors. They parked under the overpass, the commotion and roar of the storm mixed with the trucks plowing rain overhead on the interstate.

The three bikers scrambled up the concrete embankment, seeking the dry confines under the overpass and under the interstate. They held each other – Salas on the side facing the wind, Doris in the middle, Ronnie on the far end. Both men had their arms around Doris. The wind howled through the underpass, pushing Salas into Doris, Doris into Ronnie, and Ronnie to the edges of the dry confinement of the temporary shelter.

Lightning popped as a transformer exploded across the vacant plot. The sparks and flames were like miniature versions of the storm itself. They could hear a tornado siren screaming miles away. The sound wailed as it faced them, then became nearly absent as the siren went on to warn those in the south west.

Minutes passed, ten at the most, longer if you were huddled under the overpass, shorter if you were in Indiana. The rain let up, the siren was silenced, the wind eased away. The three raised their heads, their arms tight around each other. The bikes stood upright, failing to be victims to Mother Nature. Car engines ignited, each slowly progressing onto the ramp, merging with oncoming vehicles. Bruised and battered, the traffic resumed its westward destination.

"There is nothing dry on me. I am soaked to the bone," Ronnie said.

"Yeah, this GOR-TEX waterproof rain wear is bullshit. Even my underwear is wet," Salas added.

"I think my underwear was dry till I pissed them about ten minutes ago. At least I was warm for a few seconds," Doris said.

The threesome voted to forego a change of clothing and got back on their bikes. They rode in a wet mist for another hour, mostly water vapor springing from the highway. The sun was attempting to break through the clouds as the wind dried their pant legs and arms. Their torsos remained wet.

Day turned to dusk, which soon became darkness. The clock passed 9:00 p.m. when they saw the sign proclaiming that Joplin, Missouri, was 20 minutes ahead. Salas was in the lead and Ronnie was still Doris's passenger.

Salas pulled next to Doris's bike and they rode parallel. He yelled and signaled Ronnie to get them a room. On his cell phone, at 85 miles per hour, Ronnie booked a room with two double beds at the Joplin Holiday Inn Express. He used his credit card on file to reserve it. His next online order was to Papa John's for two large pizzas. He requested one cheese and one meat lovers' to be delivered to the same hotel under the name of Ronnie Higgenbotham.

Fifteen minutes later, they were checked in. Twenty minutes later, they were out of their wet clothes. Twenty-five minutes later, Salas was walking down the Holiday Inn Express hallway to the guest laundry in white boxers and a red T-shirt proclaiming that Nebraska Wrestling was number one. He put the wet clothes in the dryer and went for pizza.

He had placed the door latch to prevent the door from locking. He walked into the room without knocking. Ronnie and Doris scrambled on the bed. Both pulled the blankets to their chins.

"Damn. Can't you two go a day without it?" Salas asked.

"The use of a naked body to warm another naked body is well-documented in restoring core body temperatures," Ronnie said.

"Seriously? You need a scientific excuse to get some loving?" Salas asked.

There was knocking at the door. Evidently, the pizza guy had better manners than Salas. Doris and Ronnie stayed under the covers as Salas tipped the delivery man.

Salas placed the two pies on the desk, then walked back to check on the clothes. He returned several minutes later, clothes in hand, to an empty pizza box. Doris and Ronnie were in the shower. Probably, there was also scientific evidence that showering together increased core temperature. In addition to saving the planet.

By the time Doris and Ronnie had finished cleaning each other, Salas was asleep, with the TV on. The last thing he remembered was Sheldon knocking on a door saying Penny, Penny, Penny.

13

RJ cruised thru the streets of Vegas like he knew the city. His memory of the location was a little sketchy, but it was easier to find it riding your Harley at night with no traffic. He rode onto the parking lot of the Devil's Brothers clubhouse. It was a wooden structure, a log house with a metal roof. An odd building, even for Las Vegas.

Ronnie sat on his bike while he cut the engine, dropped the kickstand, and contemplated his next move. His Glock would be of no use. There had to be forty, maybe fifty, bikes parked in front of the building. He placed the weapon in the saddle bag on his left, burying it within raingear and extra clothes.

He swung his right leg over the backrest, adjusted his pants, unbuttoned his vest, and walked toward the piney smell. At six feet two inches and 225 pounds, RJ was ripped for a man in his fifties. His arms were solid, and his triceps and biceps flexed as he walked. He tied his hair back in place as he approached the entrance.

RJ could hear Lynyrd Skynyrd belting out the biker's anthem, *Free Bird*.

When he opened the door and walked into the main hall of the club, the music stopped. No one spoke. It was as if EF Hutton was speaking.

All eyes, at least 100 of them, were on RJ. He was the first, and perhaps the last, rival club member to enter their home base.

RJ met every eye in the room, one by one. He stood there alone, scanning the crowd. Some faces he recognized—those he nodded to. Most he did not know. There were no females present. Women had their place, but biker clubs were most likely the last bastion of male-only members. Even Augusta allowed women to join, granted at a hefty price tag, but none of the major bike clubs did. Let CNN bitch about it.

RJ walked straight ahead. The crowd parted as when Moses raced through the Dead Sea. Except RJ had no followers.

"RJ, my friend!" Manny yelled out, smiling. He entered the main hall through a side door.

The music was back on. The Devil's Brothers spoke in hushed tones, their eyes still on the adversary. The high ceiling of the large hall echoed *Free Bird*. Rojas met RJ first, looking to pat him down. Manny waived Rojas off. He met his former jailhouse roommate with a physical embrace, both his arms wrapped around RJ. The two men left the main room, a hundred eyes wondering what was going to happen next.

Manny opened a metal door and held it open for RJ and Rojas to enter. The walls of the room had the same log format as the outer structure—more fitting for a cabin in Montana than the streets of Las Vegas. A brown leather sofa faced two cloth sitting chairs. The set matched. A coffee table with a glass top separated the furniture. RJ took one of the chairs, Rojas the other.

Manny offered drinks. RJ took the bottled Busch Light, Rojas passed on the offer. Manny poured himself a cup of black coffee.

RJ broke the silence. "Manny, we need to settle this dispute you have with the local clubs. How do you feel we should end this?"

"What, RJ, you are not giving me orders? You are asking me? You not on your high-and-mighty throne above the rest of us lower club members." Manny was belligerent.

"You know that's not true, Manny. We all want peace. A turf war serves none of us. Tell me, what have you lost that has driven you to this?"

Manny opened up. He told RJ of his missing daughter, of the mysterious killing of Ramon, one of his key club leaders. He told RJ he suspected the other clubs and of their goal to shut him down, drive him out of Las Vegas. He cried to RJ as he talked about his daughter, Maria, her age, her beauty, the love he had for his little girl.

RJ listened. He allowed Manny to talk, to vent, to unleash the rage in his heart. He wanted Manny to offer a peaceful solution. Manny didn't.

"Someone must pay, RJ. Someone took my little girl." Tears were still falling down Manny's cheeks.

"It wasn't a club, Manny. Let the Pagan and the Outlaw go," RJ said.

Manny opened his mouth as if to speak. Rojas interjected.

"I agree with RJ, Manny. It is not them. We are looking at the wrong people," Rojas said. He lowered his eyes as Manny glared at him.

"Rojas, you ever interrupt me again and you will end up like Johnny," Manny said. "Give RJ the Pagan and that asshole Outlaw. Like their clubs, they are worthless." Rojas stood to leave the room. "Have Bingo drop them off on the strip."

Rojas left, shutting the door behind him and leaving RJ and Manny alone.

"Just like told times, huh, RJ? Me and you alone in a small room," Manny said.

"What are you going to do, Manny?"

"When I know more, we will attack. Who and where is up to me. Not you. You go back to Denver. You did your good deed for the day. The Devils don't need you, RJ." Manny opened the door for RJ to leave. "You accomplished what you came here to do. You got their men released. Congratulations. The mighty RJ wins again."

"I am sorry about your daughter. I will ask around. Help you all I can."

"I don't need your help. Now go."

"Manny, if I find your girl and bring her back to you, alive and well, will you do as I say?"

"RJ, you bring me back my Maria and I promise you I will do as you ask. You have my word. Now leave me be. I have a war to prepare for."

"Give me 48 hours," RJ stated as he left Manny alone in his room.

RJ stood before the crowd of Devil's Brothers. There was something about him walking into the room – the music stops. All eyes were on him.

The sea of people separated as RJ walked through the crowd of men. He could smell beer, weed, stagnant air, and body odor. He could see hate, fear, and doubt in the same eyes. The Devil's Brothers did not know what their leader was planning or what tomorrow would bring. These forty or fifty men would not survive an attack by the Pagans – much less the Outlaws, the Brotherhood, and the Angels all banded together.

RJ stood by his bike, putting the Glock back in its place. His phone buzzed. He looked at the time: just after 1:00 a.m. The call was a Vegas number he did not recognize. He swiped the Samsung to on.

"Yeah," RJ said.

"This is Rojas. We need to talk."

"Meet me at Lucky 13 in twenty." The call was over.

RJ opened the door to Lucky 13 seeing what he had hoped to see: Shelli standing behind the bar. The place was busier. At least a dozen men and five or six females crowded around the counter area, all standing in one large group. RJ went to his favorite booth as 38 Special rocked into the night.

"How was your meeting?" Shelli asked, handing RJ a Miller Light. She sat across from him in the booth.

"Another tragedy avoided. The world is safe, until sunrise at least."

"Never thought I'd see you again, much less tonight."

"The wings were pretty good. The thought of them brought me back."

"Hmmm. Not me, huh? Well, the kitchen is closed, biker boy."

The door to the bar opened again. Shelli did not look back. She kept her eyes on RJ.

"Hope not everything is closed." RJ smiled as Rojas approached. He stood by the seated Shelli.

Shelli looked to her right. She scanned Rojas from head to toe and back again. "My night for bikers."

She stood up and asked Rojas what he would like to drink. Rojas passed on the offer. Shelli looked at his vest, then laughed at the logo and the middle finger.

She turned to leave as RJ said, "I would like a Blanton's Bourbon with soda and a lime, please, Shelli."

"Aren't you Mr. Sophistication? I'll be right back." She was not gone long before she placed the mixed drink in front of RJ.

"You boys do have an effect on the crowd." Shelli walked away, pointing to the exiting former patrons. The two bikers could hear the comments about their colors and club insignias.

Rojas said, "We need your help, RJ. Manny has lost it. He will not listen to reason. We don't have the fire power or the will to go to war."

"Tell me about Maria. When did she get taken?"

Rojas explained in detail the day, the time, the house, even the address where Maria was taken. The lack of clues. No witnesses—just drunken kids at a house party. He told RJ about interrogating the Sons, the Pagans, and the Outlaws. How Manny felt it was the Angels and he was out for their blood, attacking them Sunday night.

"We have to work fast. Tell me what happened to Ramon. Manny never told me about him until tonight. Ramon was a good man."

"Parked at a traffic light a week ago, Monday. Middle of the day. Ramon was riding home to have lunch with his wife and new baby. Witnesses say an old brown van pulled up, door opened, and they shot him. Drove away. Vegas PD does not care. They never even asked around," Rojas said. "You know, the current political stance on gangs and bikers—let them kill each other off."

"Where was the shooting at?" RJ asked. Again, Rojas gave him the intersection.

"I'll talk to Scooter of the Angels. But, I know, if Manny does a hit, the Angels will do an all-out elimination of the Devils," RJ said. "Go home. Be with your wife. Sleep in late. You look like you need it."

Rojas stood. Shelli walked him to the door. He was the last of her customers. She locked the door as Rojas went outside. Locking Rojas out or RJ in.

She turned to RJ, her backside leaning against the exit door and said, "My place or yours?"

CHAPTER

14

Rashid Sadulev's home was in a gated community. The subdivision featured a six-foot-tall brick fence surrounding the twenty-something number of homes, each with their own oversized swimming pool, multiple-car garages, five- to ten-acre lots, and private security.

Abdul would laugh at the security as they made their hourly rounds; soft, overweight, diabetic retired men and women. They did not even carry a gun. The front security desk that monitored all traffic in and out did not stop any cars. They pushed the button when someone came up to lift the gate and pushed the button again to lower the gate.

Rashid's purchase of this particular home balanced on several reasons beyond the convenient wine-cellar-slash-dog-kennel-slash-prison. This lot was perched on the highest point of the subdivision, providing a clear line of sight to anyone driving up their private drive. If someone was on this road, they were either invited or were very lost. On this lot, there were no drive-bys.

Another reason Abdul liked this locale was that the brick security wall at the end of the driveway aligned with Highway 95 out of Vegas. Abdul, without permission from the neighboring subdivision and association-dues–paying members, re-designed the brick wall. Yes, it was still brick, but now it possessed rollers on a rail track.

All this hidden was into the dusty gravel and rock-adorned front yard. With a simple click of a garage door button, the brick wall separated, rolling to each side. This allowed the diplomatic-immune Middle Eastern oil baron a quick exit to the vast wilderness, emptiness, and solitude of the hot Nevada desert.

Abdul had used the secret exit on two occasions. The first to test and be sure it worked, the second to export two rotting carcasses of human flesh discarded by Rashid. Abdul proved its worth when he used the stretch limo to haul two dead bodies wrapped in plastic. The quick exit made an easy route to Mother Nature's organic body decomposition chamber called the Mojave Desert.

Abdul watched as Vegas Phil made his way up the driveway. Over a closed-circuit video screen, one of many security cameras, Abdul focused on the outside of the compound. He saw Phil park the car, and then snort something using the crease between his thumb and index finger.

He then exited the auto, spit on the concrete, and pulled his underwear out of the crack of his ass as he lifted his right leg.

Phil rang the doorbell, and Abdul yelled for him to enter the home. The two men made no greeting. Phil followed Abdul to what used to be a theater room, now occupied by the overstuffed bean bag chair, stripper pole, and stage.

Rashid leaned back with his black silk robe tied at the waist, his calves and feet looking swollen and purple. His eyes were bloodshot, barely open. Vegas Phil was amazed this man was still alive and thought he would soon have to find a new source of fast cash.

Rashid bought his dope and his women from Phil. The fat man had expensive tastes. His habits were making Phil rich.

"My friend, Phil," Rashid barked out and coughed. He adjusted his mass in the bean bag. "I have a special need."

"Tell me, Rashid. I have many sources, many outlets for you," Phil said.

"Last night, or this morning," Rashid waved his hand at the inconvenience, "I was watching that arrogant bastard with the gorgeous wife. You know, that Ballard man on the throttle that is full."

Phil looked confused, then said, "You mean the TV show, *Full Throttle?*"

"That is what I said, no?" Again, a wave of his hand. He was breathing faster, obviously the exertion from the arm exercises. "He has those dancing girls. Little girls with hard bodies. They wear leather pants with the ass cut out. Their butt cheeks smile at me. These girls, they have those tattoos above the cracks of their asses. Tramp stamps, they are called. Phil, I want one of these girls."

"No problem, Rashid. I can get you one in the next few days. This will be a little more expensive though, sir. You know biker girls hang out with biker boys, like the blonde I gave you two weeks ago. That was risky. She was a biker girl. Did you like her?" Phil asked.

Rashid looked at Abdul.

Abdul said, "The blonde, she didn't meet our standards, Phil. We are very disappointed in her. Please do not let us down again. And, no, we will not pay more. We feel you were overcompensated for the blonde."

"Right, right. Ok, Rashid, no worries. I will go with our normal fee. But you had to love the Mexican señorita, right? She was hot."

Again, Rashid looked at Abdul, this time with a questionable scowl on his face.

"We love the feisty Latina. She is perfect. I have her as a present for Mr. Sadulev this very night. She has taken much time to get under control."

"Now go, Vegas Phil. Get me my biker chick. And be quick. My appetite is strong for this one. I can see great things for her," Rashid said.

Vegas Phil showed himself to the door. He left the cool confines of the oil baron's personal strip club to the grim expanse of the Vegas sun. He took out his cell phone and speed-dialed as he got into the van.

The van's air conditioning did not work. The van was a piece of shit and even looked like a brown turd, but he liked it. It was a gift from his now-dead mother. His mom claimed she drove the van to Woodstock but the background of the picture of mommy and the VW looked more like Southern California than New York State. And the guy sitting in the van was definitely not daddy.

Phil punched a number. The answer was immediate.

"This is the sheriff."

"Sheriff, any word on the war?"

"Not going as planned. So far, my investment in you has been a bust. We need a war started before the election. I have told you. I want this current mayor to look weak. The biker gangs in Vegas are the key. Get them shooting each other in the street and the citizens of Las Vegas will cheer for me to take over."

"Damn, man. I've shot them. I ran over one. I've taken their women and they keep getting along. I heard the Devils had a meeting last night. Some guy from the Sons of Silence was there. Peace talk or war talk, I don't know. Maybe those two are joining forces. I got a lead on some clubs that will be in Laughlin for the rally. I'm going there tomorrow. I'll get another one for you. Same price?" Phil asked.

"A Son is in Las Vegas? Get those bastards involved. I want the Sons dead," the sheriff said. "Yes. Yes, the price is the same. But this is it. If the Sons are not dead and this does not get them killing each other, you are done. I will pay for another shooting or two, if you know what I mean."

CHAPTER

15

RJ woke with the rising sun. He was running on less than four hours of sleep. Shelli was locked under his arm, her hand on his chest. Slowly, he pulled his body away. Her snoring stayed consistent. She looked good asleep and even better naked.

He showered for several minutes, letting the bathroom steam over, probably draining her hot water tank. After the shower, he wrapped a towel around his waist and toured the house.

She lived in a nice home, better than the one he inherited from Deuce in Colorado. She had a large kitchen that spread into the TV room, few interior walls, high ceilings with large fans that kept the air circulating. The entire backyard was a one-lane lap swimming pool, most likely how she kept that body toned.

He stumbled around the kitchen looking for coffee and cups, and then brewing Obsidian coffee from a Keurig machine. RJ studied the pictures sitting on a mantel above a gas fireplace but below a large widescreen TV. Shelli in a white wedding gown and a tall burly guy with a brown beard, his haircut in a mullet, was holding her hand. He wore a black tux with a white bow tie and white cummerbund. Obviously a wedding photo.

More pictures of Shelli with the same guy over the years – on ski slopes, a roof top bar, a train somewhere RJ did not recognize, the couple on a beach. No pictures of kids, just the guy with the beard. RJ stared hard at the pictures and the guy with the beard.

RJ tightened the towel, venturing into her den, or maybe she called it a study or a library. Books lined the bottom to top shelves, maybe 15 or 20 layers of books, mostly hardcover. A wooden ladder leaned against the shelf, anchored at the top and could roll from right to left.

RJ took a book out at random – *Poems* by Robert Frost. He opened the front cover. It was signed by the author. *Damn*, RJ thought, *that had to be a rare one.*

He grabbed another book – *To Kill a Mockingbird*. Again, the inside cover was signed— yes—by Harper Lee. RJ was scared he would drop this piece of history and so slowly put it back.

More books. A signed Mark Twain. Leo Tolstoy – the signature was ineligible but had to be his. Robert Parker—RJ loved the Spencer series—also signed. Ten books in a series by the author Louis L'Amour, all signed. RJ sat down and stared at the collection.

"Impressive, isn't it?" Shelli's voice jolted RJ from his reverie.

"To say the least. Sorry, I was snooping, but this is unreal. I don't know where to look next. This collection is amazing. It should be in a fireproof safe, in a bank, or in the Smithsonian."

"It was my husband's. He passed a few years ago. He was a collector, as was his father. He inherited his father's collection. There is a signed *Old Man and the Sea* by Hemingway, if you want to see that. Most men love Hemingway—the man's man."

Shelli walked towards the ladder. She was naked. Suddenly, RJ was not thinking of books or the bearded guy.

"I can't take the pressure. I'm afraid I will drop the book, spill coffee, or drool all over it." RJ stood, letting his towel drop to the floor. They embraced in front of the window. "I think Ernest would rather I drool on you than on his book."

They returned to the bedroom and repeated what they did just hours before. Afterwards, they fell back to sleep. Another two hours that RJ needed.

By ten in the morning, RJ was on his Harley. He wanted to see where Maria was taken. He rode to the house address Rojas had given him.

Parking his bike across the street from the house, RJ walked the perimeter, not knocking on any doors, just surveying the area. He circled the home from front yard to back. Like the others before him, he saw nothing.

Crossing the street back to his Harley, he examined the neighbor's homes on the opposite side of the street. There, the house directly across from the one-time party house. There, above the door, a small round black dome sitting as pretty as you please. Rojas never mentioned this house. He only talked about the party house and that no one could recall Maria. No one saw her leave. No one saw her enter that house.

RJ walked several steps to the porch of the home. A white wooden swing built for two sat idly, slowly moving to a non-existent wind. The home was immaculate, new paint, new siding, new door, new swing. He pushed a silver buttoned doorbell while staring up at the black dome. He could see the "eye" inside the dome moving right to left.

The black dome housed a camera that was looking him over.

"What do you want?" A frail female voice echoed from a silver-colored bracket, pockmarked with little round holes. "What is your name?"

"Excuse me, ma'am. My name is RJ. I would like to ask you a few questions. You see, a couple of days, ago a friend of mine was taken—kidnapped—from that house across the street. I was curious to see if your security camera here may have seen anything."

"That house is nothing but trouble. You are riding that motorbike?"

"Yes, ma'am," RJ replied.

"Why you don't cut your hair? You got a ponytail like my daughter. You sell drugs?"

"No, ma'am, I do not sell drugs nor do I use drugs. I wear a ponytail, well, because I'm just too damn cheap to pay so much money to get my hair cut."

"Ha!" she yelled over the speaker phone. RJ could hear her coughing inside the house. "What did you say your name was?"

"RJ, ma'am. Do you know you—" the lady cut RJ off mid-sentence.

"What's RJ stand for? Why do you go by your initials? You have a queer first name like Rueben or Raven?"

"The R stands for R and the J stands for J. I guess my parents didn't have much of an imagination."

"Ha!"

"Ma'am, do you know your neighbors across the street?" RJ asked.

"Hell, no. Just a bunch of damn kids. They party all night. Drugs, alcohol, loud music, whores. Most of the time, a bunch of pimple-faced boys with their hats on backwards, pants pulled down, showing their underwear and their little pansy asses. Our world is going to hell." The lady coughed again.

"I agree, ma'am. That's why I would like to check your camera system to see if perhaps we can see the damn kids that took my girl."

"Ha! Ok, you can come in, but I got a gun and I have used the son-of-a-bitch before. And won't hesitate to shoot your white ass." The lady coughed out the long sentence.

RJ heard the door being unlocked. He turned the doorknob and entered the house. Inside was just as immaculate as the outside. The floor shone in the morning sun, you could eat off it.

The owner in question was sitting in a wheelchair. A laptop computer appropriately sat on her lap. She had silver hair pulled up in a bun on her head. She was wearing a bathrobe, and her skinny, wrinkled white knees pointed straight at RJ. The front of her robe was slightly adrift, exposing her left breast. She did not care. RJ did not see a gun.

"Beautiful home you have here, Mrs.…uh, I didn't get your name."

"Preston. Like Kelly Preston. You know the cute gal that married that dipshit Travolta guy."

"Mrs. Preston, my pleasure to meet you. May I look at your camera's security system?

"My, you are a big fella. Hard as a rock. That one of them biker vests?"

"Yes, ma'am. I belong to a club. Like I said, someone we care about was kidnapped and I need to find her before—I am afraid—before they may kill her."

"Here, it is all right here on this damn thing." She held up the notebook. My son is a techy little shit. Has my entire house wired with security cameras and speakers. Hell, he is watching us right now. He is texting the shit out of me, wondering who the hell you are and why I let you in."

RJ looked around, cameras were in every corner, scanning each room. Motion-sensitive, he was sure. He hoped the outdoor camera was motion-sensitive as well.

Mrs. Preston's cell phone rang. She answered.

"Cool your jets, James, you little worrywart. I can handle this. He is just wanting to look at our security tapes. He doesn't want to have his way with me." She turned to RJ. "You don't want to have your way with me, do you, big fella?" She coughed for several seconds, then hung up on her son.

The computer system was simple. Date stamped, listed by the number of the camera. The front door camera was listed as number one. And, yes, each was motion-sensitive, stored in the cloud indefinitely.

Her phone rang again.

"Look all you want. My boy is worried about me. That's him calling me again. Just ignore it. He offered to move me into his house, but it's all metal and chrome. Like the damn Jetsons. I like where I'm at. Me and my husband spent fifty years in this house. He passed a year back. My time is coming. You want a beer?"

"It's only eleven in the morning," RJ said innocently.

"Can't say you drank all day unless you start before noon. Bud or Miller? I don't have any of that fancy microbrew stuff but heard it's good. I got a Stella, though."

"A Stella would be great. Thank you, Mrs. Preston."

"Stella is my name, honey. I have a beer with me name on it." She rolled to the fridge and brought back two green bottles. She popped the top off one beer using her wheelchair as an opener. A practiced maneuver. She handed a beer to RJ.

Stella popped another and raised her bottle to RJ. She waited until he took a drink, then she drained half her beer. She looked longingly at the bottle. "My Lonnie, he was my husband. He was drinking a Stella when he passed."

RJ studied the screen.

"You know what Artois means?" Stella asked.

"Artois, you mean off the label?" RJ held up his beer. Stella nodded. "I think it is a city or area in France?"

"You're right. Pretty and smart. And Stella means star."

"Here. Found the day and the hour. I can see the party house and the kids going in but cannot see any girls. A car pulls up and a bunch of girls get out. It's really dark, but it could be her. Can make out an old, dilapidated VW van, and what looks like a jeep," RJ said, pointing to the computer screen.

He continued to view the tape, fast-forwarding and backing up. They finished their beers. RJ gave up on finding any clues.

"Sorry to bother you, Stella. This is a great security system. Your son loves you and wants to take care of you. He must be a good kid."

"Ha! Tell the techy little shit—if he can figure out how to do all this computer shit, then he should be able to figure out how to get me a grand baby before I kick the bucket."

———m———

RJ hopped on his Harley, giving it a few extra rolls of the accelerator for Stella. He exited the neighborhood, looking for a place to call, text, and email. He found a coffee shop named What Big Beans You Have in a strip mall, nestled between a boutique clothing store and a tattoo parlor. Not needing a tattoo or a lady's dress, he opted for coffee.

RJ texted Salas, "Can your computer guy check out the camera system on Havelock and Underwood in North Las Vegas? There was a drive-by shooting. A Devil's Brother taken out. No clues. Can you download the footage to me?" He included the date and time of the shooting.

Another text to Salas. "While he's at it, check a drive-by at Jennings and Wallace Ave. Also in Vegas. Two dead, both clubbers. Please send the footage." Again, RJ supplied the date and time.

A third text, this one sent to Shelli. RJ wanted to see her again.

She responded within seconds. "I've taken the day off. Meet me at the Luxor. At 2:00."

RJ was curious as to the Luxor, having never been to that casino. He responded, "Ok."

He rode the strip in dense traffic: cab drivers honking, low riders blaring music, and souped-up Toyotas with annoying exhausts and worthless rear spoilers filling the street. All of them ignorant of the motorcycle beside them.

RJ used his "get back" whip on his clutch hand twice. Once when the low rider cut him off and the other when the Toyota swerved into his lane because the driver had been looking at his phone rather than at the street. The low rider did not hear the connection due to the overzealous bass music, but the Toyota slowed to flip RJ off.

RJ whipped the metal ending again, this time a solid connection that took paint off the snowflake's car. Most likely, daddy paid the insurance.

The Toyota, riding next to RJ, faked a swerve into his lane. RJ responded with another loud swat of the whip. More paint chipped off with a dent the size of his fist on the passenger side door. Another fake swerve. RJ increased speed to match the Toyota. He pulled his Harley even with the car's passenger side window, and then withdrew his Glock and pointed it at the driver.

The kid, seeing the weapon, stepped down on the accelerator. The car swerved to the left, coming to an abrupt stop as he smashed into a concrete barrier separating the two lanes of traffic. RJ rode on.

He parked his bike on the sidewalk of the pyramid shaped Luxor. The valet did not object. RJ slipped the man a ten-dollar bill and walked into the lobby of the hotel casino. As tempting as it was to study the interior décor, bright lights, buzzing noises, and the myriad of people, RJ stayed focused on Shelli.

Shelli approached RJ in a white sleeveless summer dress, lace covering the knees. Her olive complexion highlighting her attire. The dress fit her form perfectly, accentuating her slender hips. She wore open-toe shoes with leather straps wrapped around her ankles. Her hair was pulled back by clips near her temples, her cheek bones were those of a young Raquel Welch.

Men and women noticed her when she walked by. Her smile stopped RJ as he walked towards her. His knees buckled. They met and kissed in the center lobby.

"Thought we could see the Titanic Exhibition," Shelli said rather softly. "Do you mind?"

"Can't say, I've ever seen it. So, it will be something new for me."

They held hands as they walked past slot machines and tables announcing three-card poker, twenty-one, craps, and roulette wheels. They made their way to the escalators in the main lobby. At the second level, past the food court, was the exhibit.

"Have you seen the movie *Titanic* with Kate Winslet and Leonardo Di Caprio?"

"No. Why go see it? I know how the movie ends. The boat sinks right? So why go?"

"So, not a fan, huh?" Shelli asked.

"Well, it is good timing, I guess. Afterall, it was over 100 years ago when the boat sank. April something. 1912, I think," RJ said. "Right around this time of year."

The couple spent several hours with the Titanic artifacts, then visited the Bodies Exhibition in the Luxor before jumping on RJ's Harley for a ride to the opposite end of the strip.

They had dinner at the Top of the World in the Stratosphere Casino, Hotel and Tower. Here they talked about life, business, and her late husband. RJ asked how he passed. Shelli related the motorcycle accident nearly 10 years ago. She told him she had purchased the Lucky 13 with the life insurance proceeds.

"It was an emotional purchase," Shelli said. "It's where we first met."

Later that night, with Shelli asleep in her bed, RJ returned to the living room. He stood with the lights off, the moon peeking through the windows, providing light for him to study the pictures of Shelli and her dead husband.

RJ held a ten-by-ten framed picture in his hands and slowly traced the outline of Shelli's face with his index finger, then met the black eyes of the bearded man. He knew him, minus the beard. Someone he had not seen in fifteen years. The man was a Son. His name, Zeke Townley, aka "The Sandman."

CHAPTER

16

Salas had to shake Ronnie and Doris out of a coma. How could two people sleep so soundly? Salas had shaved, showered, left for breakfast, returned slamming the hotel door, had his morning bowel movement, watched the news, and the two of them were still out like a light.

"Get up!" Salas yelled. "We got to get to Albuquerque sometime today."

Ronnie sat up. His chest, slightly sunken in, was the size of one of Salas's arms. Doris sat up. Her chest was very shapely. She was topless at the moment, unaware of her lack of attire.

"Mike, its only seven in the morning. We have all day to get there," Ronnie said.

"We got eleven hours of riding, junior. Let's get moving. We leave at eight. That gets us there in time for happy hour!"

Salas was packing his knapsack.

"I have to pee like a bitch," Doris said. She stood. Her bottoms matched her top. There were none. Salas could not help but stare. The little shit was built like a rock. She reminded him of a former fling he had with a married woman named Candy. They both looked like gymnasts; great quads, muscular arms, six-pack abs, defined lats, calves like diamonds. Like Candy, she had tattoos but not nearly as many.

Watching Doris walk to the bathroom, Salas saw the Harley tat above her bottom that read, "I'd rather ride a Harley."

Doris peed with the bathroom door open. It sounded like a cow peeing on a flat rock. She groaned, wiped front to back in a single hand gesture, washed her hands, towel-dried, and stumbled back into the bedroom. She pushed Salas to the side, grabbed a slice of pizza, took a large bite, and crawled back into bed.

"Five more minutes," Doris moaned. Ronnie agreed.

"You got 30. But no breakfast. I will bring you coffee.

Salas re-packed his Harley. He checked the oil and tire pressure on both bikes, checked emails, and called Toni. She sent more pictures – her outfit for the day and her outfit pulled up over her hips, showing Salas what he could be enjoying on her desk at work.

The two Harleys and three bikers were on Interstate 44 into Oklahoma on Will Rodgers Turnpike by 8:30, close enough to being on schedule that Salas was happy. With no rain in the forecast, barring a flat tire or engine trouble, Salas knew they could be at the Hyatt Place in Albuquerque and their hotel bar in time for free happy hour.

Outside of Tulsa, they stopped for fuel. Doris parked her bike behind Salas, filled his tank with premium fuel, then passed the hose and nozzle to Doris. While there, they checked emails, drank water to stay hydrated, and used the restroom.

"Salas, take a picture of us," Ronnie said as he stood by his lady getting fuel.

Salas snapped off several shots on his Samsung.

"Let me see." Salas handed Ronnie his phone, leaving the two for his turn to pee. Ronnie used his fingers to enlarge and scroll through the photos. Suddenly, Ronnie gasped in horror, his hand to his mouth, the color leaving his face. He placed his hands on his knees and wretched as if he were going to puke.

"Ronnie, what is it? That pizza not sitting well with you?" Doris asked.

Salas came out of the station, three bottles of water in hand. "What's wrong with you?"

"These pictures. Salas, have you seen them?" Ronnie gave Salas back his phone.

"Ah, shit. Forgot about those. Now, Ronnie do not freak out like this," Salas said as Doris took the phone, eager to see what the issue was.

"Salas, that is our captain. You have naked pictures of our captain. You will get fired for this. How did you get those? Did you hack her computer? Do you have a secret camera in her house? This is horrible, Mike. I must report this. This is a huge HR issue." Ronnie was nearly hyperventilating.

"She's a good-looking woman. Nice rack. Are these her real tits?" Doris asked.

"Ronnie, I didn't hack anything. I don't have secret cameras. And, yes, those are real tits." Salas smiled.

Doris smiled and looked at Salas. "So, you're canoodling the captain, doing the dirty deed, the horizontal bop, capping the captain. With your boss. Ever do her in her office? That'd be cool. And risky. And kind of stupid, actually, but the lady is hot."

"Ronnie, Toni and I are involved," Salas said. "We're a thing, a couple. I really like her Ronnie. We were going to tell you in Las Vegas. She's flying out to ride back with us."

"Mike, she's our boss. Like Captain Tom was. We cannot have naked pictures of our boss. How can you be involved with her? She's like my Uncle Tom." Ronnie now had his arms above his head taking deep breaths.

"This is nothing like Tom. And Tom is in prison! This is a good thing. I think, a great thing, for me. Sorry you had to find out about it this way."

They resumed their ride. Ronnie, having trouble getting his color to return, looked pale and in shock. Outside of Oklahoma City, they merged from I-44 to I-40, stopping for lunch in Clinton.

Ronnie stayed quiet during the meal, but Doris asked to see the pictures again.

Riding across the plains of Oklahoma and miles and miles of red dirt and wind farms, they crossed into Texas without noticing any change in scenery. The run through the panhandle of Texas went quick. The routine: ride 150 miles, stop for fuel, stretch, more emails, more water, more food, a restroom, and repeat. Seven hundred sixty-one miles with five stops. They made their last stop in Tucumcari, New

Mexico, at 5:00 before parking their bikes under the Hyatt canopy in Albuquerque at 6:30.

Again, one room with two beds, taking turns with the shower. Salas brought cold beer up from the lobby. They redressed in clean biker gear and walked to The Empty Faucet Bar and Grill.

The Empty Faucet was more bar than grill. The threesome found a high-top table, ordered wings, catfish fingers, nachos, and a pitcher of La Cumbre IPA. Doris ordered three shots of Fireball when the nachos arrived.

"I'm not really a shot guy," Ronnie said, holding the shot glass to his nose and smelling the cinnamon. "Last time I did shots, I couldn't remember how I got back to our car. I felt horrible the next day."

"I carried you to the car. Just don't pound six shots in ten minutes like you did in Sturgis and you will be fine." Salas held his glass up. Doris and Ronnie joined him.

"Here's to staying positive and testing negative," Doris shouted.

The three downed their shots. Ronnie, for the second time in the day, looked as if he was going to puke.

Doris shouted, "Another round!"

Three more shots arrived as the band was setting up on stage.

"To the kisses we have snatched and vice versa," Doris said, again the toaster.

Ronnie didn't drink his shot. He slid it over to Doris, who immediately pounded it down. When Salas left his on the table, Doris finished it, too. Salas ordered a round of water for the table.

The waitress cleaned away the empty baskets of food, replaced the IPA with a new pitcher filled to the top, and removed two empty glasses of water. Doris did not like water, like Ronnie did not like shots.

The band stepped up on stage, their testing and mic check complete. With a "One, two, one-two-three-four, they opened with *For Those About Too Rock, We Salute You*. The lead singer sounded and looked like Brian Johnson, hat and all. The second song was *It's A Long Way to the Top*, followed by *Back in Black* and *Stiff Upper Lip*.

After the fourth song, Doris started to dance, by herself, in the middle of the floor.

She took off her 75th Anniversary Sturgis T-shirt and tossed it to Ronnie, wearing only a red laced bra, tight blue Wrangler jeans, and black Harley logo biker boots. The crowd parted the dance floor as Doris twerked, jerked, cartwheeled, back-bent, did the slap-and-tickle and the grinding circle. She had the attention of the crowd and the band.

After a set of ten ACDC covers, the band announced they needed a pause for the cause. Doris finally downed some water. She was sweating and out of breath. When the band regathered near the stage, drinking beer and talking amongst themselves, Doris made a beeline for the lead singer.

The band members returned to the stage, each taking one giant step up to the platform, with the Brian Johnson lookalike announcing a special guest. Joining them on stage, in her red lacey bra, was Doris, microphone in hand.

The Brian Johnson lookalike announced, as he leaned hesitantly into his mic, "Ladies and gents, we are taking a big chance with this one, so bear with us. In a once-in-a-lifetime event, the Empty Faucet would like to introduce to you – Pat Benatar!"

A portion of the crowd slowly, rather awkwardly, clapped while the rest looked on, waiting for the show to begin. Ronnie put two fingers in his mouth, emitting a shrilling whistle. He stood and repeated the aggravating noise. Salas looked on in bewilderment.

"She rocks as Pat. You will love this, Salas. Doris is the best karaoke ever." Ronnie was clapping now as the band tested out their first non-ACDC song in years.

Doris paced on stage, doing her sexy walk, dipping her shoulders back and forth. She was the same size and shape—she really looked like the real Benatar.

The crowd immediately recognized the song *Hit Me with Your Best Shot*. As Doris belted out "you're the real tough cookie," the cheers of the crowd engulfed the Empty Faucet. The crowd came to life, all coming to the floor, singing and dancing along with Pat-slash-Doris.

The band did not miss a beat. One would have thought they had been practicing this for weeks. Without hesitation, they synched right into *Heartbreaker*, "…dream maker." The crowd was rioting in cheers and dancing.

Salas heard people in the crowd proclaiming it really was Pat Benetar.

Doris's third and final song was *Love is a Battlefield*. The audience stood riveted. As the music stopped, she handed the microphone to Brian, curtsied, bowed, and left the stage to a standing ovation. She rejoined Ronnie and Salas, who were well into another pitcher of the New Mexico IPA. Well-wishers and high fivers idled by their table. She got her picture taken with several men.

On her way to the lady's room to freshen up, two men stopped her. The larger man wrapped his arm around Doris, his hand landing on her butt. He pulled her in close, his lips near her ear. Doris leaned back, her back arching as she swatted at his hand, trying to pull away.

Salas was out of his seat.

The butt grabber tightened his grip as Doris pressed both her hands on the big man's chest. She struggled to get away. Butt grabber's buddy, a shorter and heavier version of the first, reached across and fondled her breasts, laughing as he did so. Doris wiggled and broke away. She swung her leg back and kicked the breast man between the legs. The guy dropped to his knees, both his hands on his crotch.

Butt grabber clinched his fist to take a swing at Doris when Salas caught the man's arm and spun him around. The two men stood face to face, fists clinched.

Butt man did not flinch. He freed his right hand, completing the punch directly at Salas. Salas saw the punch coming with not enough time to back away. He lowered his head, his forehead taking the brunt of the blow. A loud audile crack could be heard several tables away. The puncher howled as he held his right hand with his left. Salas stood dazed.

A third man stepped forward. Ronnie caught him by his bicep, stopping the man's advance.

"Is that guy your friend?" Ronnie asked.

The man nodded as Ronnie stopped him from going to Salas.

"Did you see the punch your friend delivered?" Ronnie asked. "To help you out, a little pugilist's advice. When your friend hit my friend, you see, his wrist was not locked in straight. The wrist was at an angle. That crack we all heard, I believe X-rays will show it is the fracture of his fourth and fifth metacarpals—those are bones in your hand. This break is also known as a boxer's fracture. You see, the impact of your friend's punch was taken on his ring and pinky finger as opposed to the first two knuckles. The metacarpal can easily be broken by hitting a solid object with improper technique. He is looking at six to eight weeks in a cast."

The third man looked at Ronnie, a WTF look on his face.

Ronnie continued. "Now, please watch as my friend hits your friend. Of course, my friend will utilize proper technique."

Salas shook his head back and forth, getting the cobwebs cleaned out from the blow to his head. He doubled his fist and hit the man with the broken hand in the face. The man dropped to the floor, face first. His knees crumpled under him like a wet noodle.

"Ouch. Now that will leave a mark," Ronnie said. "You see, Mike – my friend – says the key to a successful punch is not aiming for the nose but to aim six inches behind the nose. Notice how your friend is now unconscious. Please, go ahead, take a swing at my friend." Ronnie let go of the man's arm, who quickly turned and walked the other way. The man did not look back.

The two guys with damaged body parts were escorted out of the bar by a man proclaiming to be the owner and two more, rather large, gentlemen with the word "SECURITY" stenciled on the back of their T-shirts.

The music resumed, ACDC in play.

Doris continued to the restroom and returned to the high-top table with Salas and Ronnie. Several rounds of shots and cold beers awaited them, gifts from the crowd and the owner. They stayed until the drinks were emptied and the band was not only off stage but had packed their equipment and left the bar, if not the county.

Now the grateful owner asked the trio to please leave.

Phil Vega, aka Vegas Phil, was sitting outside, avoiding the sun, thanks to a Starbucks umbrella. He was drinking an overpriced cup of bitter black coffee. Phil was sweating. A nervous perspiration combined with his physical need for a little mid-morning nose-candy-pick-me-up accentuated his pulse rate.

He took a sip of the scalding black liquid, burning his tongue. The burn caused him to quickly pull the cup away. Which caused the cup to tip. Which poured hot coffee on his crotch, causing him to stand. And spill more coffee. It was that kind of day, week, and year for Vegas Phil.

He dabbed his groin with a white napkin. It would seem to those who did not witness the spill that Vegas Phil had wet himself. He rubbed the wet spot as others looked on. Noticing their smirks, he stopped rubbing and grabbed his phone.

He texted an associate. Not a friend, not an employee, not even someone he liked.

The text read, "I need a biker bitch, tonight. Smaller, hot, stripper type."

The requested response came in seconds. "Yeah, I can do that. Rally weekend, lots to choose from. Park behind the bar. Text me when you get here. Same price."

"Ok," Phil texted back, knowing the price was not money but more product for the kid to sell.

Phil had known this beach-bum–type, sandy-haired bartender called Jonesy for a couple of years now. The kid had been a regular buyer and user but was now a distributor within Phil's hierarchy. Word was, the kid had run away from Los Angeles.

Jonesy, in LA known as Petey, had been selling meth produced by a local manufacturer. It was a laced varietal. Petey's chemical addictions had resulted in the deaths of several people. Local authorities traced the drug sales to Petey, who immediately rolled over his meth connection to LA PD and the DEA.

The following day, Petey's meth man was shot and killed in an altercation with the DEA. The press coined the incident as a "standoff with the police resulting in a suicide by cop." Petey fled to Las Vegas as Jonesy.

Jonesy could easily find employment in the desert city. His first job was as a blackjack dealer at the Nugget. Next, as a black knight at the Excalibur. His third rotation, stagehand at Treasure Island. His final position was as a bartender at the Mirage.

During the last tour of duty, he was busted for stealing from the till. Word spreads quickly in the Vegas money world; thus, after that, jobs were not as easy to find. His next stop was Laughlin, Nevada.   .

The new job locale was appropriately called the Hidden Agenda, where he had an excellent position, not only tending the bar but also selling Vegas Phil's connection of weed and meth to local patrons.

Jonesy added a third part-time job to his resume by assisting Vegas Phil in satisfying the eclectic tastes of the Middle Eastern Arab know as Rashid.

Vegas Phil was particularly proud of Jonesy's snag-and-grab of the teenage twins, even bonusing the young entrepreneur for his ingenuity. Phil enjoyed Jonesy's tale of his tour of the Hoover Dam:

While within the confines of the cement structure, having just delivered a substantial amount of weed to dam security, Jonesy noticed two young ladies lazily straggling behind the thirty to forty patrons of the group tour.

Jonesy approached the two and asked how they were enjoying the dam tour. The two giggled at "dam tour" then rolled their eyes in unison, pointing at their parents who seemed to be dam enthusiasts. The bored twins complained they could not get their cell phones to connect. They willingly followed Jonesy, who called himself the "associate guide," off the official guide's path to "beat the crowd" to the end of the tour, to daylight, and the promise cell phone reception.

Jonesy offered to stay with the girls until their "dam parents" ended the "dam tour." The twins walked away from their head-phoned mother and father, who were listening to a Darth Vader voice discuss the construction of what was then Boulder Dam of the Colorado River in the Black Canyon. Later, the dark voice said the name was changed to Hoover Dam.

—w—

Phil's phone vibrated on the metal table of the coffee shop. He stared at the number as those around him issued more stares and frowns to shut the damn phone off.

"Yes," Phil answered.

"Good news. Word is, the Devils will be attacking next week. I hope they kill the Sons."

Phil recognized the sheriff's voice. "This a new number?"

"Yes, I like to switch every so often for security purposes."

Phil thought this guy was a dumbass. What good was changing phones for security when Vegas Phil keeps his phone? Maybe he should ask the sheriff for a new one.

"You still want me to get the girl tomorrow?" Phil asked, hoping for a yes.

"Of course. If they're contemplating a war now, when another club member bitch, especially a Sons is taken, the proverbial shit will hit the fan. Those crazy bikers will be shooting each other in the street. There will be blood and mayhem. The citizens of Las Vegas will be begging for more gun control and enhanced control of these damn gangs that are taking over our great city. They will blame the current administration and demand there be change. They will want a new sheriff to keep their streets safe. That new sheriff will be me. And, Phil, drop off some of my favorite recipe at the house. Cash will be in the mailbox." The line went dead.

Vegas Phil recorded, downloaded, and saved the conversation. He recorded all his conversations, texts, emails, even a few pictures of himself with the sheriff.

In the restroom of the coffee shop, Vegas Phil satisfied his mid-morning craving. His eyes watered after he took a hit, then he repeatedly sniffed at the air as he threw his head back. He looked in the mirror, just a few more scores like this biker gal in Laughlin and his gambling debt would be gone. He had not placed a bet in weeks.

Finally, his regulars were providing consistent income, the drug-money cut from Jonesy was paying off. He was only drinking a few days a week and hadn't been to a strip club in a month. His favorite prostitute was still a weekly attraction, but last time he was with her, she gave him a reduced rate. Things were looking up.

This time, he was going to turn his life around, maybe even pay some child support so he could see his kids again. This time, the guy staring back at him with the 45-year-old reflection in the mirror was going clean. He snorted another line of coke, leaving Starbucks with a complimentary refill of straight black. He was ready for the drive to Laughlin.

CHAPTER

18

Jose Orlando placed his phone in the holder of his belt. His gaze swept the official election headquarters of Jose Orlando "The Sheriff" for Mayor. The candidate's headquarters was in a nearly empty strip mall just south of Las Vegas Boulevard. The location was a convenient two-minute walk from the police precinct where he once worked.

Jose raised his head, a bright white smile on his face. His upper lip was covered with dark black hair that matched the thick wave on his head. In his mid-thirties, the former Las Vegas police officer was looking far beyond being the city's next mayor to his future role as governor, or perhaps the next Harry Reid and a life-long member of the senate.

Patience was a virtue—of which Jose had none. He wanted the whole world and he wanted it now.

Having retired from his role as police officer with the Las Vegas PD, Jose was all in with his run for mayor. With the ever-increasing Las Vegas Hispanic population driving his candidacy, Jose saw the opportunity and jumped at the chance for political advancement. He had the support of many local Hispanic businessmen, the Las Vegas Police Department, local celebrities like Mike Tyson and a non-voting Celine Dion, as well as the great Harry Reid himself.

What Jose felt he needed was not a Trump-type Twitter circus but a real city emergency, a real-time threat to the wonderful law-abiding citizens of Las Vegas. The threat of guns, the threat of school violence, increasing drug use, and the consistent danger emanating from several gangs all fed his TV, radio, and social media posts.

These threats are what scared the people of Las Vegas, not climate change. Hell, it will always be hot in Las Vegas. His community was content with employment opportunities and history had proven time and again that people with or without money could and would find a way to Vegas.

He needed a 9-11, a Hurricane Katrina, a Chicago fire, a tragic event that could sweep him into office. With his background as a police officer, it was the role of sheriff that would set Jose Orlando apart from the aging white incumbent.

"We are polling ten points behind Mayor Alfred Duke. We win this primary and we get the democratic nomination. Then we are a shoo-in for mayor," Jose said to his staff of eighteen people. He made it a point to make eye contact with each of the eleven men and seven women.

Jose was excellent at public speaking. His staff, mostly Hispanic, were sitting starry eyed, admiring their mayoral hopeful.

"The people of Las Vegas—Hispanic, White, Black, Asian—are responding to your message, Jose. They want safer streets, safer schools. We will defeat Duke!" his chief of staff yelled out. The others cheered and clapped.

"Each day, someone in this beautiful city is the victim of gang and gun violence. Get me their names. Get me their stories. That is how we will win. We must use their tragedies to promote our agenda. Now go. Find me someone, find me the story that will lift us ten points."

Jose felt energized but exhausted. He needed to relax, to clean his spirit. He drove ten minutes to his home, in the leased BMW 500 series sedan, onto the circular driveway facing his brick home. He walked to the mailbox. There on the floor of the loaf-shaped container was what he was longing for.

Jose removed the package, a small box missing stamps and postal markings. This package was not delivered by the United States Postal Service.

He stood over a black-and-gray granite countertop, the kitchen sink behind him. He opened the cardboard box with a butter knife. Inside the package he found a plastic bag containing grade A pre-rolled marijuana cigarettes. He found a Bic lighter in the top kitchen drawer among the small tools, stamps, batteries, envelops, thumb tacks, Post-it notes, and paper clips.

Jose lit the cigarette, inhaling as deeply as he could. He held his breath as long as possible, exhaling slowing on purpose. He closed his eyes and let the organic, natural drug do what it was intended to do. Jose relaxed.

A few minutes later, the would-be mayor finished his "medication." Jose sprayed himself with Axe Body Spray from top to bottom, brushed his teeth in the kitchen sink, then drove to the county courthouse for a scheduled impromptu live interview.

He parking his car in visitor parking. The roving reporter, Gloria Benson of the Live Action Five crew, met him on the front steps. The two hugged, then Gloria introduced Jose to her camera man. The "Live" interview would be covering a recent shooting at a local grade school.

Gloria checked her makeup with a handheld mirror, applied a bright-red gloss to her lips, and puffed her breasts into place. She looked down to see if the matching pair was symmetrical. While she prepped, Orlando went to the courthouse's second tier of steps.

On que, Gloria began, "Stan, thank you for letting us break into your normally scheduled broadcast." She paused for several seconds. "Welcome, Las Vegas. We are here today live for Live Action Five. Let's see if we can catch mayoral hopeful Jose Orlando exiting the Justice Center. The site of recent legal posturing regarding the shooting at Harlan Elementary. Mr. Orlando! Mr. Orlando, just a few words, please."

The cameraman zoomed his lens out, allowing Gloria to "chase" Orlando several steps. Jose stopped abruptly, seemingly aggravated by the interruption.

The cameraman zoomed back in. Gloria continued, pretending to be slightly out of wind, her chest pumping. "Mr. Orlando. They call you the sheriff. What would you recommend to prevent future tragedies like Harlan?" She pushed the microphone under Jose's nose.

"First of all, Gloria, my thoughts and prayers to the children, family, and friends of Harlan Elementary. What a brave group of young men and women. They are our future. I am so proud how these young children have rallied for their peers in spirit and action. Second, let me say this to our citizens of Las Vegas. Under my watch, the watch of Jose Orlando, we will not tolerate gun violence. We will disarm criminals. We will protect our children. Under Jose Orlando's guidance, security in Vegas will increase and with the increase in security comes a decrease in crime. Your children, our children, our future will be able to attend school as they should – in peace, in safety, and in a culture to learn."

A short pause.

"Not a culture of fear like our current mayor has allowed. With Jose Orlando, you will have a new sheriff in town. Thank you, Gloria."

The cameraman turned his attention to his anchor, with a background view of Jose walking away with his head lowered, hands clasped as in prayer. Gloria was in her bright-red dress with lowcut front made for a very pleasing closeup, perhaps negating the slumping Jose.

"There you have it, Las Vegas. Jose Orlando, the new sheriff in town, brings hope for our children, hope for our future." Another long pause. "Stan, we have time for a few Live Quick Questions if you have any Tweeters or texters."

"Yes Gloria. Stan here from Live Action Five Headquarters. We will scroll the tweet, live!"

The tweet message scrolled on the bottom of a TV screen while Gloria Benson read it "live."

"Our first Tweet reads, "We love you, Jose!" Gloria responded, "We love you, too!"

Gloria continued, "Next, we have our first text! It reads, "Jose, you talked a lot, but you didn't say anything. Mayor Duke."

The news anchor placed the microphone to her lips, her other hand on her hip as the cameraman pulled back, a full-figured view of Gloria Benson.

Gloria said, "Seems the incumbent mayor figured out how to text, still working on that Twitter account, huh, Mayor?"

A third long pause.

"This is Gloria Benson, live from Live action Five."

19

It was midafternoon when Rashid awoke, still in the same robe, lying on the same bean bag chair. He was hungry and itching for his new Latina toy. His hunger was his priority. Using his cell phone, the obese man dialed Abdul. The phone rang several times then went to voice mail. Rashid raised his chin in the air and screamed for his bodyguard.

Abdul was lying naked between the twins. Both girls were unconscious, victims of heroin injections that rendered them comatose. He had finished having his way with the teenagers and his desires had been satisfied. He was now frowning over the phone call and the incessant yelling and whining from his boss and master.

Abdul dressed, then carried the twins, one under each arm, from his bedroom to the dog kennels. He covered the girls with thin white sheets, laying them gently on their mattresses. The looks he received from the stoned blonde and revived Mexican girl were loathsome, hatred in their eyes. He smiled at his caged captives and ascended the stairs to Rashid's room.

Rashid wanted a breakfast pizza from Casey's gas station. Abdul suspected this, as Casey's was Rashid's favorite.

Abdul had several triple meats in the refrigerator anticipating the order. He set the oven to 385 degrees, cleaned and dusted the countertops before placing the pizza on the oven's top rack to be re-warmed.

He also prepared a cocktail for his boss, made of Ketel One Vodka, cranberry and pineapple juice, and two crushed Viagra tablets sprinkled into the mix. He delivered the cocktail first.

Rashid did not know of the sexual performance enhancers. Abdul added the ED drug, thinking perhaps if the fat man could perform, he would not be so rough with the girls. Abdul was liking the twins.

Two vodka concoctions and an entire large pizza later, Rashid ordered the Mexican to be delivered to his stage.

Abdul thought his boss would want the twins; they were still drugged but able to dance, albeit in slow motion.

He ran down the steps. The Latina girl named Maria was awake, hungover and detoxing from last night's injection but aware enough to ask Abdul what was going on, when could she leave, what day was it? She threatened Abdul that her father would kill him unless he released her.

Maria stepped back, edging to the rear of the cage. She did not want another shot. She wanted to stay alert. She wanted to fight back. She wanted out of the kennel and to be in the warm Las Vegas sun.

"You must take this," Abdul said, handing her a pill. "You do not want to remember what is going to happen to you."

"No!" Maria screamed. "Please, just let me go. My father will spare you if you let me go."

"Please, take this. If you fight him, he will hurt you."

"Like you've hurt me? You don't think I remember you on top of me, the pain in my groin? My father will kill you."

"Fine, do as you please." Abdul unlocked the kennel gate, grabbing Maria by the arm. He slapped her hard. She tried to fall to the floor, but Abdul held her up. "You will thank me for that. Just do what he says."

Maria stubbled on stage, her right eye swelling from Abdul's slap. Her eyes were out of focus. The man in front of her was fuzzy, a large hazy outline of a very obese man.

Maria was naked. Abdul had torn the dress off her as she went to the platform. Music was playing. Tony Bennett.

"Dance, my dear," Rashid commanded. "Dance sexy for me and daddy will treat you well."

Maria stayed still, leaning against the stripper pole, both hands gripping the metal. "Screw your fat ass."

"Oh, I love it when you talk dirty to me. Tell me more," Rashid said.

Maria slid to the floor pulling her knees to her chest, her arms wrapping them tightly.

"I like the view. Now come to me."

Maria did not move.

"I said come to me. Now!" Rashid yelled, leaning forward. With his enormous belly, Abdul could not see if the medication was working.

Maria did not move.

Rashid grabbed his walking cane, swinging it like a baseball bat. The metal cane connected with the side of Maria's head. She slowly slid to her side, her legs straightening out, then rolled to her back. Blood streamed from a cut above her ear.

Abdul left to get a towel, water, and a mop.

Rashid grabbed Maria's leg and yanked her toward him and his bean bag chair. Pulling with both hands on one of her legs, he brought her to him, her legs at awkward angles. He tried to mount her. He was not able to stand, not able to get his body on top of the unconscious girl.

Abdul returned. "Rashid, I may have to take this one to the hospital."

"Place her on me. I must have her," Rashid demanded as he laid back on his chair, not caring of his nakedness.

Abdul picked up Maria, laying her on the fat man, her blood dripping on Rashid's chest. The large man squirmed, thrusted, and grunted to no avail. He was too fat for sex.

Rashid pushed Maria to the floor, yelling in disbelief. "Take me to my bath. Take this, this whore, to the desert. I no longer want her in my house."

Leaving the girl on the floor, Abdul got the cart, something one would find at Menards, Home Depot, or Lowe's. A cart used by workmen to carry bags of fertilizer, mulch, bricks, or concrete blocks. Abdul had the flat surface of the eight-wheeled cart covered with a soft foam and cloth.

He rolled Rashid onto the cart. Pushing with all he had, he directed the cart down the hall and into the bath area. Abdul placed large soft towels on the floor, rolling his boss from the cart to the towels. When Rashid regained his breath, he logrolled into the sunken tub.

Abdul waited for Rashid's head to emerge from the water. Still gasping for air, he rolled his head to the side, his hair following the motion.

"I will take care of the girl. Enjoy your bath as I clean the stage," Abdul said.

"Get me another pizza. And wine. I want my merlot."

Abdul found Maria where he left her. He had seen cuts like that on the side of her head before, and he knew it would require stiches or leave a nasty scar. He retrieved hydrogen peroxide and white gauge bandages from a medical kit on the tool cart. He cleaned Maria as best as he could, covering the gash with bandage and wrapped white athletic tape around her head. She looked like an Olympic wrestler.

Carrying Maria to her kennel, she groaned in pain as her eyes again tried to focus just like before she passed out. Tomorrow, she would have two black eyes, a severe headache, perhaps a concussion.

Abdul admired her young, hard body. He wanted her now. The whining and screaming from Rashid once again robbed him of one of the few benefits of his employment. Laying Maria on her mattress, he gave her a kiss on the forehead, his hands examining her body. Three of his four pets were unconscious.

Perhaps the biker girl would do. He looked her over. She frowned. She was sweating and twitching. White spittle formed on the sides of her mouth. She needed a shot.

"I'll be back for you, blondie. I bet you taste better than you look," Abdul said, leaving the room.

20

A phone vibrated on the nightstand. The rattling echoed in his head, the sound of jet engines ripping between his ears. Salas was hungover. In the bed next to him, Doris and Ronnie groaned in unison, their backs facing the other's.

Ronnie asked, begged Salas to turn off the noise.

Salas sat up, letting his feet touch the floor. It took a few seconds for Salas to recall where he was, the city, the hotel, the bedroom—which, by the way, smelled disgusting.

He took inventory of the situation: he had his jeans on, the button undone, the zipper down. He wore no shirt, his left foot was in a boot, the right foot in a white sock. He could not see his other shoe.

The window curtain was pulled to the left. He could see the tops of green trees as the sun warmed the room. The TV was on Fox News, Cavuto proclaiming the low unemployment numbers and a booming Trump economy.

Salas rubbed his eyes and stumbled to the bathroom. Twenty minutes later, he emerged showered, somewhat refreshed and in need of water.

He grabbed the corner of the bedspread and sheets, then threw the covers off Doris and Ronnie, both still dressed in yesterday's clothes.

Ronnie had a pool of vomit on his side of the bed that matched the urine smell and wet spot on Doris's side of the mattress.

She was now flat on her back, snoring, with a dark blue patch over her private parts. Salas's investigative skills detected the sources of the foul odors.

Salas checked his phone, the culprit that started this new day in motion. He had a missed call from Toni, a voice mail, most likely from Toni, several texts from Toni, and two texts from RJ.

He opened Toni's texts first. More selfies with beautiful smiles. A quote "Missing someone is part of loving them. If you are never apart, you will never know how strong your love is."

Salas was falling for this woman and it appears she was falling for him.

He opened the texts from RJ. Both requested Salas to use his connections to get information. Salas forwarded the texts to Ronnie.

A soft "ding" notified Salas and Ronnie. The message was received.

"Ronnie, get up," Salas said. "We need you to do some computer work before we ride out."

"No, Mike. I'm staying here for a couple of days." Ronnie mumbled into his pillow.

"Up, now. You, too, Doris. And, guys, if I get stuck buying new carpet or a new mattress, you two are on the bill."

Ronnie did as Salas said, and inspected his surroundings while lying on his back. The room, his hands—he counted his fingers. He looked for his clothes. He looked for Doris. He slowly sat up, placing his feet on the floor.

"Ugghh, somebody threw up over here."

"That somebody was you, junior." Salas was already dressed, ready to exit the room, breakfast on his mind.

"My mouth feels like ten buffalo ran through it and the last two stopped and took a shit." Ronnie looked at Doris. "You peed the bed, honey."

"Wasn't me," Doris said in what kind of resembled English.

"Shower and do the computer stuff for RJ. I texted it to you." Salas left.

Ronnie helped Doris stand, take off her clothes, helped her brush her teeth and enter the shower. Thankfully, it was a walk-in. He adjusted the water temperature to warm, nearly hot. Ronnie felt secure that Doris was standing on her own, her left hand on the wall, right hand on her hip. While she showered, Ronnie addressed the texts.

He forwarded both messages to the laptop he carried in his backpack, easier to do research from the computer than a cell phone. Within twenty minutes, Ronnie had the video recordings for the date, time, and location given. He sent them to RJ's and Salas's phone with a link to view the video. He then joined Doris in the shower.

Salas was on his fifth glass of orange juice, his second cup of coffee, his first banana, and his sixth pancake when the phone vibrated again. He opened the text and the link.

The first video link was of a street corner and a biker sitting on his Harley. The bike was chromed out, ape hangers, fishtail pipes, custom paint. The left blinker was on. No helmet on the rider. A brown, rusted van passes, turning to the left, crossing in front of the bike.

Salas did not know why he was watching this or what he was looking for when a handgun is thrust out the van driver's side window and white flashes flare from the gun barrel. The man riding the Harley gets hit in the chest, the impact of the bullet tossing him back, forcing his hands off the handlebar's clutch and throttle.

The black-and-silver bike lurches forward with both bike and biker leaning to the right. Even in real time, the two move in slow motion, slowly falling to the ground, the biker's head bouncing off the street.

The van drives out of sight. The stop light turns from red to green. No cars move.

"You got to be shitting me," were Salas's words.

Salas watched it again, and a third and fourth time. He could not make out the license plate of the van or the exact make and model of the rusted-out brown vehicle. With each replay, Salas narrowed his focus on the falling biker, his colors, and the vest patch of the Pagans.

Another slow rewind and review. The first shot was a direct hit to the man's chest. That shot was most likely the kill shot. The second and third kicks of the handgun were shots fired, but Salas could not tell if they hit the biker or not. Salas cringed each time the man's head dribbled off the concrete like a basketball. He pushed away his remaining pancakes.

He opened the next text, again a click with a link to a video. Salas allowed time for the film to load to his phone, then hit play. The scene was dark and grainy, the camera perhaps fifty yards from the intersection.

Salas took a sip of his coffee.

Two bikers, both riding Harleys, pass in front of the camera. Hells Angels patches on the backs of both the riders' vests. One vest in full colors, the other a prospect patch. The prospect, a young man driven to prove himself to his friends, his buddies, his family. The two bikes slow to a stop, their feet settling on the pavement.

Salas could see the two men talking while waiting at the light that was stuck on red. Given the distance, the camera was not set to watch the east/west traffic. This camera was set to monitor north-to-south movements—the Harleys sitting at the edge of the screen.

On this video, Salas was prepared for the next event. The recording offered no audio, so the sudden movement of the two bikers still took him by surprise. The two men were hurled backwards, reminiscent of the prior video. Their hands leave the motorcycle chrome grips, their bodies thrown to the right, both bikes leaning, tilting, then falling to their sides as the riders' legs gave way.

The prospect was hit first, his head snapping back. This bike fell into the Hells Angel member on his right. The video captured the member biker's shoulder rolling away from the prospect. He fell with extended arms as he hit the asphalt. The biker landed chin first.

Again, Salas viewed the video four, then five times. With each view, Salas made mental notes: the way they fell, where they were shot, the vehicles in front, to the side, and to the rear of the two bikes.

Salas zoomed the video to the intersection. The passing auto, the car where the shots came from, was not visible to the camera. He could see black tires with white sidewalls and a rusted-out running board. No additional clues, no plates, no people, no help.

Salas shut off the videos. Using his phone for its intended purpose, he made a call. The phone rang twice before it was answered.

"Fort Wayne Police. Detective's unit. Gary Andrews speaking. How may I help you?"

"Gary. Salas here. Need a favor."

"Salas. You got it. How is vacation?"

"Hungover, so it must be good. Tell me, you think you can check with Las Vegas PD, ask them about a couple of recent street shootings? A Pagan and two Angels. Ask if they have any leads, witness statements, anything to work off," Salas said.

"Sure. What is a pagan?"

"A motorcycle club," Salas answered.

"What do I tell them when they ask why I want to know?" Gary asked.

"Tell them one of the guys that was shot was a relative of mine. I need some closure. It'd be nice if they could tell me who did it and why. Text me and Ronnie what you get." The call was over.

Salas gathered his ragged-looking riding partners. Doris put a bottle of Advil to her mouth, dropping several tablets in, chewing them up, then downing the chalky substance with coffee.

Ronnie was in place as the passenger on Doris' bike. He was looking at his cell phone and the videos Salas had requested.

"My ass hurts. I still have monkey butt from yesterday," Ronnie said, then showed his cell phone to Salas and asked. "Who are the dead guys?"

"Clubbers. One-percenters who did not make it. RJ wants to know what happened to them. The Vegas PD reports will be coming soon. Read them over when you get them."

Doris spoke up. "We got a straight shot on I-40 to Laughlin. Should take us seven hours or so. Five hundred miles. An easy ride."

"Should be there in time for happy hour," Salas said.

"Not me. I'm never drinking again," came from Ronnie.

"Me, neither. I might become a nun," came from Doris.

CHAPTER

21

RJ rested quietly in bed, gently kissing Shelli's shoulder, and the back of her neck. Her warm body raised more than his temperature, waking her up. Now that he had her attention, the new couple spent more time getting to know each other.

Mission accomplished.

The center of RJ's world was ready to implode while he was getting laid.

Afterwards, Shelli made coffee wearing a short silk robe left open in the front while RJ reviewed the link he received by text message from Salas. He clicked on the URL, and the videos loaded while he inspected the woman bringing him coffee.

The small screen of the cell phone made it difficult to see fine details. He hesitated, considering asking Shelli to let him use her home computer and much larger screen to view the videos. RJ pushed the thought aside, not wanting Shelli to be involved in any way.

As RJ started the videos, he again glanced at Shelli. He had so many questions to ask her. Did she know what her late husband did or what he used to do? Did she know he was a member of the Sons? Did she know Zeke was an enforcer? They had heard Zeke was killed in an accident here in Vegas years after he dropped out of the club. Did he drop out for her? Did he leave his brothers and start a new life away from the club? Was he living two lives? Books. How did Zeke get into books? What did she know? What did she want to know?

RJ paused, clicked the backwards arrow, rewinding the video. He could see men die—that was most disturbing—but not much else was visible. He did not know what he was looking for. Perhaps a large red arrow pointing to the killer.

By phone and text, RJ reconnected with Nellie, Scooter, and Soldier. The three club presidents understood Manny's desire for revenge and need to find his lost daughter. The men also agreed Manny was unstable and willing to lead his club into an all-out war over his personal loss.

Leveraging his success in getting the Pagan and Outlaw released from Manny, RJ bought more time. So far, Manny had not made a move on Hells Angels, but rumors were swirling. RJ was hoping Salas would have more insight, more intel for him to get Manny off the warpath.

RJ heard the sliding glass door open, then something falling into the pool. RJ followed the splashing noise. He walked past the open sliding glass door leading to the pool area.

Shelli was swimming laps, the breaststroke. When she made the turn, her head went underwater, her bottom flashing in the mid-morning sun. She was naked. RJ dropped his boxers and waded chest-deep into the water. He could dog paddle, maybe swim enough to save his life, but he preferred solid ground. She swam past him, gliding in the saltwater mixture.

Another turn, bottoms up, and then back towards RJ. She stopped underwater, facing him, staying there for a long period of time. Soon they were back at it, in the pool, another round of getting to know each other.

RJ showered while Shelli finished the swim workout that he had interrupted. He dressed, laced up his boots, hiding his handgun from Shelli. She met him at the door, the silk robe back in place, tied shut in front.

She followed him to the driveway. His motorcycle was leaning to the left on the kickstand. He turned and faced her. They embraced. RJ wanted to kiss his girl goodbye. He thought about the words "his girl."

He had not thought of any woman in those terms in years. They kissed a long passionate, groping, engulfing kiss that slowed passing traffic.

RJ came up for air. He looked into Shelli's eyes. "I like you Shelli. I would like us. Us, you and me, to see each other again," he said.

Shelli smiled. "After you did the Titanic exhibit, I kind of figured you had a thing for me."

"So, the Titanic was a test, huh?"

"You passed."

They kissed again.

"I have so many questions for you," RJ said.

"You knew Zeke, didn't you?" Shelli asked.

"Uh. Yes, I did. Like twenty years ago. I didn't place him at first. It was the beard. I met him several times. Then I was in and out of prison. I heard he left the club. Died in an accident."

"Zeke lived for years in Colorado, never grew a beard. Moves to Las Vegas, where it's 100 degrees half the year, and grows a beard. Go figure."

"Maybe he wanted a new look, hiding the past."

"He mentioned your name once. When I saw your vest and you said your name, I knew it was you."

"Zeke was way higher up than me. I was Deuce's guard," RJ said.

"Zeke said you went to jail for Deuce. That you saved Deuce's life. Zeke was supposed to be there. He was running late, got to the bar, Deuce was beat to shit, and you were taking care of business. Zeke said he got Deuce and got out of there before the cops came," Shelli said.

She added, "Ya know, Zeke left the club for me. He left his friends, his family for me. I don't know what all Zeke did, but he didn't like it anymore. When Zeke's father died, he inherited some money, and the books. So, he left Denver and stayed here with me in Vegas. We met at the Lucky. We had a great run. Then, one day, he tells me he bumped into an 'old friend' at the bar," Shelli said, doing the finger quotes at "old friend."

"Zeke told me that he and the 'friend,'"—finger quotes again—"had issues in the past. I remember the guy was a member of the Lifers. Zeke said they were a small gang, not a club. The next day, Zeke was killed in an accident. Rode his Harley into a building off the highway. No witnesses. Police never followed up. They said he must have lost control. No way Zeke lost control of his Harley. It was a part of him – like an arm or a leg."

"I've heard of the Lifers. Their mottos were: 'Lifestyle determines death style' and 'An eye for an eye.' Their goal was a gory, violent death to promote their gory, violent life. They lived hard, to die even worse. I heard they had closed down."

"Per Zeke, the guy four years ago still had his colors. And didn't like the Sons."

"Ever see any Lifers at the Lucky?" RJ asked.

"No. I bought the place when it came up for sale because we met there. But also because I wanted a Lifer to come in. I don't know what I would have done. But I keep a gun behind the bar. I don't know, just stupid I guess."

"Not stupid. I get it. Thank you for sharing with me, Shelli." He leaned in and kissed her again.

"Call me sometime. I would like for us to be an us, too." Shelli patted RJ on the butt when he turned to his bike.

RJ mounted his Harley, waving at Shelli as he rode away. She blew him a kiss. His destination: Laughlin. And a reunion with Mike Salas.

The hundred-mile ride out of Las Vegas started out on Interstate 11. RJ hoped for less drama than his ride to the Luxor the day before. He rarely used the get-back whip; yesterday was an anomaly.

Traffic was light, the scenery gray, overcast, and dry. RJ was in no hurry, and kept under the posted speed limits. He needed the time on his bike. Nothing like the road, the wind in his face, the concrete blurring underneath to get his mind uncluttered and refocused.

He kept to the right, merging off Interstate 11 on to Highway 95, Veterans Memorial Highway. He stopped at a Terrible Herbst for fuel, crossing the street to Gus's Really Good Jerky. He chewed on the dried meat as he rode. It was really good.

As he rode, his mind wandered to Manny' daughter, the street shootings of two different club members, the missing Hells Angel woman. Four Vegas club hits in too short a timeframe. RJ did not believe in coincidences. The events had to be related. Somebody wanted the clubs to go to war. Manny was the first to take the bait.

Turning left off 95 to Highway 163, RJ rode the final stretch to Laughlin. He rode straight to Harrah's and parked his bike in the covered parking garage. He first checked into his room, then went to the bar, ordered a Negra Modelo.

He sat and thought of the Sons, Manny, Scooter, Nellie, Soldier, then back to Shelli. He wanted her, over them. He watched the flowing border between Nevada and Arizona called the Colorado River

Waiting for Salas and his crew, RJ reviewed the videos. Again, nothing stood out to him. As the sun was setting in the west, RJ ordered from the bar menu. Korean lettuce wraps, his first real vegetable for the week. He didn't really like the thought and the necessity of watching his roughage, prostate count, and cholesterol levels. He ordered another beer.

CHAPTER

22

Manny was sitting in a rusted-out 1977 Dodge Power Wagon. He had been sitting in the same position for several hours. The Wagon's V8 motor was shut off, the truck parked under an imported elm tree not native to the area. The tree's budding leaves provided minimal shade, but the setting sun allowed the interior of the truck to cool.

He sat low in the seat, watching large men with black vests go in and out of the Hells Angels' only property in Las Vegas. The property was a one-story white concrete building with an asphalt shingled roof. Located on the north east edge of Las Vegas, it was far away from suburbia.

The subdivision featured multiple warehouses, fenced-in lots protecting large construction equipment, and several storage facilities featuring rent by the day, week, or month.

In his rearview mirror, Manny could see Rojas approaching the back of the Dodge pickup. He had brown Styrofoam cups with white lids in each hand. He was wearing a yellow hard hat and a reflective vest proclaiming to be the property of Las Vegas Public Parks and Recreation.

Rojas opened the passenger door of the truck and handed Manny a coffee.

"You been here all day, Manny. Let's go back to the club," Rojas said.

Manny ignored the comment and said, "The best time to hit this place, Rojas, is between eight and nine tomorrow night."

"We should place teams of four, here and there," Manny said pointing to the left and right of the metal gate and entrance of the warehouse. He took a sip of the coffee, pursed his lips, and blew on the lid.

"At nine, there will be the maximum number of men in the building. They are lazy, too confident. They have no spotters, no one watching the street. I say we toss those hand grenades we got from the Russians over the back fence. That way, they will be running out towards us right here. They will be in our crossfire. We hit them hard, with everything we got. Then run."

"Please, Manny. Listen to me, my friend. Yes, we will win this battle, but we will lose the war. The Angels will come back at us in full force."

"There are only twenty, maybe twenty-five, men in there. We will decimate them, Rojas."

"But, Manny, there are twenty-five hundred Angels across the United States. They will bring them all here to eliminate us. They will never give up until they track us down and kill all of us."

"They have my Maria. I must make them pay!" Manny shouted across the cab of the truck, pounding on the consul.

"They do not have your daughter, Manny. You know it and I know it. If they had her, they would want money, want our product, or tell us to leave Las Vegas."

"You know nothing, Rojas. They are sitting there nice and quiet, laughing at me. I saw it in prison. They laugh behind your back, too scared to confront you."

"No, Manny. And I'm going to prove it." Rojas got out of the Dodge Wagon. He walked away from Manny, towards the Hells Angels compound.

"Where are you going, Rojas?" Manny yelled out from the window. He then got out of the truck.

"I'm going to ask them. Enough of this guessing and planning and scheming. Your conspiracy theory is crazy talk, Manny."

Manny stayed by the Dodge as Rojas tossed the yellow hard hat and vest on the burnt grass below the elm tree. Rojas's Devil's vest was now in full view: three patches on the back, name and logo on the front.

Manny watched as Rojas walked alone towards the grounds of the Hells Angels headquarters. He walked with confidence, the swagger of the wrestler he once was.

Getting in the truck and shutting the pickup door behind him, Manny leaned to his right, opening the glove box and removing a .45 caliber Smith and Wesson handgun. He checked the weapon – it was locked and loaded. Starting the pickup, he put the truck in drive, inching forward, following his vice president.

Rojas walked past the open gate, now officially on the grounds of 81 (the "8" for H, the eighth letter of the alphabet and initial of Hell, and the "1" for A, the first letter and initial of Angels).

Rojas was now an uninvited guest on private property. An armed uninvited guest. On the property of an opposing club. A club the Devils considered an enemy. A club Manny had let known he was going to attack. A club on the lookout for anyone wearing the Devil's logo.

Manny watched as three men in blue jeans, thick boots, black vests, and dark sunglasses came out of the metal building. They were crouching low, fanning out in a straight line towards Rojas. Each Angel carried a weapon pointed at Rojas: a pistol, a shotgun, an Uzi. He heard one yell.

"You! Stop. Drop to the ground. On your belly. Do it. Now!"

Manny could not speak. He stopped the truck; he could not move. The world stopped rotating. Everything was in slow motion. Manny watched as Rojas reached with his right arm, to his rear pocket. Rojas was starting to raise the arm when shots were fired.

Rojas stood firm. Their bullets hit him in the chest, his abdomen, his legs, yet he stayed standing. His arm came up. Rojas waived a bandanna at the five men. A white bandanna swept right to left. Rojas dropped to both knees, the white flag still waiving. Rojas fell face down.

Manny screamed, "Rojas!"

His foot drove the accelerator pedal to the floor of the truck. The Dodge lurched forward, the tires squealing in protest. Manny cranked the steering wheel hard right. His left arm was out the window, the .45 barking out, the concrete spitting puffs of white chalk into the air. The three Angels fired back, splattering the rear quarter panel of the old truck with bullets and shotgun pellets.

He kept the Power Wagon at full speed, the engine grunting discomfort at 70 miles per hour as the truck climbed the ramp onto Interstate 15. Tears streamed down Manny's cheeks as he drove.

After several miles, he realized no Hells Angels were giving chase. Manny kept the Dodge at full throttle, speeding past Nellis Air Force Base, taking Highway 93 to the desert, towards Coyote Springs.

Manny turned the steering wheel hard to the right, onto a dirt side road going north to nowhere. He drove for miles, the truck jumping and jerking from side to side on the sandy road. A cloud of dust marking his trail. He was sweating, crying, screaming at no one. Manny slammed on the brakes, then shoved the transmission into park as a cloud of dust settled around him.

Without hesitation, Manny placed the barrel of the .45 to his temple. He screamed in agony as he pulled the trigger. The gun responded with a loud click. He pulled the trigger again and again. More clicks followed. The gun was empty, out of ammunition.

Manny tossed the empty handgun to the floor of the pickup. He placed his head in his hands and cried, sobbing uncontrollably.

His phone rang, interrupting his breakdown. He looked at the text message. It was from RJ.

The text read, "Don't attack. We got him. We identified the guy that took your Maria."

CHAPTER

23

Vegas Phil parked his inheritance behind the Hidden Agenda Bar and Grill in Laughlin. The sun was setting as he backed the VW van in place, the cracked side mirrors guiding his path. The van's passenger sliding door was left open, facing the bar's loading dock.

Inside the van, the rear seats were missing. Yellow piss stains highlighted the twin mattress covering the metal floor. The side and rear windows were shaded by dark adhesive tinting, secured with silver tape, both purchased at an area Walmart.

Jonesy met Phil on the dock. Phil handed his partner a grocery bag filled with enough product to meet Jonesy's physical needs and pay for his expenses for the rest of the month. For tonight's transaction, there was no cash exchanged.

Phil kept the substantial double-booking fee from the sheriff and Rashid, while the bartender settled for chump change. Vegas Phil marveled at his economic genius.

Phil followed the surfer dude inside the Hidden Agenda, taking a round barstool as a seat behind the bar. From his current location, with his back against the wall, the door to the loading dock within easy access, he could scan the floor for opportunities or an early exit.

The crowd was picking up – locales, travelers, tourists, bikers. A good mix of each. Phil studied the crowd, looking for the ideal candidate, one to meet the needs of the sheriff, Rashid, and, yes, Abdul. He knew the strong man tasted all the samples.

The two men, Phil and Jonesy, dressed in similar terms: cargo shorts with large side pockets containing their wallets and cell phones, topped off with collared polos in bright colors. Vegas Phil's shirt was yellow with a green alligator and Jonesy's tomato red sported a UNLV cowboy logo.

The full-time bartender kept sunglasses on his head, pulling his long hair back behind his ears. Phil's hair was unkempt: bedhead, helmet head, and dirty, greasy head all rolled into one. Both men had three to four days of facial stubble.

Jonesy poured Phil a complimentary pint of Boulevard Wheat, an orange slice dangling off the lip of the glass. Phil drained half the beer with his first sip. He ordered a dozen boneless wings, another gift from the owner of the Hidden Agenda who did not know and had never met the man from Vegas.

More people stumbled in as the sun disappeared over the horizon. The white glow of streetlights shone down on the red, green, and yellow neon signs of the bar, enticing people to go inside. The barstools filled first, by a row of suntanned faces, mostly men staring at their cell phones or at ESPN on flatscreens. Phil stood, occasionally looking over the head tops, scanning for bikers, men wearing their club colors.

Many entered wearing vests. Phil ignored the clubs proclaiming they were Bikers for Jesus and the Disciple Christians. There were several local Wild Hog types dressed in glossy new black leather chaps, pressed bandannas, spit-shined boots with vest patches proclaiming "Loud Pipes Save Lives," "I Rode Mine," "If you can read this, the bitch fell off," "Biker Lives Matter," and "Live to Ride, Ride to Live." Phil ignored these.

He whistled, using his thumb and index finger as a musical tool. Jonesy raised his head from cleaning shot glasses and looked in the direction his part-time boss was nodding to.

A large man with a ponytail, wearing a weathered vest showing off arms chiseled like the statue of David, came into the bar. The setting sun peaked through the door as he entered. The biker turned his back to Jonesy and Phil, pulling a table away from the wall. The back of the biker's vest, a three-patch representing the Sons of Silence.

A small, petite, yet muscular woman was hanging on the man's right arm. The woman wore tight jeans under faded leather butt-less chaps, dirty biker boots, and a pink tank top that was a size too small. She had large breasts for her size that rode high and firm minus a bra. On her head was a pink bandanna skull cap in Aunt Jemima style, with the words "Crazy Bitch" across her forehead.

Phil smiled at Jonesy and mouthed, "That's the one." He added a thumbs up. Jonesy nodded his understanding and approval.

The guy from the Sons of Silence politely asked neighboring tables for their empty chairs. He smiled as he approached, quickly garnering four stools. Two men joined the couple, one skinny with long hair who resembled Jim Morrison of the Doors, the other an MMA type, scarier looking than the Sons. Neither of the two new men wore colors. All four scanned a menu.

The Hidden Agenda's waitress staff consisted of two college-age females, perhaps students at Mohave Community College in Kingman, Arizona. The two girls looked the part, with their hair pulled back, Agenda T-shirts, and Nike running shoes. They hustled, doing the work of four as Jonesy kept drinks flowing and the cash register up to date.

Credit cards lined up on the back of the bar, names facing forward, bar tabs growing. Jonesy added phantom drinks to each card as the night played on.

Stephanie, the co-ed from Kingman, was the server for the new table of four drinkers. She took their orders, pushing the Long Island Iced Tea special. Spinning on her heals, she rushed back to the bar. Stephanie did not need to write down the orders but did anyway, more for Jonesy than her.

"Two Lake Tahoe Irish Stouts, a Pigeon's Red Eye, Cruzan Rum, and diet," Steph yelled at the bar before she turned, melting into the crowd. She was back seconds later.

"Two 16 Buds," Steph said as she picked up a round tray holding the stouts, the beer still settling from the draft, the Red Eye, and the mixed drink.

"Who ordered the rum?" Jonesy asked.

"Huh?" Stephanie asked, her eyebrows arched. Jonesy never asked who drank what and why.

"The rum? We don't get many asking for Cruzan."

"We get it all the time dude." Stephanie walked away, using her left arm as a shield, the tray held out.

Jonesy ignored the request for two Buds. He also ignored Janie, the other waitress who was asking for the whereabouts of Jack and Jim, both with diet. Jonesy watched as Steph sat the drinks on the table. The two big guys with the stouts. Made sense. The skinny guy with the Pigeon. Too easy of a stereotype. The little lady with the rum. Jonesy should have included an umbrella.

CHAPTER

24

Salas, Ronnie, and Doris rode the final 500 miles from New Mexico to Laughlin in record time. The last hundred miles, they followed a pasta rocket and rice burner, staying close at 90-plus miles per hour.

Turning off Interstate 40 at Kingman on Highway 93, the road linked to Highway 68 as the sun was setting. The pair pulled on to Bullhead Parkway, where they made a right crossing into the state of Nevada. Three states in one day.

On South Casino Drive, the two bikes followed the Colorado River to their left past the Outlet Center, Edgewater Casino, In-N-Out-Burger, the Tropicana, and Golden Nugget to Harrah's. They pulled into the covered parking garage, dropping their kickstands in an area reserved for motorcycles.

The three from Indiana checked in at the front desk. The reservation was under Salas's name. Again, they were sharing a room with two beds. They dropped their gear on the bedroom floor, refreshed with wet cloths, updated antiperspirant, and shared a can of Axe Body Spray.

Doris put on a new tank top, but the boys stayed in their riding gear. They were in the hotel bar within ten minutes of getting their room keys.

Salas saw RJ first. The two men met like old friends, a long chest to chest hug only comfortable men could enjoy. Introductions were made. Beer was ordered. Their pledges to never drink again quickly forgotten.

Happy hour at Harrah's bar included food. Salas ordered everyone sandwiches. The three men discussed the videos while Doris listened in. Ronnie ran the footage on his camera as they talked. Salas agreed with RJ that it was an attack on all clubs—separate events to get the clubs at each other's throats.

RJ surmised that the other clubs also had missing persons or dead bodies, they just did not know about them yet. Question was, who and why?

With the food gone and the sun setting, the four bikers needed a walk and a change of atmosphere. Harrah's was filling up with the over-65 crowd.

Salas was comfortable there, as was RJ. It was Doris and Ronnie who begged them to leave.

The four walked a couple of blocks, stepping into a neon-lit, yuppy-looking bar called the Hidden Agenda. Doris had her arm wrapped inside of RJ's while Ronnie had his face in his phone, reading the Las Vegas Police reports sent to him by Gary from Fort Wayne.

RJ pulled a high-top table away from the window so four chairs could be pulled around it. They sat, with Doris next to RJ. Salas and Ronnie compared notes.

Beers were ordered for everyone, except for Doris, who went for rum.

"Hey, guys. Let's do some shots!" Doris yelled.

"No!" came from Salas, Ronnie, and RJ.

RJ asked, "So, what do the reports say? Any suspects?"

"Nothing. Vegas PD has nothing on the shootings," Ronnie said. "No leads. No clues."

"What, police apathy? They don't give a shit. Bikers killing bikers. Let the clubs fight it out. One less biker to worry about," RJ said.

Salas countered, "Speaking as a cop, we don't think that way. We want justice. We do not care for whom or why. This tells me they got nothing. I'm sure they canvassed the scenes. Asked questions, took notes, interviewed everyone, and studied the same damn footage we did. RJ, you watched the videos. You notice anything? Get any ideas?"

"No. You're right. I couldn't see a thing. Only speculation and best guess. Most people will not talk if they think the shooter will come after them next. It's survival," RJ said.

"So, when you talked to the other clubs, no one is after anyone else?" Ronnie asked.

RJ responded, "Just the Devil's Brothers. Manny—the president—his daughter was abducted. No one knows by who. The Devils kidnapped some rival club members to get intel but got nothing. I was there earlier this week trying to keep the peace. I don't think it's a club hit."

Her rum was emptied, so Doris ordered another round. She could drink rum faster than the men could drain their beers. The second round of drinks arrived. Doris took a small sip then finished the cocktail with the next trip to her mouth.

Ronnie told her to pace herself. She gave him a snarl.

Doris left the three men to their discussion and walked to the DJ stationed at the left of the entrance of the bar. She requested anything by Benatar, Joan Jet, or Fleetwood Mac. After the request, she moved unsteadily to the front of the serving bar. The bartender gave her a glass of water upon request. The guy behind the bar leaning against the wall smiled at her. Doris returned the gesture, waving to him as she stumbled back to the high-top.

Standing next to Ronnie, Doris stood on her tiptoes and whispered in his ear. "I'm going to step outside and get some air. I'm feeling a little queasy."

"Ok, honey. You shouldn't drink that rum so fast. That would make anyone queasy." Ronnie kissed her bandanna-covered forehead before returning to the conversation.

Doris walked out the front entrance, bumping into people as she exited. Others stepped aside, thinking she was going to heave. She took deep breaths in and out, then leaned against the exterior red brick wall of the Agenda. She walked down the side alley to get away from the crowd, from the mocking laughter and rude comments about the drunk lady who was going to hurl in the alley.

The world was spinning way too fast for Doris when a man approached her, taking her under the arm. She tried to focus on him.

She recognized the guy as the one that had smiled at her earlier. She smiled at him.

"I don't feel so good," Doris slurred her words.

"No worries, honey. I have you. Come with me and lie down here. You need to rest." The man from behind the bar said as he led Doris deeper into the alley. He walked her to a van. The door was open. He laid Doris on her side inside the van as she passed out, her body a deadweight in his arms.

—⁓m⁓—

"I'm going to go outside and look for Doris, see if she's ok. Any of you guys get sick from the food? My stomach is churning a little. Maybe that's her problem?" Ronnie asked as he stood.

"No, I feel fine," Salas said.

"I'm good," RJ agreed.

Ronnie excused himself through the maze of people trying to enter as he tried to leave the establishment. Once outside, he looked left, then right. Seeing no one, he turned the corner at the alley. Again, his head on a swivel.

There by the loading dock of the bar, in the dim white light of a single bulb, he saw Doris going limp in a man's arms. The man rolled her into a van and slid the door shut.

Ronnie froze. He refused to believe what he was just seeing. He slowly walked forward, inching closer to the van, then broke into a slow jog, his arms up as the headlights of the van came on.

Ronnie yelled out for the van to stop. The driver went to high beam, blinding Ronnie as he approached. The van shot forward, striking Ronnie in the left shoulder as his head bounced off the side mirror. He fell hard to the ground on his butt.

Ronnie sat there as the vehicle rolled past him. He tried to focus as the van turned sharply out of the alley and out of sight.

Ronnie stood up, his nose bleeding from the impact with the vehicle's mirror. There was a red blotch on his forehead. His shoulder was numb. The driver-side front tire must have driven over his foot. It hurt to walk. He limped running back to the main street.

Ronnie looked side to side, but the van was nowhere to be seen. He pivoted on his good foot, hopping one-legged into the Hidden Agenda.

"Salas! Salas! Salas!" Ronnie yelled. RJ and Salas pushed their way to Ronnie. "Someone took Doris. They loaded her in a van and drove away!" Ronnie yelled over the crowd and the music.

"What? You got to be shitting me! Someone took Doris?" Salas asked as he and RJ followed Ronnie outside, the night air hitting them. The same dull, stagnant temperature as midday. "What happened to you? You're bleeding."

"I got hit by the van. Follow me. Right there," Ronnie said, pointing down the alley. "They took her from there."

"Slow down, Ronnie. Tell me what you saw first. Take a deep breath. What stands out to you?" Salas asked.

"He stuffed her in a van. Then I ran forward, and the van ran over me. Doris is gone. We got to get her back," Ronnie had tears in his eyes.

"We will, Ronnie. Slow down. Take another breath. Tell me what you remember. What kind of van?" Salas asked.

"An old one. Like a hippie psychedelic Volkswagen van," Ronnie said as he leaned against the brick wall of the Hidden Agenda. "I was kinda blinded by the headlights, but I could see it was an old piece of shit, blacked out with tinted windows. A rusted-out brown shitty van. With white wall tires."

"Rusted out with white walls? I've seen that van," Salas said. "I saw it in the police street videos." He checked his phone as he talked.

"Blacked out? A blacked-out van? An old, shitty van? I saw that on the video where Maria was taken," RJ said.

"Is this it? Is this the van, Ronnie?" Salas had his phone to Ronnie's face, a screenshot of the van on the display.

"It is. It's the same damn van. The same damn guy," Ronnie said.

"What else? Anything else you remember? Focus," Salas said.

Ronnie closed his eyes and thought. "The loading dock. The bartender. He was on the loading dock. He saw it all."

"Ronnie, get to your hotel room. Get online. Check every intersection stoplight from here to Vegas. Find the van. I need to know where he is," Salas said. "This is an old VW van. There cannot be many like that around. Hack into the DMV, find every owner of every forty-year-plus-old Volkswagen van in Las Vegas."

"How did he know to take Doris?" Ronnie asked. "She just wanted some fresh air. How did he know she would need that?"

"It's the bartender. He was standing on the loading dock. That motherfucker spiked her drink," RJ said. "I'm gonna kill that piece of shit." RJ walked towards the Hidden Agenda.

"No. Wait, RJ. Let me handle this. I got the badge. Ronnie, get to the hotel. Now." Salas pushed RJ to the side, walking down the alley to the loading dock and back entrance of the Hidden Agenda.

"I want to find Doris!" Ronnie yelled at Salas. "I don't want to stay here alone in Laughlin."

"We need you to find that van, Ronnie. That is how we find Doris. You find the van and you find Doris. You got the most important job. Now, go." Salas pointed Ronnie towards the hotel.

Ronnie turned, jumping and hopping on one leg towards Harrah's.

Salas raised his knee to his chest and kicked the rear door of the bar. The steel door burst open with the doorknob getting lodged in the drywall. He and RJ walked straight to the wooden bar where the shaggy-haired man was talking to a waitress.

Salas stormed thru the crowd, his wide shoulders pushing innocent bystanders out of the way. A dozen patrons sat staring at the mirror lining the back of the bar.

A dozen pair of eyes watched as Salas thrust his Indiana police detective badge in the face of the bartender.

A dozen pair of eyes watched as Salas punched the barkeep in the face with that same badge, knocking the young man to the floor.

A dozen pair of eyes watched as RJ picked the shaggy-haired man up by his blonde locks and dragged him to a backroom.

A dozen pair of eyes looked bewildered as their barman vanished. A dozen pair of eyes grimaced at a fool dressed in a blue blazer, pink polo, plaid slacks, boat shoes, and no socks step to the bar and ask, "May I have a Cosmopolitan, please."

The backroom of the Hidden Agenda once served as a storage area. Today, it was equipped with an office chair, a file cabinet, and a metal desk. A Microsoft Surface notebook sat on the flattop, the black screen facing the wall.

RJ, with nary a grunt, tossed the bartender with the shaggy hair and California suntan across the room. Jonesy bounced off the desk. The Surface crashed to the floor.

"Whoa, dude. You gotta chill, bro. What's this all about?" the bartender asked as innocently as he could.

"What did you put in her drink, asshole?" RJ asked, stepping on the computer. A crunching sound signaled the Surface's demise.

"I... I don't know what you're talking about, bro. Whose drink?" The bartender was sweating, his cheeks blushed, his neck bright red.

Salas slapped the barkeep across the face, backhanded, and asked, "What's your name, boy?"

"Jonesy, bro. Why are you doing this to me, officer?" Jonesy asked. "I don't understand. I was just minding my own. Like, you know, just serving the general public."

Salas put the badge in his front pocket. "Listen, bro, Jonesy. We are not in the mood to fuck around. We know you put something in her drink. What was it?"

"Sorry, sir. I don't know what you're talking about," Jonesy said.

Salas popped Jonesy in the forehead with an open palm. Harder than the first slap. Jonesy's head snapped back.

"Honestly, I don't know, bro. You got to chill, man. I don't know what you're talking about," Jonesy repeated.

"You got two options. One, you tell me what it was. Or, two, I let my friend here rip off your arms and shove them up your ass. It's your call. Bro," Salas said.

RJ stepped forward. He grabbed the bartender by his right arm, twisting it counterclockwise until the man shrieked in pain. He held the arm in place, ignoring the high-pitched yelps from Jonesy.

"That hurt, huh?" RJ said. "See how you like this." RJ placed the palm of his hand behind the bartender's head, then slammed it downward. The man's face crushed into the metal desk, leaving a dent in both the barkeep and the desk.

"How was that, dumbass?" RJ let his grip relax. Jonesy's head came off the desk several inches. RJ slammed it again. "I can do this all night."

"Ok. Ok. Stop. Please stop. It was just a couple roofies man. Like, she will only be out like a few hours." Jonesy said, blood running out his nose, his forehead with red blotches from the impact with the desktop.

"Why? Why her? Salas asked.

"Don't know, man. Don't know what you're saying. I thought it just be funny."

RJ grabbed a handful of Jonesy's hair, then smashed the man's face onto the table. Once. Twice. Three times.

"Stop. Ok. Ok. It was a special order, dude. For some Arab asshole. She fit the description he wanted. Please don't smash my face anymore. Its police brutality, man." Jonesy barked out as he sniffed blood back up his nose.

"I'm not a cop, dipshit," RJ said as he reintroduced Jonesy's face to the desktop.

"Who was with you? Who took her in that van?" Salas still doing the questioning as RJ cranked on Jonesy's elbow.

"Ouch! Stop it, man. I give. I give up. I will give you all I know. It was Phil. Fuck, that hurts. My face hurts. My shoulder hurts. My elbow hurts. Phil, Phil gets girls for the Arab guy!" Jonesy cried out.

"Phil who?" Salas asked.

"Just, like, you know, Phil. Short for Phillip. I don't know his last name, man. We call him Vegas Phil. He pays me and I help him snatch a few girls. I sell some dope for him, man. I'm not like a felon. You know. Just trying to make a living, man."

RJ slammed Jonesy's head to the metal desk. A white chip of a tooth flew to the floor. "You grab a Hispanic girl last week?"

"Yes. Yes. Quit it, man. I'm, like, talking, dude. I'm doing what you want. Why do you keep hitting me?" Jonesy said with a slight lisp.

"Where does he take the girls? Tell me now," RJ said calmly.

"Fuck if I know. I, like, helped with the grab, and then got out. I'm not at the delivery."

"What do you know about the Arab guy?" Salas asked.

"Phil said it. No name, though, man. I just help get the girls. I need the cash, bro, and Phil gets me some weed. He can get anything."

"You the guy been shooting guys off their bikes?" Salas asked.

"What? No, wait. I don't do, I didn't do any shooting, bro."

RJ slammed Jonesy's face three more times in succession.

"Hey, man. It was, like, Vegas Phil. You know. I was just driving the van then, like, all of a sudden Vegas Phil just shoots these dudes, bro."

"You are a piece of shit." RJ slammed Jonesy's head once again off the desktop.

"We don't have time to fuck with you. I suggest you get the hell out of town. Alaska, Vermont, I don't care. If I don't get our girl back, you will be dead. Understand?" RJ said, letting Jonesy stand. "I'm making one call when I leave here, bro. And it is to the president of the club of the member you shot. He will be here in an hour and you will be dead in an hour and one minute."

"It wasn't me, man. I was just following orders," Jonesy said, rubbing his forehead. "Don't call no one, bro. You know, I'm just trying to make a living, man."

RJ hit the bartender with a solid right. Jonesy dropped to the floor, unconscious. RJ stood over the man, took out his own cell phone, and sent a text:

"Manny, we know who the guy is that took your girl. We will get him. It wasn't a club."

RJ then texted Scooter:

"The guy who shot your prospect is a bartender in Laughlin. His name is Jonesy. Right now he is unconscious in the back of the Hidden Agenda. He is all yours."

Salas called Ronnie, who answered on the first ring. He said, "Ronnie, find what you can on a guy known as Vegas Phil. No last name given. Get into that Vegas DMV now. Find the van. And, Ronnie, see what you can find about an Arab in Vegas with tastes for women."

"Got it. I have every camera on every intersection on my screen. Vegas IT security sucks," Ronnie said. "So far, nothing. I figure he has 90 minutes to Vegas. Next few minutes we should have something."

"We're taking our bikes and headed to Vegas now. Text me what you get." Salas shut off his phone.

RJ did a group text to Nellie, Soldier, and Scooter: "We know who took Manny's girl and who did the shootings in Vegas. I let Manny know. On our way."

Within seconds, RJ had a text back:

"Too late. Manny came to our club. His man Rojas is dead. We're going after him." It was Scooter.

Another text:

"Thanks for the bartender. I will have a guy there in three minutes."

"I gave you the bartender. You give me more time. Leave Manny to me," RJ texted.

"We go at sun-up," Scooter replied.

25

Salas and RJ made the hundred-mile ride to Las Vegas in less than 80 minutes. They took an early exit to check their phones.

RJ got a text from Shelli, nothing from Manny.

Salas had nine texts, all from Ronnie:

"There are over 2,000 traffic lights in Vegas."

"All controlled by a central computer in the RTC office. They call it the FAST system."

"An easy hack. My niece could hack this place."

"So far, nothing. Damnit. He should be in Vegas by now."

"Found several old VW vans in Vegas. Searching by first name of Phil."

"Found it. Phil Vega. Vegas Phil. Has to be our man."

"Got the address. 1445 East Blackwood BLVD."

"Salas, I have the van off I-15 taking the downtown exit. He's not at the home address so do not go there. I think he is in old town Vegas. Still searching."

"Have Phil's van off the Fremont Hotel."

In the last text, Ronnie gave Salas the address to the Fremont Hotel. RJ knew the location and led the way, their Harleys bellowing in the still night air, the patented exhaust vibrating off buildings, echoing down the street.

Salas followed RJ into the five-story parking garage next to the Fremont. They found the old VW van near the exit, visible from the street. It was parked in a handicapped parking spot, a blue tag with a white wheelchair insignia hanging from the rearview mirror. The two bikers backed their Harleys into a motorcycle parking next to the van.

Both men inspected the rusted-out VW. The cloth seats were torn, the vinyl dash sun-worn and cracked. The passenger side front seat was littered with trash, empty plastic Mountain Dew bottles, Taco Bell wrappers, an In-N-Out Burger wrapper with the burger half eaten.

RJ said, "No way this piece of shit van has a security system." He brought his weapon forward, grabbed it by the barrel and smashed the rear window with the butt of the handgun. He opened the rear door. Nothing visible but the mattress. "Nothing. He had to drop Doris off somewhere before he got here. I'm going into the Fremont. I'll drag that asshole out by his ears if I have to."

"I'm going to stay close to the van. If he comes back, I got him. Keep your phone on." Salas said as RJ walked away.

Salas jogged across the street, a car honking as he cut it off. Salas waved in annoyance. He rechecked his phone and texted Toni he missed her, giving her no info on the current situation but letting her know he was now in Las Vegas.

"Oh, my darling," the raspy voice said 'darling' with the R missing, replacing it with an H. "Oh, my dahling," she repeated louder.

Salas turned. The woman wore a bright blue, red-and-yellow-striped, skin-tight dress with a yellow feather boa scarf wrapped around her neck. She had muscular legs. Her calves flexed, chiseled like stone in the three-inch platform shoes. Her face was lean, no wrinkles. Her eyes closed when she smiled. Her black skin was blemish-free—beautiful skin—with yellow eyeliner that swept nearly to her ears. Lavish glued-on eyelashes. Looped earrings hung to her muscular shoulders. She had traps and muscular delts. Her straight black hair looked smooth and solid, but it did move when she walked.

The young woman met Salas face to face, placing her arms around his neck, grinding her pelvis into his groin. She repeated "My dahling" as she looked up to meet his eyes.

Salas grinned at her as he arched back, to get a better look. She had pretty, deep brown eyes and smelled of vanilla. She leaned in and kissed him on the lips, pulling his face into hers. Salas tried to push away. She resisted. Salas was impressed by her strength.

"Oh dahling, where have you been all my life? I've longed for you."

Salas noted a protruding Adam's apple, a 10:00 shadow of stubble on her chin and cheeks. It was the slight bulging response from her, not him, as she ground her pelvis into his that got Salas's attention.

"I'm Anne. Anne with an E. My dahling lover," Anne said.

"I'm Mike. Also with an E," Salas said. Anne laughed.

The couple were still in an embrace, Salas's hands on her hips. "Perhaps were you once Anne with a D? Like Andy?"

"Oh, my dahling. You see right through me." She kissed him again before letting go of his neck.

Salas kept his hands in place. "It's my pleasure to meet you. Anne," he said it with a smile.

"Oh, that smile just melts my heart. I could take you right now. This minute. You brute. It's men like you that brings out the woman in me." Anne said, rubbing his biceps.

"Tell me, Anne. Do you know most of the regulars around here?"

"Yes, my dahling, Michael. This is my street, where I work. I know everyone." Her hands were now on his chest, rubbing it in circular fashion. She was truly excited to meet Salas. He tried to pull his hips back. "I want you now, Michael. Now. I would take you anywhere, here, the hotel, even Phil's disgusting VW." She pointed across the street to the van.

"You know Phil? Vegas Phil?"

"Everyone knows Phil, my dahling. You do not want what he offers. I can give you more than you could ever handle. I know how a man likes to be touched."

"I'm sure you do, Anne, but I really need to talk to Phil."

"Please don't tell me you're into bondage or beating women."

"No. Hell, no. Not that at all. Is that what Phil does?"

"Phil gets people what they want. Unique things. He used to arrange helicopter rides and show tickets. Now he does—how shall I say it?—other things. Hard-to-get things. He has used me once or twice. So, you see, you don't need Phil. I can do you myself."

"I'm not really in the market, Anne."

"How sweet. Oh dahling, you are in Vegas, my love. What happens in Vegas stays in Vegas. She will never know."

"Yeah. But I would know."

"Oh, my dahling. You are serious, aren't you? Oh, why are all the best men taken? You are my destiny."

"Can you find Phil for me? I need to talk with him right away."

"Oh, you and that Phil? Why do you keep asking for Phil? If you don't have a special need, he is of no use to you."

"He took a friend of mine. Kidnapped her, Anne. I'm a cop. I need to find the girl. Now."

"Oh, my dahling. I love police officers. They are so official. Is there an award? I love awards. And, yes, I would love to help you. I had heard Phil turned into doctor evil. But kidnapping?"

Another voice approached, both Salas and Anne turned. "Anne. Oh, Anne, please tell me your new beau is looking for a sweet Oregon girl like me."

This streetwalker looked like a runway model. A little on the thin side, high cheek bones, stunning blue eyes that glistened in the streetlights. He blonde hair was natural, no bleach. Very little makeup. She did not need it.

"Daphne, my dear, aren't you looking ravenous this evening? Oh, my Michael, my dahling. You, yes, you bring out the woman in me but Daphne, look at her. She is my sweet dear sunflower. She, she brings out the man in me." Anne's voice went from a scratchy medium pitch to a low baritone as she stepped toward her street friend and kissed her on the lips. "Oh! The two of you confuse me so much, my dahlings."

"Michael, I know I can help you with the release you need." Daphne said. "Anne is perfect, but I have the one thing she lacks."

The closer Daphne got to Salas, the more he could see that her pupils were dilated and that her left cheek twitched as she stood there. What was once a beautiful smile was now meth mouth with skin sores on her neck and arms. She picked at them while she spoke. A beautiful woman fading fast.

"Anne and I are looking for Vegas Phil. Have you seen him?" Salas asked Daphne.

"No, I stay away from that man. He takes girls to private vendors then never brings them back. You don't want him, Michael."

A sleek, black four-door sedan pulled up in front of the trio. Daphne opened the passenger-side door, sat in the front seat without speaking a word to the driver. "Love you, Anne," Daphne said as the BMW drove away.

"Anne, I know Phil has taken two or three ladies these past few days. He has taken innocent girls. And taken them from the wrong people."

"You are in luck, my dahling. There's your man." Anne nodded towards the opposite street. A white male, mid-forties with skinny hairy legs protruding from khaki cargo shorts was walking slowly. Vegas Phil was looking at his cell phone. "You stay here, Michael. I will get him for you. If you approach, he will run. My way will be faster."

Salas took out his cell phone, texting RJ to get to the van. He tried to not look at Anne, not wanting Vegas Phil to be alarmed.

"Phillip!" Anne yelled as she crossed the street, waving as she tried to run in platform shoes. "Phillip, my dahling. I need you."

Salas stood, cell phone in hand, his head down, his eyes up. He could see them speaking but was unable to hear the words.

Without notice, Vegas Phil raised his hand as if to slap Anne. Anne lowered her stance, left leg forward, bent at the knees, both hands held high, her fists facing Phil. She jabbed with her left once, twice, three times with amazing hand speed.

Anne advancing towards Phil with each hit. The jabs connected squarely on Phil's nose. Phil offered no defense. With grace and amazing speed on the platforms, she brought an overhand right to Vegas Phil's chin. The crisp punch dropped Vegas Phil to the Vegas street.

Anne stood over Phil; her fists clenched as she smiled at Salas.

"I have your man. All yours, my dahling Michael!" Anne yelled.

Salas sprinted across the four-lane street. "Are you shitting me? What was that?" Salas asked with his fists punching the air as he approached. A broad smile on his face.

"I was golden gloves in my prime," Anne said in her masculine voice. "One fight away from the Olympic Trials. Got caught with my pants down, literally, with the coach. Needless to say, neither of us made the team."

RJ walked into the parking garage as Salas sat Phil on the concrete floor. Phil sat on his butt, his back leaning against a brick wall. The man's legs were sprawled out like a chicken. Salas patted Phil on the cheeks.

"Wake up asshole," Salas said several times.

"Oh. Oh, my goodness. Look at him. Another one. My dahling Michael, please tell me your friend is single and looking for love in all the wrong places." Anne said, back in female mode.

"Anne, RJ. RJ, Anne," Salas said. "Anne just kicked the shit out of Vegas Phil here."

Anne greeted RJ the same way she greeted Salas. She grabbed the back of his neck with both hands pulled his head down to her level and kissed RJ on the lips.

Vegas Phil groaned. He slowly raised his head from his chest, looked at Anne and said, "Anne. Anne, you dirty little bitch."

Salas slapped Phil hard on the side of the face. "You don't talk to the lady like that." Salas said as he picked Phil up and pushed him against the wall. "You're taking us to where you dropped off the lady this evening. The lady you kidnapped in Laughlin." Salas was pushing Phil towards the VW.

"Right. No way, motherfuckers. I do that and they kill me," Phil said.

"You will and you will now, or I will break every bone in your worthless piece-of-shit body," RJ said as he grabbed Vegas Phil's hand. He snapped the right index finger like a number two pencil. The man screamed in pain.

Anne winced. "Vegas Phil, I recommend you take these boys to that Saudi Arabian dude."

"No way. I'd rather have a broken finger than have Abdul break my back," Phil responded.

RJ snapped another of Phil's fingers. Phil screamed.

Anne said, "Phil, listen to me, honey. When he breaks your toes, it will hurt even worse. Take us to this brute named Abdul."

"Give me the keys to the van," Salas demanded.

Phil reached across his body with his left hand, taking the keys out of his right pocket. He gave them to Salas.

Vegas Phil cried, "He will kill me. He will kill you. All of you."

"You let us worry about that." Salas unlocked the van.

RJ opened the side door and tossed Phil in. He heard the man's head hit the opposite door. Again, Phil screamed in pain. RJ got in the back with Phil, opened the back door and tossed the smelly mattress on the floor of the parking garage. He slammed the door shut. "Let's roll."

Salas shut the driver-side door and got in the front seat. The passenger-side door opened. Anne swept garbage to the floor of the van, some of which fell onto the parking garage concrete.

"What are you doing?" Salas asked Anne.

"You saw I can handle myself. And you said there may be an award," the masculine voice responded.

"And if these girls are in bad shape, they may need a woman to help," the female voice.

RJ looked confused but said nothing. He slapped Phil.

"Ouch! What was that for?" Phil asked.

"We need directions. They better be right. And they best be as straight of a line as you can get. If I think you're fucking with me, I will break one of your fingers with every mile," RJ said.

"You better do what he says or Vegas Phil will end up being Crazy Phil. After he done with you, you will have PSTD, that post-something disease," Anne said.

"Take a right out of the garage," Vegas Phil said.

Abdul liked what he saw. The little biker girl Phil dropped off looked like she would fun. Abdul rubbed and excited himself as he examined the female in the drug-induced sleep. A fifth dog kennel was now occupied.

Five girls would be a little much for him to maintain. He would need more drugs to keep them under control. He considered disposing of the Hells Angel that Rashid had yet to see. But Abdul liked how she performed. The young blonde was in dire need of her daily fix. Unlike the others, she was eager to keep Abdul happy. He kind of liked the girl.

Rashid was yelling, "Abdul! Get in here at once!"

Abdul rolled his eyes. He took the cellar steps three at a time, pushing open the heavy wooden door to the theater room before Rashid could muster up the air to yell again. He immediately saw the issue. One of the twins had passed out on the carpet. She was on her stomach, a pile of vomit under her chin, the goo slowly seeping towards Rashid.

The other twin sat on Rashid's belly, nowhere near the naked man's private parts. She lapped danced on his gut, in slow motion, her legs nearly in horizontal splits. The twin looked ashen. She, too, looked as if she was going to hurl at any moment.

"Get her off me. She's gagging. Her breath reeks. If she pukes on me, I want her head on a platter!" Rashid yelled as Abdul picked the tiny teenager off the fat man's belly.

Nothing and no one could help Rashid. He grew more and more impatient each day. His brain still had the cravings of a man, but his body could not accommodate his thoughts and desires. Rashid tried to strike the twin, his fat arms swatting at nothing by his sides – the short arms of a dinosaur flapping in the air.

Abdul placed a girl under each of his muscular arms, carrying both of them to their kennel. He left Rashid drinking merlot out of a bottle while he ate Chinese takeout. Vomit was still in liquid form near his feet, the smell overtaking the Chinese odor.

Rashid yelled again for Abdul to clean him.

He left both girls face down in case they threw up again. He did not want them to choke to death but knew their deaths were imminent, especially with the new biker girl in the cage.

Abdul checked his guests. The biker was still out but had rolled to her side. The blonde smiled at Abdul as he gave her two oxy's from his pants pocket. The girl engulfed the medication, dry-swallowing both tablets. The Latina looked at Abdul with hate in her eyes.

"My father will kill you. Your only hope is to ask forgiveness and let me go, you big bastard," Maria said.

Abdul laughed. "I will have you later tonight, my little brownie. You won't remember it until you go to pee tomorrow." He laughed again as he left the room.

Abdul checked his watch. Walking to the security office for his hourly observation, Abdul carefully reviewed the assortment of cameras strategically placed on the compound. He saw a van, a familiar van driving up the one-lane black asphalt. The VW took the U-shaped driveway instead of the normal garage door entrance.

"Pissant Phil probably spent his earnings and wants more," Abdul said, looking at the camera.

Abdul stood to leave, then froze. His face went pale as a large man with a biker vest stepped out of the van's side door. The man was holding a handgun.

Abdul gasped when Phil and another large man with a bald head and huge arms came walking toward the front door. This bald man also had a gun in his hand.

"Shit!" Abdul shouted as he ran out of the security room.

"Rashid, we got company. That asshole Phil brought a couple of bikers here. They're packing. We must leave."

"We're staying. I have diplomatic immunity. Tell them to fuck off."

"These ain't cops, Rashid. Two bikers and we got a biker girl here. They don't give a flying fuck about your immunity."

"What biker girl? I want to see her."

"We don't have time for that. Let's get out of here. Now!" Abdul said.

"Then shoot them, kill them. That's why I pay you. You kill what I tell you to kill."

"I don't have a weapon, Rashid. You were to get me one, but your boy Vegas Phil never followed through."

"Kill them with your hands, you overgrown child. I don't pay you to run away."

"Did you not hear me? They're packing. They got guns."

"Uuggghhh. I want my girl. I want the biker girl."

"That's not happening tonight, Rashid. We got to go."

"My cart. Get me my cart. Call our pilot. Get me to the airport. Maybe we go to Napa Valley or the Willamette Valley for an excellent pinot noir. I know, maybe we go to Mexico. I have a craving for Mexican food." Rashid covered himself with his robe.

Abdul was pulling the cart into the dance room when the doorbell rang. He ignored the buzzing noise and helped Rashid roll onto the dolly. Rashid side-rolled as Abdul pushed. They both grunted.

"Hold on!" Abdul yelled to Rashid as he pushed the cart across the tiled floor. They rolled past the front window, able to see two men at the door. Abdul kept pushing. Rashid's enormous love handles clipped the walls, eliciting yelps from the fat man. The cart gained momentum on the slick floor and servant's hallway along the back side of the home. The hallway was used to bring in groceries, furniture, supplies, and – in this case – women for Rashid.

"We get to the side door, you can roll right into the limo." Abdul pulled a set of keys from his front pocket, pressing the soft side of a black rubber fob.

The house utility door opened to the inside. Abdul stopped the cart, pulling the door open as he backed up then advanced the cart through the doorway. He looked out the door into the garage, left to right. He saw no one.

The limo was a stretch Lincoln Continental. The side door was custom built to open like a van, easier to get the fat man in and out. Pushing the fob had triggered the door to slide open.

Abdul placed the cart sideways to the servant's exit. Rashid rolled to his side, with Abdul pushing him into the limo. Rashid cried in pain as his fat slid between the door and the car's frame, getting meshed with the sliding mechanism.

The fat man bled profusely from both sides of his enormous belly. Abdul grabbed the fat, pulled, and pushed it in as best as he could and then slid the door shut.

With Rashid lying in the back in the Lincoln, Abdul leaped over the hood of the car, doing a side roll and landing on both feet.

Abdul threw open the driver-side door, crammed his large body into the seat and thrust the key in the ignition as he slammed the door shut and started the car.

27

Salas drove with Anne in the passenger seat. RJ and Vegas Phil sat on the slimy, sticky metal of the back of the van. With each passing mile and direction given by Phil, RJ would slap Phil on the side of the face.

"We get where we are going, and I don't find our girl or find out you took the long way, and I will…"

"I know. I know." Phil interrupted. "You will break my fingers. I get it. I am taking you there. Quit slapping me."

RJ slapped him again. "Don't tell me what to do."

"Right on West Desert Road."

"When we get there, Anne, I do not want you in the middle. You stay in the van until we get the place secure. Then you help us with the girls." Salas said.

"I can take care of myself. You saw that with him." Anne said in her masculine voice as she nodded to Phil.

"Red Rock to Marble Ridge," came from the back of the van.

The VW descended into quiet. Nothing but the roll of the tires on the pavement, the stagnant noise of the VW exhaust. RJ had not slapped Phil for several miles.

"Painted Feather Way. It's coming up on your right," Phil said.

"You don't have to tell me, but when are you going to make the commitment?" Salas whispered to Anne, turning on his blinker.

"Oh, my dahling," the female Anne understood the question. "I love being a man and, believe me, women love my man, if you know what I mean. But I have these inner desires. The woman in me wants out of her cage. I have been saving for surgery, but I know at this rate I will never get there."

"So, what you going to do?" RJ asked this time.

"What do you recommend, Michael?"

"I like who you are. Just be yourself. Be happy with you."

"Oh, my dahling. You see right through me. So, tell me when are you going to make the commitment?"

Salas laughed out loud. "You see right through me, too."

Phil interrupted. "Last house on the right. You can see the highway behind it."

"Got it," said Salas.

Salas parked the van in front of an elaborate home. He made note of the only exit, the multiple cameras examining the grounds, and four closed garage doors. He also made note of the Lincoln Continental limo parked next to a double-wide utility door leading to garbage dumpsters enclosed by a wooden fence. The limo was flush against the side of the home.

"RJ, you take the garage area. Me and Mr. Vegas Phil here will go through the front door. Phil, you run on me and I will shoot you in the ass," Salas said, taking his Glock from behind his low back.

"Guns and roses," Anne said, pulling the front of her dress down, a bouquet of roses on her left artificial implant. "You are my destiny," she said, smiling again at Salas.

"You stay here for now. Give us five minutes, then come in," Salas said, looking at Anne.

"Phil, where do they keep the girls?" RJ asked.

"No idea about the girls. This is as far as I get. The big Arab gives me an envelope with cash and takes the girls inside. Then I leave," Phil said.

RJ exited the van and walked to the north side of the compound. He, too, had his gun out, pointing forward. Salas pushed Phil as they approached the front door.

Salas rang the doorbell, his gun pointed at Phil beside him.

"Can you point that somewhere else? I'm not running."

"If this is all for naught and you get shot, it will be worth it. Our girl had better be here and healthy."

He pushed the doorbell again.

They waited several seconds. Hearing a noise resembling the rolling wheels of a maid's cart at a hotel, Salas looked through the window. He saw a huge man dressed in black slacks and a white T-shirt pushing a utility cart with what looked to be an obese man from *My 600-Lb Life*.

"Stand back," Salas said as he shot the lock of the arched door.

He pushed the door open and ran in, gun drawn. He heard women screaming from his left. His instinct was to chase the two men running to the right, but he went for the females.

Salas ignored the kitchen and large open family room as he looked for the source of the screams. He found black rubber wheel marks on the tile. Following those, he entered a theater room. The screen was still in place but a stripper pole and stage served as the center attraction.

"Are you shitting me," Salas said. "That is the biggest fucking bean bag chair I have ever seen. Shit." Salas looked behind him. No Vegas Phil. He retraced his steps to the kitchen then to the front door. It was a huge house.

In the living room stood Anne. She stood over the top of Phil. She looked at Salas then hit Phil several times. Lightning strike, quick direct hits to the nose and face with both her left and right fists.

"He tried to run," Anne said. "I got him. He will be out for a bit. Let's get to the girls."

Anne followed Salas past the stripper pole to the screams and wooden door of the wine cellar. Salas ran down the steps without caution, his gun still drawn. He knew the large Arab went the other way. He wanted to see Doris.

CHAPTER

28

The limo started with ease. Abdul put the car in drive as he pressed the remote to open the side gate of the house to an immediate exit to the highway. He floored the accelerator and the Lincoln's V12 responded.

Abdul lowered the glass partition separating Rashid from the front seat. He looked into the rearview mirror at a 9 MM Glock pointed at the back of his head.

"You opened the door to the limo too soon big fella," RJ said. "I was trying to break into the garage when I heard the door. Thought I would make myself at home. And, sure enough, you rolled this fat piece of shit into the back," RJ said.

"I have diplomatic immunity!" Rashid yelled.

RJ shot the big toe off Rashid's left foot. The echo of the gun blast was deafening in the close confines of the limo. Rashid screamed in agony. He tried to bend but was unable to grab his toe.

RJ turned to the driver. "Big fella, let me tell you where we're going. If you don't turn around and go there, I will shoot another toe off the fat man. If you don't care about the fat man, then I will shoot your fucking ear off. Got it? Now turn around. And do it slow."

Abdul did as he was told. Decelerating the limo, he drifted slightly to the right, checking the car's mirrors as he turned around on the two-lane highway. Abdul was thinking of his own life now, looking to fight another day or willing to give up the fat man for his own survival.

"Take 93 to Coyote Springs. You'll go a few miles, then see a couple of men on motorcycles on your right. Turn then," RJ said.

RJ's cell phone vibrated. A text from Salas.

"Where are you?"

"I got the fat man and the Arab. We're going to see Manny," RJ texted back.

After several seconds, RJ's phone lit up with several texts.

"Good. I thought they got away," Salas's text.

The next message read, "We got Doris; she is fine."

Then, "We found a young lady named Maria. She is ok. Will need help."

A third text came in, "Another victim says she belongs to the Angels. She is bad. OD on drugs. Will need a doctor."

"Set of twins. Teenagers at that. Torn apart. Calling the police and the medics."

A last text from Salas. "Vegas Phil is the shooter of the club, guys. Giving him to police."

"Where are you taking me? I demand to know," Rashid said.

"Relax, fat man. You will get your due. Enjoy the ride," RJ said. "Keep it under the speed limit!" he yelled at the driver.

Rashid yelled out, "Abdul, turn this car around! Kill this man beside me. Kill him now. You cannot touch me. I have diplomatic immunity."

RJ shot another toe off the fat man's left foot. "I don't give a shit about what you are immune to." RJ punched Rashid with the pistol. "Quit crying, you fat bastard. Abdul, if you want any chance of surviving, keep going the way I tell you."

They drove several miles in silence. RJ texted as they went.

RJ texted Scooter: "We got your girl. Ambulance will be taking her to the hospital. They drugged her bad."

Another to Scooter: "Got the guy that shot your boy. Police will take him in."

RJ texted Nellie, Scooter, and Soldier: "We got Manny's girl back. And the guy responsible. Giving him to Manny. I will take care of the rest."

Abdul did as he was requested, turning right on Highway 95 towards Coyote Springs. After several miles, two bright lights rose from the desert floor. As the limo slowed on the black asphalt of 95, a single bullet headlight bulb, most likely a soft tail, the other a double LED from a newer bagger, came into focus.

Abdul flashed the brights of the Lincoln. The bullet responded the same. Abdul took the turn, driving deeper into the desert, the limo bouncing and bobbing on a single-lane dirt, rock, and barren road. The two light beacon Harleys followed at a slow pace, their tires made for the streets of Las Vegas, not the sand and rock of the Mohave.

The limo came to a stop in front of a row of fifteen to twenty motorcycles. Abdul slowly turned the ignition, the motor went quiet. He shut off the lights, turned, and looked at RJ through the gap from the back to the front seat

"What now?" Abdul asked.

29

Salas secured the area, then dialed 911. He then texted Ronnie: "We got Doris. She is ok. Get to Vegas now."

Anne rush to the cages holding the girls. The Mexican teenager was crying, tears were streaming down her cheeks.

"You found us! I want my daddy," the teenager cried out.

Anne took a screwdriver from the red cart, using it as a lever to pop the lock and open the door to the kennel holding the Latina girl. The two hugged.

"I'm Anne. Everything is going to be all right."

Releasing Maria, Anne went to the next cage, popped the lock in the same manner as the other, her strength making it easy. She leaned over, shaking the girl with both hands. "Lady, lady, you ok?"

Doris responded, sitting upright, rubbing her eyes. "Where are we? Salas, is that you?"

Salas ran to Doris, picking her up in his arms and squeezing her tight. He had tears on his cheeks, too.

Anne tore the locks off the next three cages. The twins were unconscious, the blonde was shaking furiously, sweating, white spittle on the sides of her mouth. She tried to say, "Thank you," but no words came out.

Salas texted RJ, asking where he was and getting an immediate text in return. Satisfied with the response, he inspected each girl, checking their pupils, breathing, pulse rates. He sent RJ updates on each woman, knowing they were club members, missing loved ones.

Maria approached Salas, "I want to call my daddy."

Salas gave her his cell phone. She dialed the number from memory.

"Daddy, it's me, Maria." She then spoke in Spanish for several seconds, crying as the words slipped out. Salas did not know what she was saying, but she was sobbing. Salas recognized the word Abdul and *violacion*, Spanish for rape.

Salas asked Maria for the phone. "Sir, I am a police detective. We will be taking your daughter to the hospital, where she will be taken care of. My heart is with you and your beautiful young daughter, sir."

He gave the phone back to the young woman, who continued to talk to her father in a language Salas wished he would learn. She finished talking and gave Salas back his phone.

Anne, Maria, and Salas all looked up, hearing loud voices, boots barking on tile and granite floors, men storming the grounds yelling, "Police! Las Vegas PD! Come out with your hands raised!"

Salas yelled out, "Down here! I'm a police officer. The basement is secure. I have placed my weapon on the floor. My hands are raised. We have injured people down here. Please bring the medics."

Three men in SWAT tactical gear slowly descended the steps to the wine cellar. The men spread out in a straight line, their guns pointed at Salas, who remained motionless. The lead man kicked Salas's Glock to the side as a man in a blue blazer and khaki pants came down the steps. He was followed by four police officers in street blues, their guns also drawn.

"We have the home secured. You are a police officer, I hear?" the man in khakis asked.

He led Salas near the base of the steps. They huddled in deep conversation. Salas showed his badge as an officer spoke into a collar microphone. He voiced Salas's name and Indiana badge number. Within seconds, his identification was verified. The officer nodded to the detective in charge.

"Like I said, we're on vacation. Someone took Doris there. So, I followed them. No time to call you, sorry. I was on a motorcycle. It happened so fast. Then I saw the van by the Fremont and Anne—Anne there. She was amazing. She helped take the guy out. We knew we had to act fast, so we came straight here. I didn't anticipate any of this."

"So, the guy upstairs—he is beat to shit, by the way—you say he shot some gang members?"

"Yeah, he bragged about it. Check your street cameras. Bet you find his van in one of the videos. He also told us he took the Mexican girl and gave her or sold her to the guy that lives here."

"Yes, we have owner of this house's name. Rashid Sadulev. Where is he?" the police officer asked.

"I don't know. His friend or bodyguard got him in a limo, and they took off. I was hoping you would have passed him on the way in. I stayed here with the girls. I felt they were the priority," Salas said.

Salas watched as medics carrying stretchers and med kits came down the steps. He heard more sirens as more men and women in uniform entered the cellar. They took the Hells Angel first, the ambulance screaming as it left the home. Next were the twins.

The officer in charge said, "We have been looking for a set of twins that match their description. Thank God they're alive."

"Yes, alive, but they will be deeply messed up for years. Hopefully, with the drugs they had them on, they won't be able to remember much," Salas said.

"The medic says they were severely drugged up, evidence of rape, most likely repeatedly." The detective shook his head.

Salas watched as two medics strapped Maria to a gurney, placed an oxygen mask over her nose and mouth, then carried her up the stairs. Within seconds, another siren announced her departure from the prison she was held in.

Doris was the last of the five women to get attention. She resisted the gurney, submitting only to Salas's request that she go to the hospital for an evaluation. He told her Ronnie was coming and they would meet her at the hospital. She was asleep on the gurney before they reached the top of the steps. The roofies were still in her system.

"Salas, we will need you and Anne to come downtown with us. Lots of paperwork. You know the drill," the detective said to the two of them. Both followed the officers to a patrol car for a ride to the station.

Once outside, Salas and Anne were surrounded by the ambulance-chasing local media. Spotlights placed on portable stands lit up the front yard and driveway like a Friday night high school football field. The blazered detective pushed cameramen and broadcasters to the side.

"Miss, miss, can we have a few words?" a woman addressed Anne.

Anne stopped, several cameras and videographers pushed microphones and bright lights in her face.

"Miss, I am Gloria Benson, live with Live Action Five News. Can you tell us what you saw in that house?" The woman was in a form-fitting red dress, the hem mid-thigh, the V-neck cut exposing excessive cleavage. Her perfect smile shone under the lights and cameras.

"Look at you, Ms. Benson. I watch you all the time. I must say you are more beautiful in person than you are on the TV screen," Anne said, her smile matching the broadcasters. Gloria Benson beamed even more.

"Tell us, the people of Las Vegas want to know. What happened behind those walls of what appears to be a normal but very expensive family home?" Gloria thrust the microphone back to Anne.

"It was horrible, Gloria, just horrible. There were five women. All drugged, beaten, the poor dahlings in terrible shape. I can only imagine what happened behind those closed doors. One of the girls told me they were raped, daily, by a fat man and his bodyguard. A brute of a man from Libya, Syria, or Benghazi, one of them Hillary Clinton towns. Somewhere over there," Anne said, flipping her fingers north.

"Did you know any of the women? Were they able to walk?" Gloria asked.

"No, they weren't friends of mine. I was asked to help and came without hesitation. I am sure you would have done the same thing, Gloria," Anne said, rubbing Gloria's arm, her crotch against the side of Gloria's leg. She was twerking ever so slightly.

Anne then stopped the rubbing and grinding, she grabbed the microphone, looked into the camera, and said, "I hope the cops get that fat motherfucker."

Gloria took back her microphone. She assumed to be shocked by the words. "Miss, miss, any additional parting words for our audience at Live Action Five?"

"You are one hot little thing, Gloria Benson. You bring out the man in me, girl," Anne's masculine voice said as she gave Gloria Benson a kiss on the mouth.

Gloria broke away, blushing, her cheeks red, her lipstick smeared.

The in-studio broadcaster came online. "Gloria, Gloria, please take a few questions from our Live Action Five Quick Questions Corner. Text or tweet us your questions for Gloria's immediate response. Gloria, what do you have?"

Gloria held out her phone. "Stan, our first question comes from a friend of ours on Twitter named 'In mom's basement.' As you can see from the bottom of your screen, we are teleprompting his question live. 'If we had stricter gun laws, stuff like this wouldn't happen.' Well basement dweller, guns were not an issue in this case. Perhaps you have tweeted the wrong account."

"Stan, we have another. A text that reads 'if prostitution was legal, we wouldn't have this problem.' Texter, if prostitution were legal, it would not be prostitution. It would be called sex or marriage. This is about kidnapping and rape. Geez." Gloria shook her head back and forth.

"One last text, Stan. This one reads, 'That black lady used hate speech and is a racist. Calling the guy a fat man and from Libya. That is fucking hate speech bitch.'"

"Really. Doesn't anyone scrub these damn things before we air them," Gloria said to the camera.

"No, Gloria, we don't. That's why we call it Live at Live Action Five."

CHAPTER

30

"Get out of the car," RJ said, pointing his gun at Abdul. "You, fat fuck. You get out of the car, too."

Abdul opened the driver-side door and stood. RJ hit the open button, the door slid to the right. Rashid rolled to his side, pushing himself upright with his arms. He placed his feet on the sand. He had no shoes and the sand felt warm. He cried out in pain that his foot hurt.

Rashid tried to stand, grunting, rocking back and forth to gain momentum. He could not do it. Abdul asked RJ for permission to help. RJ nodded and Abdul reached out to Rashid with both arms, taking him by the hands. Abdul then leaned back, slowing lifting Rashid to his feet.

"I have diplomatic immunity!" Rashid cried out.

A Devil's Brother got in the driver's side of the limo, started the Lincoln, driving it several yards away from where the bikers had surrounded Rashid and Abdul.

The bikers formed a circle around the two men, their headlights on, the beams of light glaring on the two Middle Eastern men.

Manny approached. He placed his cell phone in the front pocket of his jeans. "Thank you, my friend," he said to RJ, shaking his hand. The police have my Maria. She is safe. I am forever in your debt."

"I told you I would help. When this is done, you do what I say," RJ said.

"We will do as told," Manny said, then nodded to his men.

Twenty bikers came forward, fists clinched, some carrying short metal pipes, a few with brass knuckles. They advanced on Abdul. The bodyguard swung first, connecting on the chin of a biker who dropped, lights out.

Abdul was then struck in the back of the head with a metal pipe. His knees buckled, yet he remained standing. Fists flew from Abdul and from the Devils. Another biker dropped to the ground.

Abdul picked one at a time, not swinging at the crowd. Another biker down. Abdul dropped to his knees, his hands still up, he was still swinging. Blood ran from his scalp, his nose, his ears. One eye was already closed. A large bloody knot formed on his cheek.

"Enough!" Manny yelled.

The fighting stopped. The bikers parted as Manny approached the large Arabian. Even on his knees, he was nearly Manny's height.

"You raped my daughter," Manny said.

Abdul responded, "She fought me at first. She is a tough little brownie. Then she loved it. She moved her hips. She groaned in pleasure."

Manny raised a .357 Magnum, placed it against Abdul's forehead, and pulled the trigger. The explosion quieted the desert. No crickets, no coyotes, not even the breeze moved. The back of Abdul's head washed the desert sand behind him, his body falling into the black-stained sand.

Rashid shouted again, "I have diplomatic immunity!"

Manny turned to him. "No one gives a shit, fat man. Tie him up."

Two bikers came forward. The larger of the two pushed Rashid hard in the chest, the obese man fell backwards to his butt, then flat to his back.

The two men held Rashid down, as if he could get up anyway. Four men approached, each carrying several feet of log chain. The steel chain had thick one-inch links.

Four Devil's Brothers went to work. They wrapped the chains around each of Rashid's limbs. They twisted the chain around each arm and each leg, careful not to overlap the links. The chains extended from both Rashid's wrists to his elbows and ankles, to his knees. The weight of the chains prevented him from squirming and struggling. He lay flat on the desert floor.

Four Harleys roared to life, each rider backed their motorcycle to one of Rashid's chained arms and legs. Other bikers came forward. They connected each chain by its hook to the frame of the motorcycle in front of it.

"This is called the four corners of hell, fat man. First biker that tears off one of your limbs gets $1,000 dollars!" Manny yelled over the thunder of the Harleys.

The four bikers slowly crept their cycles forward. The chains tightened around Rashid's limbs. He groaned in agony. The chains dug into the fat man's flesh. The skin quickly cracked, blood and adipose tissue leaking through the cuts.

The bikers looked back over their shoulders, as they crept the motorcycles forward. They stopped when the chains were off the ground. One of the bikes pointed east, another bike west, one north, and one bike south.

Manny waved his hand. The four bikers laid on their throttles.

Braaaaaaap. Braaaaaaap.

The chains squealed as they tightened, snapping into a locked position, squeezing Rashid's arms and legs. He screamed long wails of pain. Each biker went full throttle, dust and dirt shooting backwards from each tire, coating Rashid in desert sand.

Rashid's left arm snapped, the radius and ulna succumbing to the pressure of the torque on the chains. A fibula cracked – first the right leg, then the left.

The eastbound biker relaxed his throttle, rolled back a few feet then laid on the accelerator shooting forward. Rashid's left arm snapped and popped, flying off his body, separated at the elbow. Blood pumped out with each beat of Rashid Sadulev's heart. Yellow body fat glistened in the headlights of the sitting bikes. Sheets of grease mixed with the dirt of the Nevada desert. Rashid cried out louder than before as the winning biker raised his hand in triumph.

The other three bikers continued their assault on Rashid's body. Within seconds, the biker headed south tore Rashid's right arm off, also at the elbow. More blood spurted into the night air, mixing with the dust.

Rashid was still alive, screaming, while the Devil's Brothers shouted encouragement to their buddies on the bikes. The biker headed north adjusted his direction to go straight opposite of his partner pulling on the other leg.

What sounded like a rug being ripped off the floor was Rashid's pelvis being torn in two.

Rashid went quiet.

Manny yelled at them to stop. The bikers shut off their motors. No one spoke. The desert became quiet.

Manny checked the fat man's pulse at the neck, standing in a mixture of blood and yellow lard. Very little blood came out of Rashid's torn off appendages. The large man had bled out. Rashid was dead.

"Bury him in a shallow grave. Leave the chains on him. Let the coyotes and hawks eat for a few days. Take the limo to Danny's garage. Chop it out tonight. Give RJ a ride back to Vegas. Get him to his Harley," Manny said. His men responded to his orders.

RJ spoke, waving off his escort. "Manny, come with me." The two walked out of hearing distance from Manny's men. "Manny, here's the deal, or the Angels will retaliate for your attack on their compound."

"But we didn't attack. Rojas just wanted to talk to them."

"You, you yourself shot at them, Manny. Yeah, they shot Rojas, but you were on their turf. After you let everyone know you thought they took your daughter and that you were going to attack," RJ said.

Manny lowered his head, knowing he would take whatever sentence RJ gave to him.

"Your club is done, Manny. You can patch over as a group or as individuals to any club you want. But the Devil's Brothers is over. Burn your colors. You either take this or you all will be dead. You got your daughter back, Manny. Let her have her father. She needs you now more than ever. You got till sun-up to let me know."

"I don't need till sun-up, RJ. We will do this. I promised you. Consider it done. I am done," Manny said to RJ. "And thank you, my friend, for saving my daughter. As I said, I am forever in your gratitude."

31

Salas and Anne gave their statements to the Las Vegas Police Department. What could have been a nasty situation for a fellow officer of the law was overlooked given the current safety of five abducted women and the takedown of a sex-trafficking operation.

Vegas Phil blamed everything on Rashid, that he was a victim forced to abduct women or be beaten by Abdul. He claimed he knew nothing about the biker shootings. No one bought it.

A patrol officer gave Salas and Anne a ride in a Chevy Lumina with the word "Police" written in bold black letters on each side. The patrol car had a cattle guard on the front. They rode, minus the sirens, to the Fremont Hotel.

Salas was surprised to find RJ's Harley missing. He hoped RJ had it and the bike was not stolen.

The police sedan came to a stop. The driver unlocked the rear doors with the driver-side's unlock button. Anne and Salas exited by the door adjacent to the sidewalk. The officer drove away, leaving Anne and Salas alone in front of the parking garage.

Salas turned to his partner. "Thanks for all your help, Anne. I told the police to contact you if there was any reward. You deserve it. You took out the major villain here in Vegas – Phil. He will be going to jail for a long time."

"Oh, my dahling. Are you really going to leave me? We must keep in touch." They exchanged phone numbers. Salas dialed Anne's to be sure the connection worked.

"What now, Anne? Back to the streets?"

"I love the street, Michael. I'm thinking of making the change, a full metal jacket conversion."

"I like you just the way you are, Anne. My girlfriend is flying in to meet me at the Bellagio. I'm headed there next. If you got time tomorrow, call me. I would love for you to meet her."

"Yes, we both need to commit."

Anne stepped forward, jumped into Salas's arms and wrapping her legs around his waist. She squeezed her thighs tightly together, putting Salas in a move known to wrestlers as the body scissors. He squirmed in pain.

"Oh, dahling," she moaned before she kissed Salas on the mouth. The sound of horns honking and passing cat calls told them to get a room.

Salas said goodbye as they untangled, then walked to his Harley while checking his phone.

"Oh, Michael, my sweet Michael, I totally forgot!" Anne yelled again.

Salas stopped. Anne ran to him.

"Here. I took this from Vegas Phil. I thought you might get more out of it than the nasty po-po." Anne handed Salas a cell phone.

Salas stuffed the phone his is front pocket, swung his right leg over the saddle of the Harley, turned the barrel key to on and pushed the start button. His bike roared to life. Looking both directions, Salas turned right and headed for the strip and the Bellagio. He waved a two finger salute to Anne as he rode away.

After exchanging texts with Toni, Salas checked into the Bellagio, reserving a separate room for Doris and Ronnie. In his sixteenth-story room, Salas showered and shaved. He needed sleep before Toni arrived. With a white hotel towel wrapped around his waist, he leaned back against the headboard of the king-sized bed, his legs crossed, a bottle of Miller Light on the nightstand.

Salas used the remote and the television came on. Elevator music. He pushed the channel button to a local news channel and opened Vegas Phil's phone. The battery was 75% to capacity. There was no password. He viewed the most recent calls. Three missed calls from "Sheriff." He opened the contacts file, only to close it after scrolling through to the C's. Too many names he did not know.

Salas opened "My Files." Here he found images, documents, downloads, audios, and recent voice mails. He tapped the voice mail icon. The first voice mail was the last missed call from "Sheriff."

Salas listened: "Where the hell are you? I don't have my dead biker. You have till morning, then I'm coming for you."

He tapped open the recorded audio tab. The same voice came on. He listened to the phone exchange while watching TV.

Salas said, "You have got to be shitting me."

CHAPTER

32

Ronnie waited impatiently for Salas, RJ, or Doris to call, text, email, or make any type of communication while he sat alone in Laughlin. He tried to sleep, but his mind was on Doris.

Room service trays were in the corner by the door, stacked white ceramic plates scarred with ketchup and mustard. Empty plastic water bottles filled the trash can by the desk. A half-empty bottle of Advil looked at him. He grabbed it, taking four 200 milligram tablets and emptying another bottle of water to wash the tabs down.

He stood looking at his foot. It was not that swollen. Perhaps the Advil and ice packs were working.

Ronnie placed his foot on the carpet, heel first. The pain was not too bad. He stood there balancing; the majority of his weight was on his right foot. He leaned left. Not bad. He balanced stepping forward with his right foot, exposing his left to serious pressure from above. The foot collapsed; he fell to the floor.

He touched the top of his foot, tracing the bones going to his toes. From the big toe to his third digit, it hurt like hell to touch, even more so to squeeze them together. The van must have broken at least three of his toes, metatarsals, when it ran over the top of his foot.

Ronnie heard his cell vibrating on the nightstand. He crawled to the bed, lifted himself to sit upright, the bad foot dragging behind him. Finally, a text from Salas. They had her! His Doris was ok. Salas telling Ronnie to get to Las Vegas.

Ronnie hopped around the hotel room, throwing clothes into bags, packing Salas's and Doris's belongings. He was more careful with his laptop, being sure to power it down before he placed it in his backpack.

He checked the room for phone chargers, toiletries, and socks, and then hopped out the door into the hallway. Loaded with three bags and the backpack between his shoulders, Ronnie used the walls for support. He was sweating by the time he made it to the elevator.

In the lobby, a doorman came to his aide. The two men walked to the parking garage, Ronnie's hand on the doorman's shoulder while jumping on his good leg.

In the garage, the doorman gladly accepted the five-dollar tip from Ronnie and left him standing by Doris's Harley. Ronnie used extra bunging cords from the saddle bags and strapped the gear to the back seat and backrest of the motorcycle. Feeling the gear was secure, he balanced on his right leg, swinging the injured left over the bike.

Ronnie placed his hands on the handlebars, his feet flat on the ground, the bike still leaning left, the kickstand firmly supporting the Harley. He pulled out his cell phone, went to Google, and typed in: "How do you start a motorcycle?"

After watching a four-minute YouTube video, Ronnie assessed the machine. Clutch on the left, accelerator on the right. Shifter on the lower left, by the left foot, rear brake on the lower right by the right foot. Front brake on the right hand. That made sense: squeezing the front brake negated the accelerator.

Ronnie turned the barrel key to the right; the headlight came on and the front dash had red and green lights shining at him. A bright green N looked at him. Ronnie stared back at it. Per the video, he squeezed the clutch in and, with his left thumb, he pushed the start button.

The bike roared to life, growling at him as he moved the accelerator back and forth. He was still leaning to the left. Ronnie smiled. He knew from Doris that the green N met neutral. Ronnie released the clutch hand. The bike did not move.

Ronnie kept the engine idling as he googled, "How do you put a Harley in gear?"

Taking a deep breath, Ronnie pushed with his left heel while leaning right and pulling with his right arm. He got the bike to sit up straight. Again, with his heel, he pushed the kickstand under the bike and settled on the seat. Both feet on the ground, the bike balanced under him. He rolled the accelerator, the bike responded. Ronnie smiled again.

Per the directions, he squeezed the clutch. One down and five up is what the video said. Ronnie pushed down with his left toes to put the bike in first gear. He grimaced in pain with the effort. The broken bones screamed their displeasure with the force applied on them. Tears fell down his eyes as he released the clutch. The bike lurched forward and shut off.

Ronnie planted his feet. More pain, but the bike stayed upright. He did not let the bike fall.

The second attempt to go forward went as planned. Ronnie restarted the bike. This time, he slowly released the clutch, giving some acceleration in a coordinated effort. Man and machine crawled forward.

Both of Ronnie's feet skimmed along the concrete floor of the parking garage. He turned right at the exit. Thankfully, no cars were coming. It was a wide turn, but he adjusted into his lane. Ronnie turned the accelerator down, giving the bike more fuel. The new couple went faster, the engine whined as he needed to shift to the second gear.

He slowed, going 10 to 15 miles per hour. He did not want to shift. He knew if shifting down was painful, shifting up would be worse. Ronnie decided to just go slow for a while. He leaned back, straightening his arms and swerved back and forth, practicing control of the bike. He slowed nearly to a stop, then accelerated. He rode in the right lane, near the shoulder of the highway.

Ronnie crept along. Cars honked as they passed him. He saw a sign in the distance. Before he passed it, he did the math in his head: Las Vegas 97 miles. At 15 mph, it would be a seven-hour ride. Ronnie took a deep breath, raising his toes. He put the Harley into second gear. A slight whimper emitted from deep inside himself.

Shifting to third through fifth was easier than the first two gears. Ronnie learned to pronate his foot and drive it inward. This placed more pressure on the outside and upper aspect of his foot. He could downshift with his heel.

Ronnie rode along at over 70 miles per hour. The wind blew his shaggy hair back over his shoulders, his cheeks fluttered against the wind. He was riding a Harley.

He rolled into Vegas in under two hours. Downshifting with his heel, he blended in well with traffic. Ronnie rode slow, staying in the right lane, knowing that would be the lane to run into the hotel.

Ronnie came to a full stop in the Bellagio garage. He pulled next to Salas's Harley, the front tire snug against the concrete wall. Ronnie struggled dropping the kickstand, finally bending over and extending the stand with his hand. He cut the engine, the bike safely leaning left. He hugged the gas tank.

33

Gloria Benson stood before the camera, the palm of her right hand smoothing any wrinkles in her form-fitting dress. There were no wrinkles. The dress looked as if it were spray-painted on. Her eyelashes shaded her cheeks, her lipstick a bright red AOC look. She held the microphone in her left hand. Eagle talons for fingernails were painted the same shade as her lips.

The cameraman whistled. Gloria raised her head to see her assistant with his hand raised, palm open, five fingers extended. He was counting down, mouthing the words five, four, three as he closed one finger at a time into a fist.

"Good morning, Las Vegas! I am Gloria Benson with Live Action Five News. We are still here at the North Vegas home of Rashid Sadulev, where just last night a major sex-trafficking organization was uncovered."

Salas, sitting in bed, sat a little straighter. He shut off Vegas Phil's phone, all eyes and ears on the TV and Gloria Benson.

"Per our anonymous source inside the Las Vegas Police Department, the case was broke open by a police detective. An Indiana Police Detective who was here on vacation! My question is: Why wasn't the Las Vegas Police Department able to crack this case? Only current

Mayor Duke can answer that question," Gloria pontificated as she turned to her right. The cameraman went to a wide-angle view.

"Joining me is current mayoral candidate, Jose "the Sheriff" Orlando. Thank you for joining us, Sheriff Orlando," Gloria said placing her microphone under the chin of Sheriff Orlando.

"My pleasure to be here, Gloria. First, let me say congrats to the Las Vegas Police Department for their fine work on this case. Yes, it took an outsider to break the case open, but, but this is of no fault of the current brave men and women of LVPD. If the current mayor would take sex trafficking more seriously, if he would properly fund the Las Vegas Police Department, we would be far more successful in preventing these types of sex-trafficking organizations."

"Mr. Orlando, as the new sheriff of Las Vegas, or—please correct me—when you are elected as the new mayor of Las Vegas, what additional concerns do you have with the current mayor's approach to protecting the citizens of Las Vegas?"

"Gloria, one of my major concerns is the increase in crime orchestrated by the numerous motorcycle gangs invading our fine community. Just recently, we have had not one but two biker-gang–related shootings on the streets of Las Vegas. Two shootings, several murdered, and no arrests. Not one arrest has been made. This is unbelievable. This is unacceptable. I promise you, mark my word, as your mayor, this will not happen. We will run these bikers, these Sons of Silence gangsters, out of not just Las Vegas, but out of all of Nevada! The Sons of Silence must be destroyed. Our officers will have direct orders to remove them."

"There you have it, Las Vegas. The firm commitment from the new sheriff, Jose Orlando." A long pause. Then Gloria looked directly into the camera. "Mayor Duke? Where are you? Why are you so quiet?" A close-up of Gloria Benson. "This is Gloria Benson of Live Action Five."

Salas was dressed. He laced up his boots and called RJ. "Hey. We need to meet."

RJ rode past the fountains to the Bellagio entryway, his hair pulled back into a bun on his head, dark sunglasses protecting his eyes from the Vegas sun. Under the huge, open-air entryway of the hotel, porters hustled with suitcases and luggage carts. Car attendants whistled, taxis responded as people moved in and out of the hotel.

The pipes of RJ's Harley echoed in the cave-like structure. He parked his bike in the shade, a few feet from the valet's podium. Salas was there to greet him.

"I take it you handled the Arab and his bodyguard?" Salas asked.

"Let's say they're taking a long desert vacation," RJ responded.

"Here," Salas said. "This is that Phil's phone. Listen to the voice mails and audio recordings."

"What's the CliffsNotes version?"

"Vegas Phil and the mayoral candidate for Vegas were trying to start a biker war. Phil killed those bikers. Some guy named Orlando, he calls himself the sheriff, ordered the hits."

"As you say, 'you got to be shitting me,'" RJ said. "Thanks. I will take care of this. You good?"

"Yeah. My lady is flying in. We will ride back tomorrow. Meet you in St. George, Utah, at noon. We're taking the Denver route home."

Thirty-two minutes later, RJ rode by the same tree Manny Escamilla parked under, the tree in front of the Hells Angels compound. He stopped his bike by the curb facing the structure. Two men slowly walked toward RJ, meeting him in the street. The three of them talked in low tones. One man turned and went into the building. Scooter came out, waved at RJ to enter.

RJ and Scooter listened to the recordings on Vegas Phil's phone.

Scooter said, "I'll take care of this. I have men in Vegas PD to handle Phil. I'll give this Sheriff Orlando my personal attention." Scooter took a deep breath. "And, hell, to think, I was going to vote for that guy."

RJ said to Scooter, "He specifically mentioned the Sons and we are not even in Vegas. I want to know why. Count me in."

CHAPTER

34

Ronnie met Salas in the Bellagio lobby. They ate a midday lunch after both men had a few hours of sleep. They enjoyed a cold beer at the lobby bar as they waited for Toni to arrive by taxi and Doris by police escort. Doris had spent the night at a local hospital for observation.

They heard Doris before they saw her. She yelled as she walked into the room, "Ronnie! Your crazy bitch is here!"

Ronnie limped from the carpeted bar to the granite floor of the lobby. Doris jumped in his arms, both legs wrapped around him. The couple kissed for over a minute. Salas watched, ordering another beer.

"We will be right back. Going to take her to the room for a change of clothes," Ronnie said, Doris still attached to him in the front-leg lock. She was biting his ear.

Moments later, Salas got a text. It was Toni. She, too, was in the lobby and, curiously, in need of a change of clothes.

The two couples met outside. Ronnie approached his boss.

"Hello, Captain Harrison." Ronnie could not look his captain in the eyes. "It's great to see you with your clothes. On. Well, you know. I did not mean to see you with, you know, that way. It was an accident. I felt terrible. I mean, you looked very good. Not that I really looked at them very long. I mean you look nice with your clothes off. And on.

You look nice with your clothes on. I just wasn't ready to see you in that way," Ronnie stumbled over words.

"It's ok, Ronnie. Mike told me about it. We should have told you about us. But I order you to forget what you saw," Captain Harrison said.

They started their walk. Salas and Toni were in the lead, walking hand-in-hand around the Bellagio Fountains. The 1,200 waterjets shot choreographed streams of H2O over 400 feet into the air. Broadway tunes played above the noise of the falling water.

Ronnie regrouped. "The Bellagio is actually built where the historic Dunes Hotel once sat. The entire Bellagio project, conceived by Steve Wynn, was inspired by Lake Como in the town of Bellagio, Italy. The artwork inside, that is where we should be sure to visit. Dale Chihuly's famous Fiori di Como features over 2,000 hand-blown glass flowers."

No one spoke as they walked, so Ronnie continued, "There are nearly 4,000 hotel rooms inside the Bellagio. Construction was completed in 1998 and it was just sold in 2019 to the Blackstone Group for over $4 billion. But Blackstone rents it back to MGM for over $200 million dollars a year. What most people do not know is that the Bellagio was robbed in 2010 of $1.5 million in chips. They caught the guy and he got 27 years in prison."

Doris stopped Ronnie as he limped along. She took his face in her hands and kissed him. "Did you read that while I was on the toilet?"

They finished the circle of the eight-and-half-acre pond, turning right walking towards Aria and the Waldorf. They could see the Eiffel Tower of the Paris Hotel down the street, Planet Hollywood, and the MGM Grand in the distance. They walked along Las Vegas Boulevard. The air was hot and dry. Salas was sweating. Ronnie was limping, using Doris as a cane.

A car horn honked. The driver lay on the horn. A blaring noise in the middle of the strip. All the walkers froze, expecting a massive collision.

"My dahling! My Michael!" the words echoed off the concrete.

The four watched as a sky-blue Chrysler Sebring convertible, the top down, flew by them. The brake lights shone bright red as the car made an immediate U-turn in the middle of the boulevard. More horns honked as offended motorists expelled profanities.

Salas and Doris pulled their partners away from the street, against the metal fence of the Bellagio fountains. The Sebring jumped the curb, onto the sidewalk, coming to a stop in front of Salas and Toni.

"My dahling! My dahling! I found you." Anne jumped out of the convertible, not bothering to open the door. She wore a pink miniskirt that barely covered her groin, a yellow halter top showing off six-pack abs and wore no shoes. She ran to Salas and, as Doris did to Ronnie, jumped into his arms with her legs wrapped around him.

"Anne. Great to see you," Salas said trying to pry Anne off his chest. She kissed him hard on the lips as Toni stood there in awe, her mouth open, her hands on her hips.

"Toni, this is the Anne. The lady I was telling you about," Salas said as Anne's feet went back to the ground, her arms still around his neck.

"Anne, please meet my girlfriend, Toni."

"Oh, my. Look at you, my lovely. Michael, she is even more beautiful than you said." Anne looked her up and down. She took Toni's hand and turned her a full 360 degrees. "Ohhhhhh. Oh. Look at this, as she patted Toni's bottom, her voice changed. "You bring out the man in me, woman."

Switching back to the female voice, she turned back to Salas. "Michael, you were right. I am rich. There was an award for rescuing those twins!"

"It's called a reward. That's great news, Anne. Now, you can apply that to your medical bills," Salas said softly.

"Oh, no. I bought this convertible instead! A Sea Breeze! Don't you just love it?" Anne exclaimed as she ran her hand over the hood of the car. "I like who I am. Now get in the car. All of you. I have a great plan! In. Get in."

Doris jumped over the door into the back seat. Ronnie opened the door and dragged his left foot into the car, sitting sideways in the rear seat to give his broken foot more room to move. Toni sat in the front seat. On Salas's lap. The seat belt stretched snug over the two of them.

"So, where we going, Anne? What's this plan you have?" Salas asked.

"Oh, my dahling," Anne said. "Trust me. We are going to do what you told me you wanted to do in Las Vegas!"

CHAPTER

35

Vegas Phil stood alone in an eight-foot-by-eight-foot cell, wearing an orange jumpsuit. The pant legs were six inches too short, termed highwater pants. His shoes were slip-on white canvas boat shoes, maybe two sizes too big. Highlighting the back shoulders of the orange ensemble was the word "PRISONER" in large black letters.

His left eye was swollen shut. Both cheeks were black-and-blue. He was missing a front tooth.

Phil had been incarcerated before – for possession of a controlled substance, distribution of a controlled substance, solicitation of prostitution, assault with a deadly weapon, grand theft auto, passing forged checks, failure to pay alimony and child support, just to name a few. He knew two of the four other gentlemen in neighboring cells, both with similar histories such as his. No one spoke.

Having spent the night in a jail cell was not new. Sitting in a jail cell without being interviewed, talked to, or been given his rights was new. This made him nervous. They did feed him an early morning breakfast of stale donuts with cold coffee. He did not complain as it was his first meal in two days.

At 11 a.m., two armed security guards escorted the prisoners for an outdoor break. A little exercise in the sun before the Vegas heat made it a health hazard. Phil stood to leave and assumed the position by the cell gate.

Back to the iron, legs spread wide, hands behind the head, fingers interlocked.

But Phil was not invited. As the second guard, the rear guard, left the room and shut the metal exit door, Phil finally released his hands and faced the locked gate.

The front door then opened. A short, large woman entered. She wore a white lab coat that draped below her knees. She had short hair like a guy, but no sideburns. In her left hand and to her side, she carried a small plastic tray filled with syringes, test tubes, cotton balls, and purple elastic ties. The nurse-slash-doctor-slash-lab-tech made a showing of snapping on white plastic gloves.

"I need some blood," she said loudly. "Please place your arm through the bar, your face against the metal." She talked to the needle, but it was loud enough for Phil to hear.

"Blood? Why you want my blood? I have been here before. No one has ever asked me for blood. What I need, doc, is some pain pills. See my hands?" Phil put both palms up. Two fingers on his right hand were not pointing in the same direction as the others. "The fucking cops broke my fingers. I need X-rays, a cast, some pain medication."

"I'm not a doctor. I'm just here for some blood samples."

"I don't give a shit what's in my blood. Give me some oxy."

"I don't write the orders, sir. I just carry them out. Please do not make my job any more fun than it already is. Your left arm, please."

Phil placed his arm through the bar.

"Further, please. And do not jerk or try to do anything. It will just hurt you and we will come back with more people, and they won't be as gentle as me."

The nurse inspected Phil's arm. She patted a purplish vein on the front of the elbow and returned to her bag. She slowly rotated her body, at the last moment exposing a syringe she stuck into Phil's triceps. She deftly pushed the plunger. A white cloudy substance once inside the barrel of the syringe quickly disappeared into Phil's arm before he could back away.

"Ouch. You gave me a damn shot. I thought you were taking my blood?"

The nurse did not respond as she placed the empty syringe in her bag. She removed the gloves and tucked a wisp of hair behind her ear. She smiled at Phil, a crooked empty smile. She left without saying a word.

Phil rubbed the side of his triceps, then winced and gently shook his right hand. The injection site burned. He was leaning against the far blocked wall when the guards brought the four prisoners back to their cells.

"Hey. Hey, guard!" Phil yelled out. "Some nurse just came in and gave me a shot. What the hell was that all about? What was the shot for? What I need is some pain meds. I want to see a doctor. Look at my eyes, man." Phil asked as he approached the gate of the cell.

The guard locked each prisoner into their temporary new home. "We don't have any nurses here, man. This ain't the county lockup. We don't give you no doctor and we do not give no shots. Do we look like a fucking urgent care to you? Now sit your ass down and shut up," said the guard.

Phil felt dizzy, unsteady. He sat on the edge of the cot then lay down, one foot still on the floor of the cell. He placed his head on the feather pillow and closed his eyes. His heart stopped beating.

—ᴍ—

Scooter and RJ rode in silence as the Ford Astro Van made its way along Interstate 15, turning right on Interstate 215 behind McCarran Airfield. Spirit Air was at a sharp upward trajectory above them. Scooter maintained the speed limit. Both men stared straight ahead. Neither spoke.

Finding Jose Orlando's house was an easy Google Search. Finding out if Orlando was at home was even easier. RJ called the campaign headquarters and asked for Jose. They said he was home preparing for a debate with Mayor Duke.

Bad news: it was broad daylight and Orlando lived in a normal, middle-income suburban neighborhood, so lots of neighbors.

Good news: it was nearly 100 degrees. No one would be outside, and all curtains would be drawn to keep the interior of their homes as cool as possible.

The only real precautions: both Scooter and RJ abandoned their club colors and wore over-sized long-sleeved denim shirts with a large emblem on the back promoting A1 Air Conditioning. Both wore matching blue denim baseball caps sporting the same company logo. They arrived in a van, not in their Harleys.

The bright yellow Ford pulled into the driveway of Mr. Orlando's ranch-style home. The front yard featured a rock lawn and a lacebark elm tree that appeared to be in the final stages of a slow death by dehydration.

The two men exited the van as a silver Dodge Charger cruised slowly by Orlando's home. The driver, an elderly man with silver hair in a military buzz cut made eye contact with RJ. RJ tipped his hat in acknowledgement. The Charger did not slow, and moved on down the street. RJ watched as the car turned right and left the neighborhood.

RJ opened the side panel door of the van, reached forward, removing a black rectangular toolbox. The toolbox was missing wrenches, screwdrivers, and electric tape but did contain a stolen Ruger 22 pistol with a blue handgrip.

The toolbox had a latch for easy opening and the Ruger was locked and loaded.

Scooter rapped his knuckles on the door, announcing A1 Air Conditioning was wanting in the house. They could hear someone walking toward them, bare feet on a hard floor, a man's voice instructing the knockers to hold their horses.

Jose Orlando opened the door without hesitation and said, "What's up? I didn't call anyone."

Scooter stepped forward into the entryway, lightly pushing Jose back with a finger to the chest. "We heard you had a problem with some bikers and was looking for Phil. We're sorry, but Phil couldn't make it."

RJ shut the door as Scooter pushed the sheriff onto a leather couch. Orlando was wearing golf shorts, and the back of his thighs squeaked as the skin caught on the couch. He fell on his side, then pushed himself upright.

"What are you talking about? I don't know any Vegas Phil," Jose said as beads of sweat suddenly appeared on his forehead.

"Who said anything about Vegas Phil?" Scooter said.

"Vegas Phil. You said Vegas Phil?" Jose Orlando asked, looking right to left within the confines of the house.

"Sir, Mr. Orlando, please meet my air conditioning apprentice. Mr. Apprentice, did I say Vegas Phil?" Scooter asked RJ.

"No, boss. You did not," RJ said.

Orlando tried to stand. Scooter put a hand on his shoulder, forcing him back to the couch.

"Listen to me. And, please, let's talk as professionals," Orlando said as he crossed his legs and spoke with his hands. Again, he looked over Scooter's shoulder as if wishing for someone, anyone to come to his rescue. "This Phil character. He means nothing to me. An end to a means. I'm going to be the next mayor of Las Vegas. I take it you two are bikers. Let me tell you what I can do. I can have you guys run out of town. Or I can give you this town. How does that sound?"

"Mr. Apprentice, would you please do a quick recon of the house. Appears Mr. Wannabe Mayor is expecting someone. And check for any surveillance cameras," Scooter said to RJ. He turned back to the sheriff. "Ok, Jose." Let's talk professionally."

"First. My home is not wired. I am, I was a police officer. I am the security system," Jose said with confidence. "Second. About the city. With my administration, I can guarantee you that I can exterminate your competition. What gang, sorry, what club do you two represent?"

"So, you *are* offering special deals. Tell me, what's in it for you?"

"As with any mutual partnership, there is quid pro quo. Let's say, 15—no, 10—percent of your gross. For that, you have my word. Your competition will be in jail, detained, raided, and harassed until they decide to leave Las Vegas."

"Sounds tempting. Tell me. I read in the paper of three different biker clubs, their men were hit in drive-by shootings. Was this by your guy named Vegas Phil?" Scooter asked as he sat in the high-backed chair across from Orlando. A coffee table with a glass top separated the two men.

"In a way, yes. But no harm, no foul, right? We're professionals. We do what we have to do, to get the results we desire," Orlando said. "Just as you are here today. A small sacrifice for you to lose one man to enrich several. Don't you think?"

"Another club had one of their ladies taken. You know about that, too?"

"Women. Nothing to worry about. It was a business transaction. Totally replaceable. Probably did the poor fellow a favor. Am I right, Mr.—? Excuse me, but I never did get your name."

"My friends and club members call me Scooter."

"Scooter. How unique. Your club?"

"We go by Hells Angels. Ever heard of them? Cuz the lady you took was one of ours. And one of the drive-bys… was one of my men."

"I can sense your frustration. My apologies. Again, all for the greater good. Just think of what I can do for you and your club. Think big picture, Scooter."

Scooter asked, "And, Mr. Apprentice…" RJ was back in the room. "What is the name of your club?"

RJ spoke up, "The Sons of Silence. We know you've heard of them, Mr. Orlando. You mentioned us on TV."

The sheriff demonstrated his first signs of panic and fear. Sweating was normal in the 100-degree heat. Lip quivers, teary eyes, and shaking hands, not so much.

"Do you need a recap on what you had to do? The end to the means?" Scooter stood over Jose.

"You have one chance to tell me. What so special about the Sons?" RJ asked as he opened the toolbox and removed the Ruger. He handed the weapon to Scooter.

"All of a sudden, you're kind of quiet, Mr. Wannabe Mayor." Scooter held the weapon in his hand, the barrel pointed at Orlando.

"Gentlemen, please, let's be men of common sense. You may run a club, but you are still businessmen. I can make it that you will have the city to yourselves. Your businesses will thrive. You will be rich beyond imagination. Every club dreams of having a man on the inside. You two will have it. Tell you what, let's do 5 percent, not 10." Orlando's knee was moving up and down as he nervously twitched his foot.

"I think you had better answer his question." Scooter nodded to RJ. "Why mention the Sons? What they ever do to you?" Scooter tapped the barrel of the Ruger on the tip of Orlando's nose.

Orlando bowed his head. "It was just the first club I could recall. That's all."

"No. You seemed pretty hell bent on the Sons. And, given your former position with the Vegas police, you know the Sons do not have an operation in this town."

"It was a long time ago. I was just a boy. It's old news. You cannot hold this against me. Your club, the Sons of Silence," he looked at RJ, "they brutally beat my father. It was years ago. My father, he never fully recovered. I had to respond in kind. You know, an eye for an eye."

"So, you're a Lifer," RJ said.

Orlando grew quiet. He seemed more secure. "Yes. How did you know? My father started the club," Jose said with pride.

"You ran him off the road, didn't you? Zeke. It was you. Were you in your patrol car at the time?" RJ asked.

"Hah! Yes, I forgot about that. Total transparency, right? That's how you build trust. We are businessmen. Let's come clean and build this relationship built on transparency and trust."

"If we are going to be business partners, then yes. Sounds like a plan." Scooter still had the pistol pointed at Jose.

"I take pride in that hit. Your Zeke. He was the one that gave my father the beating. And, lucky me, my first year on the force, one of our Lifers sees Zeke in a bar. He called me and I did the payback. That man deserved to die. But I honored him and your club. I honored him by letting him die on his Harley and not in a convalescent home like my father did."

RJ grabbed the toolbox. Closed it and left the house, leaving Scooter and Jose alone.

Orlando sat up straight, with more confidence. He did not speak, as Scooter had placed the end of the gun barrel against his temple.

"Think about it, Scooter. You will own Vegas. You will rich beyond your means."

Scooter pulled the trigger.

Wiping the gun with a bandanna, Scooter placed the weapon in the palm of Jose's hand, making sure the gun was covered with Orlando's prints. He dusted off the high-back chair with the head rag, checked the carpet, and leather couch. He also wiped down the door handle.

Outside, RJ was waiting in the Ford van, the air conditioner on high. He watched as Scooter exited the house. The two men left the area the same way they had come. As the van climbed the entrance ramp to the interstate, they passed a silver Dodge Charger parked on the shoulder of the road. The buzz-cut senior citizen, who was leaning against the side door of the van, nodded at RJ as the two men passed him.

36

The drive to 1717 Las Vegas Boulevard was loud. Anne had the speakers of her new "Sea Breeze" maxed out. She had Spotify synched with her car, with *Cupid Shuffle* leading the way but cut early because Anne could not dance and drive at the same time.

Anne took a sharp right, and everyone leaned into the curve. She shut the engine off in a spot reserved for the handicapped. Kool and the Gang was playing on Spotify, celebrating a good time. It was a special request from Salas. What can he say, the '80s were good to him.

"What's this place?" Ronnie asked.

"The Chapel of the Flowers," Anne said. "Carmen Electra and Dennis Rodman got married here! It's the place for all things married."

"Well, you know," Ronnie said, "There are over 300 weddings a day in Las Vegas. That's 10,000 ceremonies a month, 120,000 in a year. Vegas is unique. They do not require a blood test, no waiting period. All you need is an ID, one witness, and $77. Now, a misconception is that you can get married when intoxicated in Vegas. You can be drinking, but 'drunk' is actually illegal." Ronnie went on, "Who's getting married?"

Toni and Salas exited the Chrysler first. Salas shut the door before Ronnie could get out. Salas turned to Toni, "I know this is fast. I haven't even told my daughter, Sami, about you yet. She may be pissed that she wasn't invited, but I know she will love you, too."

He dropped to one knee, "Toni Harrison, would you do me the honor of being my wife? Toni, will you marry me?"

"Oh, my Lord," Doris elbowed Ronnie in the ribs.

"My James will be mad, too." Toni grinned. "And you know that when we get home as Mr. and Mrs. Mike Salas, the first thing I will have to do is fire your ass?" She paused a few seconds. "And, yes, I will. I love you, Mike."

Doris and Ronnie stood in the back seat clapping and cheering while Anne played Bruno Mars's *Marry You*.

The fivesome entered the Chapel of the Flowers. They were immediately greeted by a tall skinny white man in a perfectly fitted tux. The black bow tie was crisp, the pants with an ironed crease and the shirt heavy on the starch. He introduced himself as Roger and guided the group to the Magnolia Chapel.

Seems Anne was so confident that she had prepaid, had the marriage license ready, and pre-arranged the ceremony.

Toni, Anne, and Doris, in high-pitched squeals, entered the ladies' dressing room. Ronnie and Salas went the opposite direction to the men's.

Anne dressed the ladies in matching pink chiffon thin-shoulder-strap dresses with the backs exposed. Anne was a whiz with a needle and thread, paper clips, and a stapler to get the dresses form-fitted. Doris's dress had the most to adjust, as Anne had thought she would be taller.

In the boy's room, Salas and Ronnie found black blazers, white flipflops, and long black over-the-knee basketball shorts with the Nike swoosh on the side. The white shirts were huge, with long sleeves, but no ties. Both men tucked the excess material in their new shorts and made their way to the chapel.

Roger pinned a red rose boutonniere on the groom and best man. The two stood side-by-side, waiting for the bride.

Toni held a handtied seven-pink-rose bouquet. The three ladies, to the music of *Canon in D*, made their way to the front stage of the Magnolia. Doris on Toni's left, Anne on Toni's right.

Roger, the greeter, was also the pastor. He said, "Who gives this woman to be this man's lawful wedded wife?"

"I do!" yelled Anne as she grabbed Salas by the back of the neck and planted a kiss on his mouth.

"Anne, you have got to stop doing that," Salas said.

Anne followed up by kissing Toni, also on the lips. This kiss a little longer than the Salas kiss. Anne then turned toward Doris, who backed away, hands out, leading Anne to a standstill.

Roger led the ceremony, telling both the bride and the groom what to say. Vows were exchanged and the unity candle lit. Roger then pronounced Salas and Toni man and wife.

The prepaid reception included Champagne in plastic flutes, a keg of beer, mini hot dogs, fried chicken and biscuit sliders, and a veggie platter.

After the group of five had danced twice to *Cupid Shuffle*, Salas requested Chris Stapleton's *Tennessee Whiskey* and *Starting Over*. Roger then shuffled the newlyweds out of the chapel, and back to the Bellagio for a night cap.

CHAPTER

37

The two couples were on their Harleys and on Interstate 15 by ten in the morning. Mr. and Mrs. Salas led the way, with Mike watching Las Vegas disappear from his side mirrors.

It was Toni's first experience on a motorcycle. The first few minutes, she sat perfectly still, her arms tight around Salas's waist. After 30 miles, her squirming increased. Her rear was not accustomed to the tiny seat of the Harley. Salas was already planning a bike upgrade to the passenger convenience of the Ultra.

Near Mesquite, a lone rider on a Harley passed the two bikes on their left. It was RJ. His hair flew behind him like the mane of a quarter horse at the Kentucky Derby. His dark glasses protected his eyes from sun, while his cheeks were spread wide from the force of the wind.

RJ saluted to Salas as he passed, pausing slightly to check out the lady hanging on for dear life to Salas.

At St. George, the trio stopped for fuel. Salas updated RJ on his surprise nuptials. Ronnie, RJ, and Salas assured Toni that her biker's butt would get better before it got worse. They were lying.

RJ said nothing about Vegas Phil's phone, Scooter, or the late Sheriff Orlando. He did agree with Salas that, in Vegas, love was in the air and made plans to return to Sin City within the month.

Near Sulphurdale, Utah, the bikes leaned right, taking Interstate 70. They rode hard at 85 and 90 miles per hour through the wasteland of Utah and Colorado. They arrived in Grand Junction as most people were getting off work. While parked under the canopy of the Love's Travel Stop, they voted to spend the night in Grand Junction rather than ride the Rockies at night.

Salas made a sharp turn to treat Toni to her first taste of motorcycle gear at the Grand Junction Harley Davidson. They left with a leather jacket for Toni, a helmet for Toni, a silver Harley ring on Toni's wedding finger, and a 2018 Electric Glide CVO Ultra Classic.

Once Toni sat on the Ultra, Salas knew he had a new bike. The chromed-out Burgundy Cherry Ultra with GPS, heated seats, Bluetooth, and 117 cc motor were inconsequential against the comfort of Toni's butt and that rear seat.

The group was seated at a round high-top table for six. The U-shaped bar, guarded by a dozen high-backed wooden bar stools, served as the focal point of Applebee's Bar and Grill. The restaurant was nearly empty; their arrival doubled the number of customers.

RJ faced the main entrance, while Salas and Toni had their backs to the door. The waitress took their orders. Salas informed the crew he was going to retire from the Fort Wayne Police Department.

His plan was to get on with the Allen County Sheriff's Patrol, maybe contact the Roanoke or Huntertown police departments or perhaps open an office for Mike Salas Private Investigative Services.

RJ interrupted Salas. He stood, reaching behind his back. His weapon missing – it had been comfortably stuffed in the saddlebag of his bike. He rushed forward, pushing a bar stool to the side as a shot rang out. Splinters of wood pierced RJ's cheeks and neck as the back rest of the bar stool shattered. He dove for the carpet as more shots filled the air.

Customers screamed; some ran out the front door but most dropped to the floor. The bartender dove behind the safety of the bar.

Salas instinctively dragged Toni to the carpet, covering her with his body. His handgun pointing to the door. He told his wife to stay down as he logrolled to the left, looking for the shooter.

More shots rang out, this time from the back of the restaurant. In the prone position, Salas quickly fired two rounds. The man at the door fired again as he fell to the tiled entryway.

Ronnie yelled out. "Two shooters! One shooter down, one left by the rear exit. I'm on it." He ran out the front door, hurdling over the first shooter as he went. He carried no weapon.

RJ and Salas brushed shoulders as the two hovered over the first gunman. Specs of blood and wooden splinters pockmarked RJ's face. Salas kicked the man's weapon across the entry's floor.

Blood was seeping from the silver-haired man's chest. RJ recognized the shooter.

The older man lay flat, his breathing heavy, small bloody air bubbles percolated from his nose and mouth. He wore a faded blue denim jean jacket. A small round patch covered the left pocket. It said: "Lifer."

A low-neck tattoo peeked out of the man's shirt. RJ tore the white T. Under the chin, in dark ink, it read "An Eye For An Eye." The old man was smiling.

"An eye for an eye. You got Orlando, I got you." His eyes turned to Salas. "You got me. My boys will get you."

Ronnie re-entered the building, joining Salas and RJ. "I couldn't find the second shooter. No sign of anyone running or a car racing away. He had to be parked out back. I called 911, they're on their way."

RJ slapped the man on the floor. "Who was your partner? Was it your boy? I know you are Lifers. Who was it?"

The dying man forced out a "Screw you, Sons. Sons of bitches." Drops of blood shot upward. The spittle settled on the man's face and chest.

Salas grabbed the Lifer, turning him slightly. He removed the man's wallet from his left rear pocket and took out the driver's license, letting the man slump back to the floor. Salas handed Ronnie the ID.

Ronnie read aloud, "Harvey Weston. Belle Fork, Forch-a, South Dakota?"

"Belle Foosh is how it sounds. But spelled different," RJ said.

"I've been to Rapid City and Sturgis, South Dakota. Where is Belle Foosh relative to that?" Ronnie asked.

"It's twenty-five or thirty miles west of Sturgis, just off Interstate 90."

Harvey coughed; more blood jumped into the air. His eyes widened as the pupils slid backwards, the white of his eyes filling the sockets. His chin rose as his neck arched, the air leaving his body. It was his last breath.

"Mike... Mike." It was Doris's voice.

Salas turned. Doris was sitting on the floor, her back against the base of the bar. Toni was lying on her back, her head in Doris's lap. Doris was stroking Toni's hair.

"She covered me, Mike. She pulled me over here and lay on top of me. She saved me. She got shot. I heard it hit her. It was a low, sinking, sucking sound. It should have hit me. She's not talking. She's not moving. Toni isn't breathing." Doris sobbed softly as she continued to caress Toni's hair and cheeks.

Salas made his way to his new wife where she lay in the arms of Doris. Toni looked as if she was taking a nap, just resting. She looked peaceful. Salas went to his knees and checked the pulse on her wrist. Nothing. He put two fingers on her neck. He could not feel anything.

Slowly, Mike turned Toni to her side. Her new leather jacket had a small tear, a hole between her left shoulder blade and spine. It looked like a simple snag, a rip in the leather.

Doris began singing quietly to Toni, "Amazing Grace, how sweet thou art..."

Salas ran his hand up Toni's back, under her jacket. She was warm, her back damp. He removed his hand from under the leather. He stared at his palm. It was covered in blood.

Ronnie was talking. Salas could not understand what he was saying. RJ said something about Toni. Doris was singing. The waitress was screaming. Police sirens got louder and louder.

Salas pulled Toni to his chest. He kissed her. He held her. He cried.

Ronnie and RJ guided Salas through the rest of the evening. Police interviews. The dead man. The guy that got away. Doris in shock as she continued to sing. Salas's gun. Salas's badge. Toni's badge. Toni in an ambulance, Salas by her side.

The sun still rose from the east. Life moves on, even when you don't want it to.

Salas, RJ, and Ronnie sat in the breakfast area of the Holiday Inn Express.

"Mike, I've got my boys coming to get your Harley. Don't worry about it. We will get it to your house. You go home with Toni, back to Indiana," RJ said. He lowered his head into his hands.

"This is my fault, Mike," RJ said. "These guys must have followed us from Vegas. I saw them there. This group, a shithole bunch of guys with a long history of resentment against the Sons. I should have seen them. I should have taken them out in Vegas."

"You did nothing wrong. I don't blame you. I blame them, the Lifers." Salas slapped the table with his fist. Heads turned, a man and wife switched tables.

"You need some time off, Mike. I will work with the department for you. Make sure you get the bereavement time you are due. You take all the time you need," Ronnie said.

"I'm quitting. I told you, I'm quitting the force," Salas said as he took a drink of coffee.

Ronnie spoke, "Mike, that was before. You have lots of time to think this over. Let's just go one day at a time. No need to make any decisions right away. This will take time, but it will all get back to normal."

"Yeah, Mike. You just rest," RJ added.

"Today, I'm taking Toni home to her son. Shit. I haven't even met him yet. I've got to call him today. He deserves to know."

"Mike if you want, I can handle that for you," Ronnie said, adding, "We don't have to talk about the wedding."

"I want her son to know she was loved. I want him to know me," Salas said, his voice raised. The husband and wife with the free cinnamon rolls and orange juice stared at them. They moved another table away.

Salas went quiet. He drank more coffee. Those staring went back to their rolls.

"I'll take care of Toni. Then, I'm going to South Dakota."

"No, Mike. The Lifers are mine. They are the Sons' issue. I will take care of them. Please let me handle this," RJ said.

"You can go with or without me, but I'm going to South Dakota."

"Mike, you left me alone in Laughlin. There's no way you're leaving me alone in Fort Wayne. Count me in."

"Boys," RJ looked at Salas and Ronnie, "looks like we're headed to Sturgis."

38

The first few days in Indiana, Salas met Toni's son, James. Sami drove over for the funeral, still unsure as to who, what, and how it all happened. Salas shared with Sami his feelings about Toni, his new friend, Anne, and the Vegas wedding. They laughed over Kool and the Gang and getting married in baggy shorts. They cried as Sami's dad told her of Doris singing *Amazing Grace*.

The days and weeks following the funeral were a foggy haze. Ronnie was wrong; nothing went back to normal.

It was late on a Friday afternoon when Salas emailed his resignation to the interim captain-in-charge, Richard Chastain. Chastain was the Fort Wayne captain before Green; his retirement had placed Green in the leadership position.

Salas had always gotten along with Chastain, but the detective and officers called their captain Dick, and not because his name was Richard. With Chastain as the new chief, Salas confirmed his time was over.

There was no retirement party, no golden watch or one last tour of the floor for handshakes and goodbyes. Just the email. Salas placed his personal belongings from his five-by-five cubicle in a cardboard box. There was not much to pack. He tossed most of it: papers, a coffee cup, a day planner, and business cards. He packed a Jack Reacher paperback by Lee Child and a hardcover Joe Pickett novel by CJ Box.

Salas's prized possessions were the pictures of Sami – a couple of framed photos and several pictures printed off the station's color printer. Sami posing on the campus of Notre Dame, Sami on spring break, Sami at a Fighting Irish football game, and Sami with her boyfriend, Tripp.

Salas liked Tripp. Hell, he was the one who introduced them when he rode to Daytona and she was in Panama City Beach.

Salas left his badge and service revolver on Toni's—Chastain's—desk. He stroked the desktop's wooden veneer. He had good memories on that desk, which prompted a smile.

Checking in the Ford Taurus and handing the keys to the motor pool desk clerk was the final nail into his official retirement. Salas opted to walk home over catching a ride or an Uber.

The last few blocks of the four-mile jaunt were in a light rain. Water beaded on Salas's bald head, with more soaking into his jacket, blue jeans, and leather biker boots.

Arriving home, he stood in his entryway to remove his coat and strip off his shirt as water pinged off the tile floor. A small puddle crept its way to the carpet.

As Salas checked his phone, there was a knock on the door. Three loud raps.

"Yeah. Just a sec. On my way!" Salas yelled. He stepped off the carpet, the rubber heel of the boot catching the edge of the puddle. His legs shot forward as his butt went to the tile. As he fell, a blast torpedoed wooden fragments and iron shotgun pellets through the door and over Salas's horizontal body.

Salas rolled to his belly, crawling on all fours to his bedroom as another blast blew the door open. A third and fourth round from the shotgun took out the hallway window.

Another shot was fired, hitting the door jamb of his room as Salas reached under his bed.

He grabbed his weapon, a Mossberg 590 twelve-gauge tactical shotgun. He could hear the gunman swearing, the sound of a shotgun shell dropping to the floor. The attacker was reloading.

In his prone position, Salas could smell the bedroom's carpet. He leaned into the hallway, Mossberg first. He fired. The first round removed the attacker's tibia and fibula from the knee down. The man fell against the wall, blood flowing out of an arterial hose.

Salas fired again and again.

Chastain, Ronnie, three EMTs, a dozen city police officers, and two from the State Patrol invaded Salas's home, front yard, and driveway. Neighbors stood in the rain as two men pushed a gurney carrying a body bag into the ambulance.

"Got your email. How are you liking retirement so far, Salas?" Chastain asked.

Salas ignored him. "Ronnie, who was it? You got anything?"

"No identification on the guy. The car, a silver Dodge Charger. We guess it's his car in the driveway, has no registration, no insurance ID card, no luggage. But the VIN leads us to South Dakota and a Mr. Harvey Weston. I'm thinking this is one of his boys."

"The eye-for-an-eye bullshit. The old man said it would happen."

"Enjoy the rest of your evening, Salas. Thanks for ruining mine." Chastain walked away.

"Are we headed to Sturgis? I'm ready when you are, Mike," Ronnie said, watching Chastain duck his head to get into his car. "I'm feeling good on my Road King and have lots of vacation time."

Salas opened two beers. They sipped on Guinness in the kitchen as a light breeze from the missing window ventilated the scene. They watched the forensic techs take pictures and gather blood and tissue samples.

"I'll call that cleaning crew the department uses. They can place some boards over the window until you get a carpenter in." Ronnie paused before asking, "Anything from RJ?"

"He's back in Vegas. I just need to make up my mind."

Later that evening, Salas made the call. "This goes against everything I stood for over the past twenty-five years as a police officer. I don't want justice, Ronnie. I want revenge. I've been waiting and wanting to get over this feeling. Now, today, they attack me in my own home. I want the Westons. Don't feel like you have to come, Ronnie. I'm going off the reservation on this one. I don't care if I come back."

39

Elected state officials banned fireworks due to a statewide drought, fearing their use would be an unnecessary fire hazard. Neighborhoods were rattled awake as Ronnie and Salas's Harleys *hupt-hupt-hupted*, spat, and banged through the city. It would be the only fireworks Fort Wayne would get on this fourth of July.

The bikers accelerated on Highway 30, racing to Gary, Indiana, where the two would merge onto Interstate 90, I-90 being the path that flowed the entire way to their final destination. The 1100-mile ride was just the prelude to meeting the Weston boys of Belle Fourche, South Dakota.

Ronnie briefed Salas the night before on the results of his internet search of their new nemesis. He found that the Westons owned a 10,000-acre ranch north of I-90, near the unincorporated Fruitdale, South Dakota, and the Bell Fourche Reservoir. Per the Butte County Treasurer Office, the property was a few miles off Highway 212 and operated as a cattle feeding business.

The vast majority of the property's acres were listed as rolling grasslands with two alfalfa fields under Reinke center pivots. Ronnie further discovered that the Westons once owned over 20,000 deeded acres. The dead Harvey had sold down to the current size over the past eleven years.

Ronnie guessed financial troubles or perhaps a family spat forcing a land sale to stay afloat. More public records relayed Harvey and Betty Weston as having seven children. Five boys and two girls. The five on the ranch and the two in Colorado. Ronnie believed one of the boys to be the dead man in Fort Wayne. So, four boys were still in Belle Fourche.

Traffic through and around Chicago never slowed down. No matter the season, the holiday, or the weather, it was always busy. The interstate system was faster than cutting across rural America, but the heavy traffic of a major city was far more intense when on a motorcycle.

Salas and Ronnie rode in a close pack, speed steady at 65 mph. They remained in the right lane, following a silver Mercedes. The two were always watchful for merging traffic and an occasional glimpse of Lake Michigan.

Traffic thinned as they passed Schaumberg, Illinois, and the bikes were urged to go faster on the plains from Gilberts to Madison, Wisconsin. It was Salas's first long ride on the new Ultra he had purchased for Toni in Grand Junction, Colorado. RJ's crew had delivered the CVO to his home in Fort Wayne, arriving before Salas did.

He did a couple of test rides around the neighborhood and short excursions with Ronnie and his new bike. Ronnie was getting the feel of riding on his own. Gone were the days when he rode on the back of Doris's Harley.

Salas loved the Ultra, the balanced feel of the ride, the large fairing diverting the wind, the sound system, and GPS. Ronnie went old school; no windshield on the Road King, with ape hangers holding his hands slightly above his shoulders.

If the duo stayed on the chartered course from Indiana to South Dakota, no helmet was required but both carried their lids in the saddle bags of their bikes.

The first night on the road was spent in an American Inn and Suites near the Madison Harley Davidson store. There was no shopping nor any drinking. After takeout burgers, Salas spent the night cleaning his handgun, a .38 Cobra Colt Special. He kept the revolver in an ankle holster on his left leg, making it accessible while he rode.

The new toy for the trip was a Winchester Model 94 Trails End Takedown. The .30-30 Winchester with a lever action design was broken down into two components for easy storage in the Ultra's Tour-Pak.

One more handgun was safely locked in the right saddlebag of the Ultra. In a specially designed foam conceal kit, a 9 mm Sig Sauer P226 with one magazine was snug and tight. It was also locked and loaded.

In a trance, Salas broke down and reassembled his weapons while Ronnie tapped the keyboards of his laptop.

When Ronnie spoke, Salas flinched. "I'm perusing Facebook. Never understood why people like this. Anyway, I've found Mrs. Weston, Betty's Facebook page. Inside her photo album is a polaroid picture. The clip has the likeness of Harvey Weston and a man captioned as a 'dear friend' named Jesse Orlando." Ronnie looked at Salas. "That was the guy in Vegas that RJ mentioned."

Ronnie twisted the computer, so Salas could see the screen. Two men saddled on their Harleys, looking over their right shoulders, both smiling. Each wore leather Lifer vests with red-on-black embroidery proclaiming: *Lifestyle Determines Death Style.*

Harvey and Jesse, both now deceased. One of Harvey's boys dead and Jesse's son, Jose, a victim of suicide from the stress and rigors of the mayoral race in Las Vegas.

Salas kept cleaning. Ronnie kept typing and talking.

"Surprisingly, very little information on a motorcycle club called the Lifers. Jesse Orlando and Harvey Weston pop up several times. But mainly for petty theft in and around western South Dakota. Get this. Harvey had stint in the state penitentiary."

Salas looked up. "Really? What for?"

Ronnie said, "The high crime of the 1800s. Cattle rustling. Harvey spent five years in the South Dakota State Pen."

Ronnie typed some more. "Here we go. A new one. The 'Grave Digger,' formally known as George Watson, is mentioned here in the Spearfish Newspaper Obituary section. A total of three paragraphs sum up his life. With the highlight being his friends within the Lifers Club and his 2015 demise from complications due to cancer. No surviving relatives. Other than that, the last of the Lifers mentioned was found in the archives of the Rapid City Journal. Thanks again to obituaries, we have found the infamous Lifer, Norman Lancaster. Norman died when the John Deere tractor he was driving was hit broadside by a farmer hauling manure. Seems none of the Lifers had a very glorious lifestyle for their death style."

Minutes later, Ronnie's snoring was in sync with the rise and fall of his chest. Still in his riding clothes, Ronnie's personal sidearm, a .40 caliber Smith and Wesson semi-auto, slept snuggly beside him in his Bianchi waistband holster.

As the sun rose on day two of the trip. Both men had their bikes loaded and on the interstate. Their next stop for the night was scheduled for Sioux Falls, South Dakota.

CHAPTER

40

RJ opened his eyes. The clock was past 6:00 a.m. He planned on sleeping in, again. Shelli's body was too warm and too soft to even think about getting out of bed. He liked his new home. His two weeks in Colorado were long enough to sell Deuce's house, give the reigns of My Three Sons Construction to the three doing all the work, and transfer his club's presidential power to his second-in-command.

He now considered himself semi-retired. No one never really leaves their club, but they can slow down and transfer authority to the young guns.

Unlike in Salas's case, the club hosted RJ a party, complete with kegged beer, smoked brisket, handshakes, and hugs. His plan was to marry Shelli, work at the bar, sleep in more often, and maybe learn how to swim.

But, first, he was going to Belle Fourche, South Dakota, and eliminate the last of the Lifers. He owed this to Salas and Toni. He owed it Zeke and to the Sons. But, mostly, he felt he owed it to Shelli.

Like Salas, RJ had an 1100-mile ride to Sturgis. Given his later-than-planned start, as he still wasn't out of bed or done with Shelli, his first day ride on Interstate 15 would end in Salt Lake City, Utah.

The six-hour ride was far shorter than most trips but duty called, and that duty was to Shelli. His last ride to Utah, and the railyard meeting with Manny Escamilla, seemed like centuries ago.

RJ watched Shelli's chest rise and fall. She snored lightly with an occasional snort. She rolled out of his arms to her left side, in the fetal position. RJ scooched down to spoon.

His ears perked when he heard the sliding glass door leading outside to the pool slide open. RJ knew the sound.

He deftly rose to his feet, slipped on his boxers and tiptoed out of the bedroom, gently closing the door as he left.

None of the floors in the house were carpeted – tile, wood, and granite flooring being the standard in Las Vegas. Still on his toes, RJ turned to enter the kitchen. He caught a movement in the corner of his eye: a slight movement, an arm raised. Stepping forward to the left, RJ leaned back, his left shoulder down, his right shoulder twisting with his movement.

The attacker did a round house swing, the blade of a knife glistening in the morning sun. RJ palmed his left arm forward, pushing the attacker's arm up and back. The blade of the knife caught RJ's right deltoid. The muscular hump on his right shoulder tore open from the cut. Blood quickly oozed out from the gash.

RJ stayed on his feet, his fists clenched. He had both hands up in a fighter's stance. His opponent squared to meet him, holding a serrated hunting knife in his right hand, blood dripping from the blade.

RJ didn't wait for him to settle into position. He shot out a front leg kick that connected with the attacker's left lead leg just as the man was stepping forward. The snap of the cruciate ligaments could he be heard as the leg buckled and the man fell to the floor.

There was no yelling, no screaming, no threats to kick ass or kill anyone. The attacker tried to stand, but the knee was not cooperating. He swung his right arm back towards RJ, hoping for some part of the blade to connect. It didn't.

RJ stepped forward with a side kick to the man's head. The top of his foot connected and created a loud crack that echoed off the tile. The man's eyes rolled back. RJ grabbed him by the nap of the neck while bringing his own knee upward.

The tip of the man's nose smashed into RJ's knee. More snapping and cracking as the attacker's nasal bones were driven upward into his brain.

The man fell to the floor as his last gasps for air escaped him. RJ twisted the man's wallet out of his rear pocket. The driver's license read: Wyatt Weston, Butte County, South Dakota. He was listed as five feet nine inches tall, 175 pounds, with brown eyes and blonde hair. His thirtieth birthday was last month. He was an organ donor. RJ ripped open the man's shirt, the top of his chest read in black ink "An Eye For An Eye."

RJ made one call. Within 20 minutes, Scooter and three Hells Angels carried Wyatt Weston out of Shelli's house. The dead man with the double crushed skull was stuffed inside a large plastic trash can. The can strapped was to a utility dolly.

RJ watched from the living room window as they drove away. He quickly cleaned any blood splatter off the floor and kitchen counters. He also cleaned his own wound. He patched it with a dish towel and silver tape from Shelli's toolbox. He was already dressed and sitting at the kitchen table, drinking coffee, when Shelli entered the room.

"Morning, honey. I slept like a rock. Been up long?" Shelli asked.

—⟋⟍—

RJ packed light, not expecting to be in Belle Fourche more than a few days. He knew what he had to do and was more than prepared to get it done, especially after the home hit by the Westons. He had a Glock 9 mm hidden in his bike, with plan A and plan B in his mind for the family in South Dakota. His only concern – how many Lifers were still Lifers.

After a night's stay in SLC, the exit to the railyard was a blur in his side mirror as RJ raced through the ever-growing and expanding Salt Lake City metropolis.

Taking Interstate 80 to Rawlings, Wyoming, RJ then turned to highway 285 for a direct route to Casper, stopping on I-25 in Gillette. The oil town had low-priced fuel, high-priced gas station burritos, and an exit to Interstate 90. The final leg, a 115-mile sprint to downtown Sturgis.

RJ passed the exit to Belle Fourche and the first exit to Spearfish, South Dakota. He loved the Spearfish Canyon ride. He thought maybe, if all goes well, he would lean into the curves before heading back to Shelli.

After many years, RJ was planning a future for himself, and not for others. He could not escape this. It was his duty to Salas. He had committed to the memory of Toni Harrison and a bit of revenge for Shelli. Since his release from the Colorado Federal Prison nearly a year ago, he had taken a few lives, lived on the edge, all while claiming to go legit. This was it. After Belle Fourche, RJ would be done with this life.

A few miles from Sturgis, RJ leaned right, taking an exit onto Laurel Street, the gateway to Whitewood, South Dakota. The sun was setting as he rode past Howdy's Plaza and the block plant to Meade Street. He parked his bike, taillights facing Bullwacker's Saloon.

Air conditioning greeted him as he walked through the door, a luxury fairly new to the bar, considering it served its first patron when Grover Cleveland was president. RJ faced the front bar as he sat at a high-top round table. A LED television hung at an angle above him, the sound off, a baseball game on.

A rotund barmaid in a tight V-neck shirt made eye contact with RJ. She leaned against the high-top, her breasts pushed up and out.

"Evening, big fella. Know watcha drinking?" she asked.

"Yeah, I'll take one of those IPAs from the Crow Peak Brewery."

"We got the 11th hour IPA. That do you?"

"Yes. Please. Say, do you happen to know the Weston family over in Belle Fouche?" RJ asked.

"Honey, if you live here, you know those boys. They no good. If you a friend, please don't call 'em and have 'em come over. Deal?"

"Deal. And they aren't my friends. But I heard they were trouble."

"You got that right, big fella."

RJ's phone rang; he was expecting Shelli. It was Scooter.

"Yeah," RJ said.

"Just an FYI. One of my boys brought a little lady to the club last night. Pretty little blonde. She looked good and wanted to please. You know how some of the boys like the groupies. Well, she was willing. Partied hard for an hour. Went to the can, came out, and wanted to leave. Seems she had enough. She was sprinting out of the building, my heartbroken boy hot in chase. Bones was next in the toilet. He was a Nam vet. He came running out, yelling 'C-4 and its hot!' We all followed Bones, who was following the blonde. She was still running when Bones tackled her. The explosion took out the half our building. No one hurt, thanks to Bones."

"You got a name?"

"Yeah, the blonde bomber is Brenda Weston. You know her?"

"It was her brother you emptied in the trash."

"They didn't have a very good Vegas vacation," Scooter said.

"Any tattoos on her?"

"I take it you want to know her logo? Yeah, above her left breast is "An Eye For An Eye."

"Thanks for letting me know. I'm here in South Dakota to stop this. I'll let you know how it goes."

"I don't think lover boy or Bones will be letting her go back home, if you know what I mean."

CHAPTER

41

The ride through Minnesota was straight. No curves, no hills, a 70-mph speed limit. Sprouting corn winked at the two bikers with fields of wind turbines waving in their side mirrors. To say this stretch of Interstate 90 was boring was being polite.

Ronnie and Salas headed southwest past Rochester, crossing under the Des-Moines-to-Minneapolis I-35 express in Albert Lea, Minnesota. They rode parallel to the Iowa border for what seemed like 100 miles longer than it was. Fuel in Worthington, Minnesota, had them arriving in Sioux Falls three hours earlier than expected.

The two wasted little time in discussion and continued westward. The scenery changed from a farmer's perspective of fun to a rancher's dream of a lush wavy grassland.

Lunch at Culver's in Mitchell led to a must-stop-and-see Al's Oasis in Chamberlain, South Dakota. They didn't know why they stopped except for the one-too-many billboards telling them to do so.

With the break, they topped off their tanks with premium only to fall to the same marketing campaign. Bypassing Kadoka, they stretched their mileage and landed in Wall, South Dakota, and the infamous Wall Drug.

Seventy miles and less than an hour later, Ronnie followed as Salas took the right lane to the second exit into Sturgis, South Dakota. The 76th annual Sturgis Rally was nearly eight weeks away.

The town was an empty shell of what it would transform into come the first week of August. Gone were the vendor tents, thousands of bikes, thousands of people, and the roar of Harley exhaust.

Salas gassed his bike. It responded with a quick thrust that jerked Salas's head as if nodding approval to the acceleration. A year prior, when Salas rode Lazelle Street, bikes were tire-to-tire in rows of two going east and west.

Today, Lazelle was empty. The only bikes were Salas's Ultra and Ronnie's Road King. He took a right on 3rd, followed by a left on Main Street past the Sturgis Police Station. The brick building triggered memories of Salas riding Doris's bike, and Albert Christiansen killing the county deputy with a screwdriver.

They made a U-turn in the middle of Main Street. No oncoming traffic was in view. They stopped and backed their bikes to the curb of the Oasis Bar. The sun was gone from view, and darkness settled on the small South Dakota town.

The front door of the Oasis was open, with Jamey Johnson singing "*...that's how I don't love you,*" his voice echoing into the empty street. Salas and Ronnie locked their bikes and entered the tavern.

Salas ordered two Coors Lights as they walked past the bar, settling into an empty table for eight. Three cowboys in white sweat-stained straw hats sat at the bar, their backs to Salas and Ronnie. One wore spurs with ten-point rowels, another with cow-shit-stained boots and pant legs. They drank out of brown longneck bottles.

Ronnie ordered wings, Salas the same. Two more Coors Lights went down like the water it tasted like. From his cellphone, Ronnie made online reservations at the Super Eight located off the exit they just rode in from. The sound of another motorcycle made the U-turn on Main, the headlight scanning the interior of the Oasis. The rider gassed his engine one last time before he killed the motor.

Salas and Ronnie both stood as RJ entered the bar.

Salas, Ronnie, and RJ compared notes.

Ronnie spoke first, "Four Westons are no longer active members of the Lifers Motorcycle Gang." Ronnie held up a finger. "Gone is the father, Harvey." Fingers two and three popped up. "Gone are sons Wade and Wyatt." A fourth finger rose. "And daughter Brenda has left this world, courtesy of the Hells Angels. All victims of their eye-for-an-eye motto."

Salas said, "That leaves three boys: Willie, Webster, and the youngest boy, dubbed 'W.' We assume those three are still around, along with the mother, Betty, and daughter Barb. Though we think she's in Colorado."

The men made their plans for the following day. Salas was to ride west to Belle Fourche, then take Highway 212 to the Weston ranch. He wanted to check out the proverbial lay of the land.

Ronnie and RJ were to ride east of Sturgis, then north to Bear Butte Mountain, turning west before Newell, South Dakota. The three would meet on Highway 212 at the Nisland bar by noon.

Their goal: to scope out any road construction, roadblocks, or delays before the three went full force to the Westons.

The two teams left the hotel at 9:00 a.m. Temperatures were in the mid-sixties, with a projected high of 84 for late afternoon.

Salas took I-90 west. The 25-mile ride cleared his senses as he took the north exit and Highway 85. The Cenex station provided premium fuel and the exit east on 212.

Salas slowed near Fruitdale, South Dakota, population 64 and dropping. A dirt road across the highway of the Belle Fourche Reservoir exit marked the entrance to the Weston ranch. A large metal sign of six cowboys riding horses stated that "Weston Angus" was a quarter mile south.

Salas sat on his Harley. He cut the engine and looked at the Weston homeplace. He could smell ammonia from uric acid and the pungent odor of cow manure as it drifted northward from the gust of wind.

Cedar trees provided the log-cabin home with a northern and southern windbreak. East of the home was a row of concrete feed bunks stretching over 50 yards. The bunks connecting the cedar trees from north to south had concrete slabs extending 20 yards west from each bunk. The concrete had to provide year-round solid footing for the 400 or more black Angus cows fenced in the yard.

Far too many cattle for one feedlot, or so Salas thought. The cattle were too crowded to move. A green tractor with six-feet-tall black tires pulled a grain sled that was dumping feed into the bunks. The cattle bumped and bellowed as they hustled to the east to grab a feeding spot.

South of the lot, Salas saw two center pivots shoot water out of sprinkler heads high above the green topped alfalfa.

The man in the John Deere stopped his northern-bound journey, the spray of feed and grain growing hesitant with the tractor's speed. Tractor and Harley stared at each other. Salas could see three people on the front deck of the log home. Arms were waved and fingers pointed in Salas's direction. One of the three on the deck was now missing.

Salas started his bike as a black pickup kicked up dust west of the home. He placed the bike into gear, looked left on Highway 212 for oncoming traffic, popped the clutch, and sped east on the two-lane.

Riding a few miles above the 60 mph limit, Salas watched in his side mirrors as the black truck grew larger. He slowed to under 50, riding the white line as the truck was now within inches of his rear tire. He could feel the heat from the Dodge's motor and see the eyes of the lone occupant of the truck. The man was smiling.

Salas sped up as he moved the Harley to the center yellow stripes. The truck kept pace.

With his bike in the center of the two-lane, Salas watched as the Dodge advanced to his left. Salas anticipated the driver's goal of forcing him off the road to the right.

At 75 mph, and the miles long ditch of five strands of barbed wire fencing, Salas would more or less land in the hospital for months or in the morgue for good.

As the pickup approached Salas's left shoulder, Salas slammed on the front and rear brakes of the Harley. He fought to keep the bike going straight as it burned rubber to a halt. The Dodge shot forward, leaning into the right lane and narrowly missing Salas and his motorcycle.

Salas geared down to first, then shot forward, going through gears one through six in seconds. He was now on the trail of the Dodge, closing the distance nearing 100 mph.

He reached down, rotated the REVO ankle holster, and unsnapped the leather locking. Salas drew the weapon, aimed, and fired. The .38

Special was not the ideal weapon of choice for shooting anything at that speed or distance, but firing the weapon made him feel better. The third round shattered the Dodge's rear window.

The driver of the truck tried Salas's trick and slammed on the brakes. Salas reacted in time and slowed the bike faster than the Dodge could brake.

The two sat idling on Highway 212, both units facing east – five yellow lines separating them. Salas dropped his kickstand and knelt beside the Ultra's fairing. He expected shots to be fired through the shattered rear window.

No shots came.

He looked behind him, as a pickup sporting a Ford logo on the front grill approached his bike and came to a halt. The Dodge came back to life, slowly regaining speed and heading east. Salas placed the Colt back in the ankle holster before he stood. He walked toward the Ford as the Dodge got away.

Salas tried to approach the passenger window. Three men were in the truck, two in front, one in the rear seat of the four-door F-250. Salas was not able to get any words out because the truck pulled into the left lane and sped forward, leaving him in the wake of the diesel's exhaust.

Salas got on his bike and followed the two trucks chasing the eastern horizon.

Ten miles later, he came upon the scene. The Dodge was on its side in the right ditch. Several wooden fence posts had snapped mid-post, others had been uprooted. Barbwire surrounded the truck and rolled in curls along the highway.

The Ford was parked, overlooking the carnage. Two men stood over the driver of the Dodge, who lay face down in the green grass once fenced in by the wire. Both men wore black leather vests embroidered with red-and-white Sons of Silence logos. They were facing Salas.

One of the men straddled the prostrate man, one hand cupping the man's chin, the other gripping the side of the man's head. He rotated his hands hard from right to left. The Dodge man's neck snapped. The Sons threw the dead man to the grass, stepping on his spine as they walked back to the Ford.

The neck snapper yelled out, "That was Willie!"

The other man said, "Ride safe."

They both climbed into the Ford, slammed their doors as the driver turned the truck towards the west and drove away.

Salas rode east to the Nisland Bar.

CHAPTER

42

Salas stopped on Highway 212 in Nisland. The "bar" was a former gas station. Now, minus the gas pumps, it housed five tables, a dozen chairs, and a wooden counter. He parked his Ultra next to two Harleys.

RJ and Ronnie were sipping coffee. The bartender was in the cooler, busy stocking shelves with canned and bottled beer. Salas could see the man through the glass doors.

The beer stocker yelled from the cooler, "Help yourself to whatever you want! I'll be out in a bit."

Salas grabbed a white ceramic cup from the tabletop. It read "Proud Sponsor of the Sturgis Scoopers." He poured black coffee from a glass pot.

The three sat in blue, green, and yellow plastic chairs surrounding a round metal table. The establishment's walls were four feet high. There was no glass in the windows, providing an open view of Highway 212. The side walls and empty window ledges were covered with cryptic messages courtesy of black magic markers: "75th Sturgis Rally," "Big Jim was here," "for a good time call 5551212," "Nebraska is windy because Kansas Sucks and South Dakota blows," "GBR," "Kelly loves Rhonda," "You got Groffed."

The bartender refilled their cups with steaming black coffee as a brown-and-white ambulance with headlights flashing and siren screaming zoomed past the bar.

"Huh," Salas said loudly, "I just rode in from that way and didn't see a thing."

"Police scanner says a one-vehicle crash west of here. Probably a biker not paying attention or on his damn cell phone. It will only get worse as we get closer to the rally. Some guys just don't know how to ride," the bartender said. "Boys, they call me Buck. You all want today's special?"

"Sure, Buck. Bring us three of them," RJ said.

"Wait, what's the special?" Ronnie asked.

"Shit on a shingle," RJ said, pointing to white words on a black chalkboard that hung from the wall behind the cash register. Shingle was spelled "shingel" and priced at $6, which included coffee.

"Sausage?" RJ asked.

"Yeah, sure," Buck answered.

"What is?" Ronnie started to ask.

"You'll like it. Just eat it," Salas said.

Salas spoke softly as Buck went through a door, to what Salas assumed, was the kitchen. He told the two about what happened to Willie, the car crash, and the Sons. RJ acknowledged he had a little help on the lookout and was surprised Salas had not noticed them.

Back on Highway 212, a black four-door sedan with "State Patrol" painted on the side door roared past in a blur—no flashing lights, no sirens. The Dodge's V8 pitched a deep cough.

"Can you believe all this, it started in Laughlin? Doris getting abducted. The sex traffickers Abdul and Rashid, some guy named Vegas Phil. Anne. Hell, I got married. Harvey Weston in Grand Junction. Toni. The Weston guy in Fort Wayne." Salas leaned back in his chair as he spoke.

"All actions have reactions," Ronnie said. "Our world, as spontaneous as we would like to think it is, is actually governed by causal relationships stemming from physical laws of the universe. We would like to think spontaneous events cannot be predicted; however, they have a cause.

It is the individual decay of events that cannot be predicted and are therefore truly random."

RJ looked at Salas and said, "Yeah, shit happens."

"Let's eat. Then I say we go to the Weston ranch. We try and talk some sense into Mrs. Weston. This has to stop," Salas said.

Ten minutes later, the specials arrived. Ronnie hesitantly tried his first bite; the second and third forkfuls were without a pause.

Buck picked up the dirty dishes, balancing the three plates on one forearm as he carried the silverware in the opposite hand. He left and returned carrying a fresh pot of coffee. He stopped and said, "Oh shit." Buck was looking at the parking lot.

Salas, Ronnie, and RJ followed Buck's stare as a white Chevy Silverado skidded to a stop on the graveled parking lot. Dust found its way into the bar. A blonde-haired woman wearing blue jeans, brown cowboy boots, and a white button-up shirt tied in a knot over her belly button had jumped out of the truck and was stomping their way. She was carrying a shotgun, and the gun was pointed inside the bar.

Ronnie said, "Ya gotta love South Dakota ladies. They carry shotguns around like city girls carry a purse."

"This ain't no lady," Buck said as he sat the coffee pot on the counter. "That's Barb Weston. She has hated me since I dumped her ass the night of our senior prom. The woman is bat-shit crazy."

"Barb! Barb, put that 870 away. You ain't gonna be shooting my bar up again!" Buck shouted.

Salas, RJ, and Ronnie dove to the floor as the first shot from the 12-gauge blew their metal table out the back windowless window. The second shot shattered the cooler's glass doors. Beer cans burst open, and beer fizzed and foamed like an indoor sprinkler.

Salas stayed on his belly and waited, hesitant to pull his .38 from the ankle holster. Was she after them or the bartender? Ronnie lay beside Salas, his weapon also still secure and hidden.

RJ crawled toward Salas and mouthed, "I don't have my gun."

Salas pointed to his .38 and said, "There's an extra in my saddlebag, if you can get to it."

Buck picked himself off the floor. He reached under the counter and pulled out a double-barrel 20-gauge shotgun.

"Barb, put your gun down. Don't make me shoot you."

Barb fired again, the pellets, in a tight pattern, punched a large hole through the black chalkboard. The sign swung left to right on the wall, but stayed in place. It now read "Shit $6.00, includes coffee."

Salas yelled out, "That's three shots! Grab her before she can reload!"

A fourth shot blew the coffee pot off the countertop, with more pellets attacking the innocent beer. Buck cussed the hot coffee and glass shards that stung his arms.

"She's packing five!" Buck yelled as he pulled both of the double barrel's triggers.

Barb Weston flew backward, her body doing a backflip on the gravel as her Remington fired its final round into dirt. She lay flat on her stomach as the dust settled around her.

The four men walked slowly out of the bar and surrounded Barb's dead body. They stood there, watching her blood pooling at their feet. Ronnie gently turned the body over as was his duty to administer CPR if needed.

Her eyes were open. They were a soft pale blue. A gaping hole exposed what he thought may have been her heart. A small black ink tattoo was over her right breast, her white bra now a more crimson color. The tat read "An Eye For An Eye."

"What the hell was that all about?" RJ asked, knowing it was them she was after.

"I don't know. She hasn't done that in years. Last time she fired a gun at me, hell, I deserved it. I haven't talked to her in over a year. I thought she moved to Denver," Buck answered as he dialed 911.

Salas could hear Buck tell the dispatch about the death of Barb Weston and the dispatch's response about two Westons in one day.

And the day was not over.

CHAPTER

43

The Sturgis ambulance made a return trip to Highway 212, this time without any flashing lights or a siren. Evidently, when you know the person is deceased, noise and lights are no longer important.

Buck took control of the scene. He had coffee for the officers ready when they arrived. Salas, Ronnie, and RJ gave statements, phone numbers, and email addresses to the state and county police. Each story matched Buck's and his attempts to get Barb Weston to drop the shotgun. Buck shared with the officers he was convinced the attacked was motivated by their hostile breakup in April of 1980.

The state patrol officer commented on the car accident and tragic death of Willie Weston just a few hours prior to his sister's demise.

"Willie must have lost control or overcorrected. His body was thrown from the truck and his neck was broken, nearly twisted off. These kids have got to learn to wear seat belts." The officer droned on, "Poor Mrs. Weston. You know she lost her husband just a few weeks ago. He was shot and killed in Colorado. Now this – two kids in one day."

Salas, RJ, and Ronnie watched as the ambulance and police officers left the gravel parking lot. Still no sirens or flashing lights. Salas hoped the South Dakota law enforcement didn't match their names from the Weston shooting in Colorado and the new death of a Weston in South

Dakota. The odds of the same people being in both locations was too small. Plus, once they identified the Weston body from Salas's house, well, it would create a trail of deaths too difficult to talk themselves out of.

RJ received a text from his boys. They had yet to leave South Dakota and were following Webster Weston. The text told them Webster was buying ammo at the Runnings Farm Store in Belle Fouche.

RJ texted them back to keep Webster in Belle Fouche, and that he was on his way there. He wanted Salas and Ronnie to have a chance to talk to Betty and W Weston at the ranch before more ammo was delivered.

Salas left Buck a $20 dollar bill. Buck protested but did slip the bill into his front pants pocket.

The three Harleys started the *hupt-hupt-hupt*, taking left turns out of Nisland towards Belle Fourche. Five miles east were two men in a grassy field, gathering fence posts and untangling barbwire. Fifteen miles east, RJ kept riding as Ronnie and Salas turned onto the dirt road going south to the Weston Ranch.

RJ met his boys in the Running's parking lot. He parked his Harley by the driver-side door of the Ford F-250.

"You guys blend in. Great driving that Ford. You should be pulling a horse trailer," RJ said.

"South Dakota is fun for a visit, but we don't think we could take all the quiet," the driver said, pointing his finger straight ahead. "There he is, your boy, Mr. Webster Weston. Scrawny little shit, ain't he?"

They watched as Webster left the farm store. He pull his pants up with his right hand, then took keys out of his front pocket. His blue jeans were one size too big for his waist and two sizes too long for the length. His shirt was red-and-black plaid, with the sleeves cut off at the shoulders. His arms looked abnormally small compared to his chest. His hair was long and oily. He kept tossing his head to the right to get the bangs out of his eyes.

RJ got off his bike. "Take my ride. All of you, follow me." He tossed the key to his Harley through the open window and the waiting hands of the driver. He walked toward Webster. He saw the blinkers flash on a Platinum Ford F-150 in response to Webster pushing the key fob. RJ approached the vehicle from the passenger side, opened the door, and sat down as Webster entered from the driver's side.

"What the fuck? Who are you, old man? Get out of my truck," Webster said as he placed the key in the ignition and started the Ford. "Out now before I call the cops."

"You won't call the cops. In fact, I'm going to do you a favor. You aren't going home for a while. You and me are going to take a little ride." RJ pointed his weapon at Webster, the barrel of the gun resting on RJ's lap. "Let's take Highway 34 to Aladdin." RJ motioned with his other hand, "That way." He pointed south. "You know how to get there. Don't make me tell you twice."

"What you gonna do? Shoot me while I'm driving? And wreck us? Asshole." He pulled his hair back with his right hand then whipped his palm on his pant leg. It left a grease mark.

Without warning, RJ snapped the pistol across the bridge of Webster's nose. "You going to drive or cry?" RJ said as tears welled up in Webster's eyes.

Blood surfaced over the indent on his nose. Webster cleared his eyes with the base of his shirt.

"You are so dead, man. An eye for an eye, bitch. Me and W will hunt you down like the dog you are. When Wade gets back, he will make you squeal like a pig." Webster made the turn onto Highway 34.

"Wade is dead, Webster. He was shot and killed in Fort Wayne, Indiana."

"Bullshit. You are a fucking liar."

They drove several miles in silence.

"One question for you, Web. Why is your family doing all of this?"

"It's our creed, old man. An eye for an eye. It's how we live. It's how we been raised. It's what folks around here know about us. That's why no one fucks with us." Webster laughed. "What, you gonna kill me? I don't think so. We own this area, man. The Westons dominate around here."

RJ said, "Pull over, Webster. Put the truck in park, shut it off, leave the keys in the ignition, and get out of the truck."

RJ got out of the truck as Webster shut the driver-side door. The Sons parked behind them on the shoulder of Highway 34, now called

Wyoming Highway 24. Two Sons exited the Ford and stood next to Webster.

"What's wrong, old man? You don't have the guts for dying? Going to go back home to your mommy?" He stuck his chest out like a pigeon, his chin high in the air.

"Dump him and the truck on the Wind River, Rez. He ain't worth saving. Then you guys get on home." RJ got on his bike, did a sharp turn facing the cycle back to the east and Belle Fourche. He rode off. He could see Webster's neck snap in his side mirror.

44

From the highway where Salas had watched the homestead earlier that morning, they could see two people exiting a barn and walking toward the house.

Ronnie parked his Harley in the shade of the cedars on the north side of the feedlot. The smell of manure was stronger than earlier in the day, the result of hundreds of cattle eating and shitting for 24 hours.

Salas opened the rear luggage compartment of his Ultra and took out the Winchester .30-30 Trails End. He quickly reassembled the weapon and loaded it with five rounds of .30-30 ammo. He handed the rifle to Ronnie, and then reloaded his .38 and placed it back in his ankle holster.

"You've shot a rifle before. This one is just as easy. No need to shoot unless you see me shoot or I wave at you. Hopefully, the woman will want all of this to stop as much as we do. I'm going to park on the east side of the feedlot and yell out to them at the house. The cattle will separate us. You stay in the cedars and keep me covered. They won't expect you to be there."

"You know, Mike," Ronnie said, looking at the weapon, "there are over 12 million cattle on feed in the United States, with the state of South Dakota having over 100,000 feeder cows in feedlots at any one time." He pumped a shell into the firing chamber. "The typical cow enters the feedlot at nine to eleven months of age, weighing in at around 900 pounds. The cow will stay in the feedlot anywhere from 60 to 200 days and gain from 400 to 600 pounds."

"Ronnie. Remember." Salas used two fingers, pointing from his eyes to Ronnie's eyes and back. "If I start shooting at them, then you start shooting, too. Got it?"

"Yeah, sure. Don't worry. And, the average daily weight gain of a cow in a feed yard is over 3.5 pounds per day. Amazing." Ronnie had Salas hold the rifle as he climbed over the four-strand barbwire fence to enter the cedar trees.

Salas then handed him the rifle. Again, he did the two fingers to the eyes and back.

Salas straddled his bike, started the engine, and rode to the middle of the eastside of the feed lot. He sat and revved his engine. The roar of the motor pushed the huddled mass of cattle west and successfully got the two people at the house to look east.

Salas shut off the motor. He climbed over the concrete feed bunk, standing on the concrete slab, and waved a white bandanna in the air. He could see a man and a woman leave the porch and get into a side-by-side four-wheeler. They crossed a cattle guard and entered the feedlot, slowly driving through the herd of cattle towards Salas.

A red Polaris Ranger crept toward the feed bunks. Salas watched the silver-haired woman behind the wheel talk to a buzz-cut young man, more of a boy riding in the passenger seat. The Polaris had a roll bar and black headrests with a hardtop roof. The windshield was folded down. A synthetic rope hung from a winch attached to the front main frame of the four-wheeler.

As the Ranger came forward, clumps and chunks of a mud-and-cow manure concoction jumped off the knobby tires. The woman stopped 30 yards away from Salas, fifty to sixty cows standing between them. The boy, carrying a bolt action rifle, stepped out of the rig, the weapon folded across his arms as he walked toward Salas.

Salas looked to his right to see if Ronnie was in position. He couldn't spot him in the thick, dark green entanglement of cedars.

Ronnie peered through the branches. He could see a four-wheeler creeping through the brown sludge of the feed yard. He struggled as the cedars grabbed at his arms and legs, preventing him from making any forward progress. Ronnie turned his back and pushed, his legs driving him through the onslaught of cedar tentacles.

He heard the sound of teeth chattering, then felt multiple sharp pains shoot into his calf. Ronnie bent his leg and looked back at his ankle. Several white sticks stuck out from his pant leg and into the leather of his riding boots. The pain intensified as he looked at it.

Ronnie watched as a small rodent swatted its tail, leaving a small patch of quills in his tibia.

"A porcupine?!" Ronnie said aloud. He took his Winchester, poking the barrel against the rodent's head. The porcupine waddled off as blood darkened Ronnie's pant leg. He grabbed a quill and yanked. It tore his pants and his skin. A burning pain shot up his leg.

Ronnie knew he had to get to the edge of the cedars to help Salas. He buried his head and trudged forward. Now, just a few feet from the open space, he raised the rifle, setting the barrel on a branch, his eyes on the man in the Polaris.

Ronnie took a deep breath, his focus on the rifle's site. He heard a soft *wummmpf.* The smell of sulfur engulfed him. His eyes burned. He looked down as a skunk slipped under the cedar's branches and skuttled away. He had just been skunked.

The spray forced Ronnie to fall back into the trees. The barrel of the rifle went down and, to the left, a shot rang out. He had accidentally fired the weapon.

The bullet from Ronnie's Winchester landed a few feet to the side of Salas. The impact of the .30-30 bullet sent fragments of concrete up Salas's leg, piercing his skin and embedding chunks of cement into the jeans over his buttocks. He grabbed his thigh and jumped into the feed bunk.

W yelled out, "Momma, its Wade! He's back!" He raised the bolt action and fired at the feed bunks, his shot hitting one of the black angus cows in the back hip. The cow dropped, struggling to stand. The animal brayed and bawled in pain.

W ejected a shell and fired again, hitting the feed bunk.

The blast of the Winchester .30-30 being fired triggered the cattle. The herd responded by running away from the sound. Hundreds of startled and scared black Angus cows thundered from the northern end of the feed lot to the south.

W's round confused them even more, encouraging a panicked stampede. The animals ran into and over each other. W was trapped. He dropped his weapon and turned to run towards the Ranger. A large steer lowered his head, sending W face-first onto the muddy, crappy floor of the feed lot.

Another steer ran over W, the hooves stomping on W's back and burying him in the muck. W rose. He saw a brief opening to get to the four-wheeler. As he stood, a 1,200-pound running ribeye kicked back, his hoof connecting with W's skull. Again, the boy dropped face-first. More cattle ran over him, crushing his skull. Broken ribs protruded through his flannel shirt.

Betty Weston sat in the Polaris, both hands on the steering wheel as the mass of cattle bashed into the Ranger. The four-wheeler tipped and turned but stayed upright with all four wheels on the ground. She reached into the toolbox attached to the back deck. She removed a .44 Magnum Colt Anaconda revolver.

Betty held the walnut grip with one hand and aimed at the feed bunks. She fired. The impact of the bullet hitting the bunk sent concrete dust flying in the air. The bunker responded with a large crack extending downward from the hole it created. She fired again and again, with each round shaking and rocking the Polaris under her.

Salas pulled the .38 from his ankle holster. He had raised his weapon when the first round of the .44 crushed through the bunker just inches from his head. Startled, Salas accidently dropped the .38. Another round from the .44 prevented Salas from reaching for his gun as he crawled backward. Two more rounds further separated him from his only form of protection. He waved, trying to get Ronnie's attention.

Ronnie fired the Winchester. The skunk dropped dead in its tracks. He was trapped inside the cedar cage. Large dark brown and green branches kept swatting him in the face, shoulders, and legs. His face was scratched and bleeding. He smelled of sulfur. The tear gas burned his eyes.

The shooting stopped. Salas thought he had counted five shots from the cannon Betty Weston was shooting. He knew most .44s held only six rounds, but he didn't know if she had more ammo or another gun, and he wasn't willing to raise his head to find out.

"Betty! Mrs. Weston, can we talk?" Salas lay on his back as he shouted from the feed bunk.

"I ain't got no words for you!" Betty yelled back.

"Please, Betty, listen to me. This eye-for-an-eye thing – it has to stop. No one wins. You have lost oved ones and so have I."

"When my boys get here, we will see who wins."

"Betty, Harvey died on the floor of an Applebee's in Colorado. Your son, Wade, I killed him. He died on the floor of a shitty $125,000 one-bedroom house in Fort Wayne, Indiana. Wyatt and Brenda. You will never see them again. They are on a permanent Vegas vacation. No one will ever find their bodies. Today, Willie died alone, in a ditch. Your daughter, Barb, she died in the dirt-and-gravel of a bar's parking lot. And Webster – you will never see him again, either. Let's say he is on reservation time. And W, you see him lying over there, don't you? He died in a lake of piss, mud, and cow shit. Your lifestyle determines death style doesn't say much for your life now, does it?"

Betty didn't respond.

The sixth round of the .44 magnum exploded. The cattle bellowed as they stretched the fencing on the west side of the feedlot.

Salas peeked over the feed bunk. He saw Betty Weston's body leaning off the driver's side of the Polaris Ranger. Her left arm dangled in the mud as the seat belt strained to keep her upright.

"Damn, what is that smell?" Salas yelled.

"It's me," Ronnie said as he walked through cow shit towards Salas. "I got skunked." Ronnie stopped and shot the wounded cow in the head.

"Damnit, Ronnie, you shot me."

"Technically, I shot the concrete. I do apologize for that. But it was that skunk. And about the skunk, did you know the skunk's spray is from their anal glands and they can shoot it accurately over three feet? It is a yellowish, oily aerosol composed of sulfur and thiols. Thus, the rotten egg smell."

"Good to know. What's that in your leg?" Salas asked as he dusted himself from the grain and feed in the feed bunk.

"Well, that is from a different incident that happened before the skunk. Seems that groves of cedar trees are home to several different species of rodents. These are porcupine quills and they hurt like hell. Quills or spines, as they are called, actually inspired the invention of hypodermic needles and the modern-day suture."

"Are you are shitting me?" Salas asked. "While I was getting shot at by an old lady with a cannon you were messing around with a skunk and a porcupine? Didn't you think with all that shooting it was possible that I could have been killed?"

"Mike, possible refers to what can be done or what can occur, whereas probable refers to what is likely to be done or likely to occur. Thus, when you say possible, you are expressing far less confidence in the outcome than if you would have said probable."

"You should probably shut up."

The two men left Betty and her son, W, in the feed lot. They both limped to the bunks and slowly climbed over the concrete wall. Salas started his motorcycle, then turned the cycle back toward Highway 212. Ronnie joined him in the passenger seat. They rode together as far as the cedars and Ronnie's Road King.

Salas turned to Ronnie. "Take off your shirt and throw it in the ditch," he disassembled the Winchester and stored it in the travel pack.

"But it's my favorite T-shirt. You got it for me in Daytona."

"Throw it. You got to get rid of that smell before it becomes a permanent part of you." Salas handed Ronnie his pocket knife while he removed small rocks of concrete from his side.

"Now cut your jeans above the quills and throw them in the ditch, too. We need to get you to a shower."

"I'm riding into town wearing nothing but my boxers?"

"Yeah, you probably won't be the first guy to ride into Sturgis wearing only your underwear."

45

Salas slid a five-dollar bill into the kiosk of the self-serve car wash. Their Harleys stayed outside of the concrete block building while the two bikers entered.

Salas held the spray nozzle, shooting from the hip as it sprayed out warm water. Then, with a click of a knob, he switched to soap suds that came through the same hose, followed by a second click for a degreaser. Salas hosed Ronnie, careful to avoid the inflamed porcupine quills in Ronnie's calf and shin.

After the car wash, Ronnie smelled more of soap than sulfur. It was now safe to take him to the Sturgis Hospital emergency room. Twenty-three porcupine quills later, the physician's assistant announced it was her third porcupine incident of the year. The hospital was not advertising their porcupine specialty clinic.

In his rear, the PA gave Ronnie a shot of the antibiotic, ceftriaxone. She also gave Ronnie a free tube of Neosporin for the spear marks and the cedar-induced facial cuts. Ronnie got to keep the quills.

Still wearing only his boxers and the sulfur-smelling leather boots, Ronnie paid his bill at the front desk with a credit card and filled out a claim form to send to UnitedHealthCare.

Ronnie and Salas rode a few blocks north to Main Street, then took a right. The two walked into Sturgis Harley Davidson off Junction Avenue. The boots and boxers went into the trash, with Ronnie leaving the establishment fully clothed.

They rode back down Main and parked their bikes next to RJ's Harley in front of the Oasis.

Salas and Ronnie joined RJ at the bar – Salas on his right, Ronnie on his left.

No one spoke for several minutes, as beer was the priority.

"You smell like cow shit," RJ said, looking at Salas. He looked at Ronnie and added, "You smell kind of like soapy shit. But with new clothes."

Salas spoke next, "You know, all of this, it started at Laughlin. Now I've been to three bike rallies. And really haven't gotten to experience any of the traditional rally stuff. Hell, my first time at Sturgis I was chasing a serial killer. I didn't even know what Sturgis was. Then in Daytona – RJ, your bike was stolen. That Lopez guy and the alligators. Then all of this. Seems like someone is always shooting someone or chasing someone."

"Tomorrow, my friend, we ride Spearfish Canyon and Needles Highway. Then let's get drunk as hell at Saloon Number Ten in Deadwood. You can't get more rally-ish than that for Sturgis. Ronnie, get us a room at the Mineral Palace," RJ said.

"You got it," Ronnie said as he pulled out his cell phone. "I know where the Lake of the Ozarks has a rally in September. It is called Bike Fest. They had over 100,000 bikes there last year."

"Never been there. Heard the Ozarks are beautiful. Count me in," RJ said, sipping his beer.

"Missouri, huh? Let's try it," Salas said, looking at Ronnie. "What could possibly go wrong in Missouri?"

The End

ABOUT THE AUTHOR

JJ Spain

JJ Spain is a 25-year veteran of Bike Rallies, including Daytona, the Sturgis Rally, and Laughlin. His captivating crime are set at his favorite venues, bringing the Daytona ride and experience to your fingertips.

Take the ride. Enjoy the rally.

ALL BOOKS IN THE MIKE SALAS SERIES

IF YOU ENJOYED THIS BOOK OR FOUND IT USEFUL I'D BE VERY GRATEFUL IF YOU'D POST A SHORT REVIEW ON AMAZON. YOUR SUPPORT REALLY DOES MAKE A DIFFERENCE AND I READ ALL THE REVIEWS PERSONALLY, SO I CAN GET YOUR FEEDBACK.

THANKS AGAIN FOR YOUR SUPPORT!